Nostalgia

DERRICK L. SMITH

PAGE PUBLISHING
Conneaut Lake, PA

First originally published by Page Publishing 2022

ISBN 978-1-6624-5891-0 (pbk)
ISBN 978-1-6624-5892-7 (digital)

Printed in the United States of America

I dedicate this book to my mother, Mary Ann Smith. It was her love for reading that led to my love for reading. I wish that she was here to read this book. I love you, momma.

ances that the necessary ballrooms will be paid for through my foundation. In addition, the foundation will cover the opening night bar
and catering. The stipulation that they must agree to is that it must
be the Friday and Saturday night of the same week of the ISF that I
will be attending in Chicago two years from now. If that can't be met,
then let them know that the donation unfortunately would not be
available from the foundation. Let me know when this is completed.
Thanks."

"Ms. Benson, is there a cap on that amount?"

"Yes, but tell them before anything is secured by them that we
must have their best estimate to the amount of the foundation total
outlay. This should guide them in their approach a bit."

"Yes, Ms. Benson." With that, Nick exited as smoothly as he
had entered into the spacious office. This inner office was surrounded
by the outer office that Nick worked in and further surrounded
by the entire floor of the Baschcomb building here in downtown
Washington, DC. It was in this building that Valerie not only chaired
the foundation that was started by her grandfather, Howard Benson,
but she also ran her own business, International Safety Services. It
was this business that drove her to phenomenal worldwide success.
Her father, Howard Benson Jr., currently served as her only adviser
on this business, and she had been running it for the last five years.
Prior to that, she served as his number two. She didn't come into
the business as his number two. She came to be his number two by
a path of hard and dedicated personal and professional work and
achievement.

After finishing high school at Bishop Noll in Hammond,
Indiana, she was off to Harvard undergrad and studying international
business. Upon finishing it in three years, she went to Columbia
University in New York City for law school. When Valerie completed
her three years of law school, she worked at the United Nations for
two years before taking on a director's role at International Safety
Services, a position that had a great deal of distance between the position her father had in running the business. Still, over the next seven
years, she outworked everyone, including her father, in pushing the

business's growth and structure. At the end of those seven years was when she earned the position of CEO and president of the business.

With all that she had accomplished for International Safety Services, in the short ride from Chicago's O'Hare Airport to downtown with all the importance of the public and private meetings at the International Security Forum that she was heading toward, all that Valerie could think about was whether or not he would be coming into town.

CHAPTER 2

Being nostalgic was a commonplace for Ron Winston to find himself. He lived his life in a day-to-day manner, not because of his financial resources but because of the manner in which his financial resources were accumulated. It began over twenty years ago while he was still in high school. His home environment did not lend itself to great financial resources. His parents both worked and worked steady in providing all the necessities for Ron and his three siblings. Ron was the oldest and, at a young age, knew that anything that he wanted outside of the bare necessities was only going to be achieved through his own work. Ron would use the family lawnmower to complete his yard chores early on Saturday mornings when he was as young as twelve and in the sixth grade. Before he finished sixth grade, he had started to get lawn maintenance work with others in the neighborhood block that he lived on to earn his own money. Ron never spent anything at this point in his life. He was all about accumulating money for what he thought would be a path to his happiness later.

In the summer between the eighth and ninth grades, he maintained the lawn maintenance work of his family's yard, the others in his block, and also the surrounding blocks in his community. On top of that, he had found part-time work through a community center for four hours per day during the week for the summer. Ron enjoyed the hustling and goal setting for where his savings could go. It was at this time that he set his first high-price purchase in mind, and he knew that it was still two years away: a car. He knew of older kids that worked at the mall, which was a twenty-minute car ride from where he grew up in Gary, Indiana. He was thinking about working there during the school year since his lawn maintenance was not a yearlong endeavor. He figured after the football season in his freshman year of high school that he would look to get work at the mall. He figured that he could get a ride with some of the older kids in the neighborhood to get there. He knew with the busyness of his parents' schedule that they would suggest he did something more local. The economic community of Gary was not thriving, and as a result, the work that was available in the community was neither plentiful nor desirable in his mind.

In many respects, Ron was looking forward to starting high school because he would already be involved in football before school started, and the transition to high school would be on the way even before the school doors opened. He was also looking forward to playing football with his best friend. His friend lived in the same block that he lived in, and he was very talented in school and any sport that he tried a hand at. Ron knew that when football practice began in mid-August, he would be on the same field with his best friend. Ron was an outstanding natural athlete himself. Fast, strong, quick, smart, and hardworking were how coaches would always describe Ron. It turned out that Ron and his best friend would not play football together. His best friend was pursued on an academic basis (and athletics basis) to have his tuition paid at the private catholic school, Bishop Noll. While they never played football together, they did remain best of friends and cheered for each other the best that they could.

Ron had never sought out large gatherings like the ISF, but it was something that he was aware of and wanted to learn more about the type of companies that would come to this type of convention. It wasn't that his business was competing with the companies that were going to be on display and presenting the industry that lured him into coming to this convention. Ron's thoughts were that perhaps it was time to get out of the local business that he was in and join up with a national or international organization. The fact of the matter was that he probably had taken his business as far as it was going to go at its current makeup. He still found it ironic that he got to the point that he was in life through lawn maintenance, working at a mall, selling small quantities of marijuana in high school, selling larger amounts of marijuana while in college, joining the police academy out of college, serving as a policeman for four years before getting shot in the line of duty, and then setting up a private investigator service specializing in electronic and physical surveillance to support folks seeking divorces primarily in the Chicago suburbs. During his drive from the western suburb of South Elgin, Illinois, to go to downtown Chicago for the ISF, Ron couldn't help but think of how he got to this point this day and how much he still missed his best friend, whom he hadn't seen since they both finished high school.

It was during the time that they were both at different high schools that really solidified their relationship. They would spend time with Ron's friends from his school, and they would spend time with the kids at Bishop Noll. They would also get with kids from the other high schools in Gary, and they always had a good time. There were always guys around, and there were always girls around when they wanted to be with girls. Ron remembered how his best friend would introduce him to the girls that he knew. Ron knew he had a lot going for himself even besides being a small-time marijuana salesman, yet his friend always introduced him to other folks by building him up even more. His friend introduced him to girls, and those girls treated him very well because of his friend. There was one girl that he was introduced to; however, his friend made clear that this girl was special and was not a groupie like the others.

Ron saw something different about her himself. First, it wasn't that she was his friend's girlfriend. They didn't show affection like that for each other. They showed an affection of respect, honor, care, concern, and trust with each other. They showed love for each other in a way that did not involve any of the high-school silliness that was found at that age. Ron met her when they were sophomores in high school and didn't quite understand the distinction that his friend made about her after the first meeting in pointing out that she was Jewish. Ron knew what he knew. Every family in his neighborhood was either black or Hispanic, and every student at his high school was the same. He saw her many times over the years from that first meeting as sophomores to the high-school graduation party at her home. While both his friend and this girl was very able to socialize with whoever would be in any room, they would always gravitate back to each other. They never proclaimed that they were boyfriend and girlfriend; they just showed love for each other. For that matter, his friend never proclaimed any girl to be a girlfriend. This didn't seem odd. Ron knew that he liked girls because he saw him with girls. Ron thought that he didn't proclaim a girlfriend because then that might limit the number of girls that his friend would or could spend time with by having an identified girlfriend.

The graduation party was the last time that Ron saw his best friend, and he couldn't help but think about him as he was coming into Chicago from the west on the Eisenhower Expressway and seeing how some buildings stood so much taller than others. He knew that wherever his friend was today, he was still standing taller than others, not only physically but also from a character standpoint as well. Ron thought just then, *What was that girl's name, and where is she today?*

CHAPTER 3

Rick Smalls preferred to drive when possible. It provided time to think. It provided space to himself. It provided a solitude to planning for the work ahead of him that he truly treasured. Many closing sales arguments were structured during a drive somewhere. Over the last five years, his drives were mostly domestic to the United States. In the years after college, he bounced around and used whatever mode of transportation was the right mode for the assignment in front of him at the given time. Today, his drive was bringing him north on Interstate 65 from the Indianapolis, Indiana, area to Chicago. He knew that he would drive through and past his hometown of Gary, Indiana. He supposed that once he got into that area, he might get off the interstate and drive through town just to drive around the town that he remembered from growing up there. He hadn't spent any real time in town since leaving it for college after high school. He left two weeks after graduating high school or, the way he liked to remember it best, two days after a wonderful party. Rick knew that he came from a background of a family that provided a great deal of inconsistency into his life. He was an only child. He found his best relationships outside his family. He recognized that his parents did not prepare themselves much for adulthood, for a married life, or for having a son. The result of this was a great deal of living by the seat of their pants. One day, there was a family car and food in the refrigerator. The next week, you might have neither. There was no counseling from his parents to prepare for the future. It was because of his athletic abilities that he was able to get a different education than what was presented in the Gary public school system.

This education was not book based only. By being a standout athlete in football, basketball, and track for the school and in baseball in summer leagues, he met a different group of people than he would have at the inner-city high school that he would have gone to. At the public high school, there would have been very few kids from backgrounds where their parents were professionals or salaried and educated. The vast majority of the kids that he would have gone to school with would have parents that were laborers in the steel mill, small-project construction workers, or retail workers. The kids whose parents were teachers or administrators in the school system were about as professional as it got in their community. Rick remembered that there were the exceptions as well of a family that had a parent as a doctor, nurse, lawyer, or business owner. This was the exception. The student base at Bishop Noll where Rick went to attend high school had parents who were professionals, and the working-class folks were the exception. The administrators, teachers, and the other students' parents embraced Rick. He knew that it was most likely because of his contributions to the sports teams that he was a part of for the school. If it mattered to Rick, he would wonder how many of those same parents knew that his other interests in school was math, computer coding, and the debate team. Rick was well-rounded.

Rick used the school and its environment just the same way that the school and the environment used him. They got all the athletic abilities out of him that they could. In return, he got education in smaller classroom sizes, advanced math and science courses, and structure and counseling from folks that had gone to college and became businesses themselves. He understood from this environment that his living environment was not the world. He used them all for knowledge. There was one person at the school that he never looked to use, and he believed that she never looked to use him. It was with this thought that Rick got a shiver. His last sight of her was three years after high school in Boston. She was telling him that she was about to move out of town. They promised to stay in touch. They figured it would be easy. Being in touch for the four years of high school was easy since they were at the same school and social-ized quite a bit together outside of school. They went to different colleges but in the same town, not by plan but by life-path choices. Rick had come to Boston to study at the Massachusetts Institute of Technology. He figured he could get the undergraduate work com-pleted and the masters in four years because of the program that was available to him. She was at another school in town for the studies that would support her life's path.

They made it a point to see each other in Boston for the three years that she was there. It wasn't high school, and they knew that their growth in their chosen fields of study would come first. Whenever they got together, it was always good. It was his best rela-tionship ever at that point of his life and to this day. The relationship had times of intimacy, but it wasn't based in intimacy. The intimacy only rarely was sexual, yet it was probably more intimate than most marriages of twenty years. He thought about twenty years since it was twenty years since they left high school together. Rick's trips in nostalgia would take him back to his time with her and with his friend from the neighborhood. While he last saw her seventeen years ago, it had been twenty years since he talked with this friend. He did see him from a distance twelve years ago. As Rick was approaching Merrillville, Indiana, traveling north on Interstate 65, he knew he would need to make a decision soon about his driving path to go by his childhood home, which would allow him to see his friend's home as well and then to go past where she grew up in Munster, Indiana, before going by his high school in Hammond, Indiana. He also knew that he was going to take a chance first to see if one of his all-time favorite roadside restaurants was still open for business. It was worth a shot to see.

CHAPTER 4

Now off Interstate 65, Rick was travelling west on Interstate 80/94. It was about now that Rick realized that the sunny day coming north out of the Indianapolis area from the June sunshine had turned into what he realized after leaving this area after high school, the perpetual gray skies of the greater Chicago area. Exiting the highway to go south on Grant Street from the interstate, the local feel of Gary settled back into Rick's memories. Besides the cloud cover, there were the truck stops on both the east and west side of Grant Street, just like it was when he left twenty years previously. Continuing to head south, there was still no structure greater than one story tall in sight. On both sides of the road there were small storefronts, some open for business and others boarded up with no indication that it would be opened ever again.

Nevertheless the appearance of the community right here, Rick was headed farther south for eight blocks to see if Ray's Shrimp House was still in business. As he approached the site where he remembered it to be, he saw a car parked on the side of it and assumed the best. Rick pulled in beside the other car and began to walk around front to see what was there now. Rick was dressed comfortably in jeans, a collared golf shirt, and his favorite shoes of all time for nonathletic purposes, a pair of lace-up black Ecco shoes. He was pleased to see the sign flipped on the side stating that they were open and to please come in. Rick went inside and saw two people sitting at a table eating at a small tabletop while seating in vinyl-covered chairs. Some things never changed. Not changing also was the chalkboard with the daily special written on it and the posters with pictures of different items that you would see on the menu. The menu was the same type of menu that he remembered from those years ago, where you spelled out the words that you wanted with the block letters that fit on the surface. Some letters had fallen from what Rick wanted, yet that did not stop him from knowing that they were still serving what he wanted. He stepped toward the bulletproof glass that separated the restaurant staff and the customers that enter into Ray's. Rick was asked what he would have. "I'll take a half order of fish and chips with mild sauce on the side and red cream soda," Rick said with the confidence as if he had been there just yesterday.

"We don't have the red cream soda today. Would you like a white cream soda?" the clerk asked.

"That will be fine, thanks," Rick replied while thinking, *Wow*. He hadn't been in this restaurant in twenty years, and it was so clear to him what he wanted. Now it was a matter of it meeting the memory standards. Rick was told the price. He slid a $10 bill into the slot and told her to keep the change. She slid a chit with his order number on it and then stated his order number to him.

"Your order number is sixty-two," she said with the enthusiasm of someone working behind bulletproof glass for maybe ten years.

Since there were only the two customers inside and they had their food, Rick was surprised to see that the deep fryers were all in use already even before he made his order. He looked above the deep fryers and saw three order slips hanging above the fryers. Folks must have called in orders that they would pick up. Maybe it was being "Ubered" to folks as well. Instead of taking a seat to wait for his order, Rick backed away from the window and leaned on the wall about halfway between the door going outside and the bulletproof glass. Rick began scanning his emails on his phone. As he was scanning his phone, the door opened, and three new customers came in. It was one man and two women. They were continuing their conversation that they were having outside as they entered Ray's. The man actually wasn't much involved in the conversation with the two ladies. They were conversating with themselves and directing things at him. He smiled and looked back toward the menu, which was on the wall that Rick was leaning on and to Rick's left. As Rick was looking toward the man without staring, he recognized something about him but kept to himself. The man turned to the ladies and asked them if they knew what they wanted. They told him, and he ordered and paid for all of them.

After getting his chit, the man noticed that the ladies had taken a seat, and he told them their order number and told them that he was going outside for a smoke. He began patting his shirt and pant pockets, as if searching for a light. He looked up and asked Rick if he had a light. "Sorry, I don't," Rick replied.

"That's okay, I found it. Thanks anyways," the man said while pulling a light from his back pocket. "Hey, are you from around here?"

"I'm not," Rick said matter-of-factly.

"You really look like a guy that was from here some years ago. He was a kid then. He lived here and went to high school in another town near here. The people were really proud of him because he was from here. He was something else in football and basketball. That boy could play."

"How are the sports for kids in this area doing these days?" Rick asked to begin some redirection of the man's conversation.

"Not like those days. The kids aren't staying in school. There are fewer schools because there is no tax base, and nobody seems to care about the kids."

"Jerry, leave that man alone. You only thinking about Rick because there was an article in the paper about him today, and that man you bothering is about how tall Rick was!" one of the ladies that came in with him yelled across the room. "Go outside and smoke your cigarette and leave that man alone."

"I'm sorry to bother you, but she is right. There was an article in the *Gary Post-Tribune* today talking about this kid—well, he's a man now—who was something else. Nobody really knows what happened to him. When he left, there was no information on what he was doing in sports in college. They said he was smart, so we all thought he went to college and would be playing sports. He was real good."

"No apologies necessary. It seems wherever I go, somebody thinks I'm somebody that they know."

"See, I was two years behind him. We didn't go to the same school though. I played sports at another school, but I lived in the house on the street next to him. I even remember when his parents died in that car accident. I didn't really know them. I guess they was good people. People talked about them a lot after they died 'round here because of their son Rick. There was a lot in the paper back then about him, wondering where he might be and why he wouldn't come to his parents' funeral. A lot of people went to the funeral probably 'cause they thought they were going to see him and find out what was going on with him. There was a lot of people living their lives in some ways through him when he was in high school."

"I'm sorry to hear that about your friend."

"Oh, I wouldn't say that we were friends. He talked to a lot of people but seemed like he only had a few friends."

"Jerry, leave that man alone, please. Sir, let me apologize for my brother. Rick was all right. My brother is making him out to be something that everybody didn't see."

Jerry turned toward the woman and away from Rick and said, "Tina, most people did like him. You still don't like him just like you didn't like him then because he wasn't with you but with that white girl instead!"

"Order sixty-two?" was the call from behind the bulletproof glass.

"Excuse me," Rick said to Jerry and stepped toward the window. And Jerry stepped to go outside and began lighting his cigarette before getting all the way outside. As Rick turned from the window with his order and began moving toward the door, he waved toward the ladies and said, "You ladies have a good afternoon." Once Rick got outside, he saw Jerry over near what was the third car in the parking lot, smoking. Rick waved and said "Take care" to Jerry.

Jerry returned the wave and said, "Here, take this paper." He pulled it from his back pocket. "There is a big four-page article in this about him. I guessed they timed it with his twentieth-year high school reunion. He is missed, or maybe he is just missing."

CHAPTER 5

Again, working on memories and former habits, Rick got in the car and drove back toward the interstate. About halfway between Ray's and the expressway, he turned right on Ridge Road. He went about four and a half blocks east and parked to eat. There were some two- and three-story apartment buildings on his right and the Glen Park Golf Course across the street on his left. This was a public course as Rick remembered it, and he never played it. He spent a great deal of time running on the path outside the fence that surrounded the golf course. It was just under two and a half miles for one lap around the course. Rick wondered then how many hundreds of miles he had run around this golf course. Rick parked here out of habit because that was part of the routine of getting Ray's. He never ate it inside nor could he remember ever taking it home. Today, he parked his Toyota Sequoia here on Ridge Road to eat his lunch. The white fish was as he remembered; the chips or fries were only okay to his memory. The sauce was still great. The cream soda unearthed memories all by itself. While finishing up his meal, he found the page-two story about himself that the *Post-Tribune* had put in print this day. It had many recounted stats from his playing days in all sports, it had coaches who were directly and indirectly involved with him quoted, it had subjected accounts as to what had become of him, and it had the open-ended account of what might have happened on the evening of his parents' accidental death in their car. Some folks quoted on that speculated that the accident didn't seem right at the time and that they still worried about it today.

All in all, Rick found the story to be a wonderful account of someone that he used to be. Because when he left Gary twenty years prior, he left with arranged paperwork showing him as Michael Dixon. However, there was an aspect of the article that got him stuck on being Rick Smalls once again. That was the open questions about the death of his parents.

CHAPTER 6

Done eating, Rick—or it should be said, Michael—began his drive toward his old neighborhood. He really believed that he drove there blindfolded from where he was because he knew he made a U-turn on Ridge Road to go back west. He turned right on Grant Street to travel up to Twenty-First Avenue and then turned right on Taft Street. He would ride Taft Street up to Eighth Avenue to turn left and, one block later, turn right onto Taft Place. A few short blocks later and he knew he would be in the middle of the five hundred blocks of Taft Place and in front of his parents' home, where he grew up. He had no reason to believe that he couldn't identify the point that he and the guys had identified as the starting point of their forty-yard dash that finished at the pole that had the street light on it between his parents' home and Mrs. Campbell's home. He could drive there blindfolded. He didn't drive blindfolded but might have done just that. Because his mind was clearly somewhere else, he was not clearly looking at the road, as was evidenced by him drawing the horn of another vehicle that was travelling southbound when he was making his left turn onto Twenty-First Avenue from his northbound travel on Grant Street to go west. After getting through the light without incident, Michael turned right onto Garfield Street and pulled over. Why were people here still thinking about Rick Smalls the way that they were, and what was the truth about his parents' death?

Michael realized that earlier in the day, the thought of Ray's, riding through familiar neighborhoods, and passing his old high school would be pleasant. The thought of the accompanying nostalgia was completely gone now and replaced with a very empty feeling of wonder.

CHAPTER 7

Valerie arrived at the Chicago Hilton Towers just before two in the afternoon. Her Uber driver removed her luggage from the trunk of his car. She had gotten out of the car, tipped the driver, grabbed ahold of the handle on her suitcase, and placed the other bag on top of the suitcase up against the handle and maintained a hold on both the straps of the bag and the suitcase while not missing a word that was being said to her on the phone. She shook her head from side to side to the valet that was waiting nearby, indicating that she was okay. When she got to the counter to check in, she simply slid a business card to the clerk. Valerie was not looking to interrupt her phone call to check in to the hotel. The clerk understood this perfectly and held up a room key for Valerie to see and then raised one finger followed by a second finger. Valerie lifted one finger in response. As Valerie began to turn away from the counter with her room key and bags, the clerk spoke up to say that they had placed in her room the welcome package from the ISF along with the hotel's welcome package for their diamond members. Valerie nodded and slightly smiled as she turned again toward the elevators. Once on the elevator and after steadying her suitcase, Valerie pressed the number 29 for the top floor, where the larger suites were located. When the doors opened on 29, Valerie looked at the wall straight in front of her to get some bearings for which way to go now that she was off the elevator. She saw the plate indicating that rooms 2925 through 2950 was to the right. Valerie went right until she approached room 2948, which was her room.

Once Valerie was in the room, she left her bags, nearly fifteen feet, in the room up against a chair, and while still talking on the phone, she walked through her suite. She had entered into the first sitting area that had two chairs and a sofa with two end tables and a coffee table. Mounted on the wall, there was one television. To the right of the television was a door to a bathroom with a shower. About halfway across the room on her left was a sink with a countertop. On the countertop was a coffeepot with insertable coffee brews next to it. Cups were there along with glasses. Below the countertop portion was a refrigerator. Above the coffeepots and behind the cabinet was the minibar. Directly across the sink and countertop was the opening to the sleeping area. Valerie didn't go in there just yet. Instead, she continued across the room and toward the windows that looked out on Michigan Avenue. Grant Park was across the street. In that area of the room was a dining table that could seat four. Valerie then went into the bedroom area and sat on the bed. She checked the bed in that area while bouncing with her backside on the mattress three or four times. She was satisfied with the feel and got up and opened the closets and then went into the bedroom's bathroom. It was spacious and well laid out.

Now at the end of her tour or inspection of the room, she said to the person that she was talking with on the phone, "Nick has made a reservation for us outside of the hotel for dinner at seven tonight at Gibson's. I'll meet you in the lobby at six forty-five."

CHAPTER 8

From slightly after two that afternoon until six thirty that evening, Valerie was on the phone, unpacked some of her belongings, read and responded to emails, showered, unpacked some more, made more phone calls, answered more emails, readied herself some more, and looked at her keynote speech for tomorrow evening. Making one last assessment of her preparedness to leave the room, Valerie looked in the floor-length mirror on the bathroom door while still using the mirrors over the bathroom sink. The lighting was good, and Valerie was now stretching her mouth to know that her lipstick was properly placed. Valerie hadn't grown an inch since she was fifteen. The only height that she controlled was in her shoe choice. Barefoot, she was five five. Tonight, she would be five eight in public. Those three inches would come from her favorite Christian Louboutin Mandolina pumps tonight. Her dress was a simple black dress with a belt that carried to just below the knee. It was sleeveless with a round collar, which was perfect for the pearl beads that she wore this evening. She turned back and forth from the half mirrors above the sink and the full-length mirror on the door. Satisfied, she smiled at herself. She was ready to go. The dress fit well, but not too well. It was not her intention to give folks reasons to think of her as nothing other than a confident, strong woman first and foremost. She knew she was thirty-eight and appeared a bit younger. She worked hard to maintain that look. She worked hard at everything that she did, and it showed. Before turning off the light in the bathroom, she took one last look at herself, and the thought crossed her mind that she had gained less than ten pounds in the last twenty years. She smiled with that thought. By the time that she grabbed her purse and room key and made it to the inside portion of the door to room 2948, that smile had vanished. She thought of the lack of a family and quickly wondered if there ever would be one.

She headed down the hall to the elevators and pressed the button to go down. At this moment while her countenance was down, she simply wondered if he was going to come this weekend. And she smiled as she got on the elevator. Once on the lobby level and walking toward the lobby sitting area, she saw Dale Langford stood. After he stood, he headed in her direction. Dale extended his hand to shake hers and said, "How are you tonight, boss?"

"I'm fine. We've got a few things to review tonight for the contacts that we will be making here at the forum. Is the car out front? I didn't want to eat here because there will be many folks on the property that are here for the forum, and I want to guard against folks listening in our conversation. Imagine that? I am guarding against conversations being overheard at a security conference. Ironic, huh?"

"Your instincts are probably right, as they usually are. I have talked with others from our team, and they are prepared for their meetings as well," responded Dale. Dale nodded toward the exit doors and extended his left hand and arm to indicate to Valerie the direction to the car.

Dale had been a longtime employee of International Safety Services. In his current role of senior vice president of strategic implementation and operations, he was Valerie's number two. Valerie could remember seeing Dale with her father when he came home for the weekend from Washington, DC, to northwest Indiana on those fast weekends when she was a teen. His loyalty was, without question, to both International Safety Services and to Valerie. Dale had suffered an injury while on an overseas work assignment before Valerie joined the firm. She was told by her father after she joined the firm that related to his work, there was a steam explosion in a utility area that burned and scarred Dale. Dale was in the area because he was scouting a path for a future client's covert exit plan. The burns and scars had caused Dale to have limited use of his right hand through his shoulder. The burns and scarring showed publicly on the right side of his neck and face. While the right side of his face might cause someone to try to look away to avoid staring, it seemed that the logical turn to looking squarely on his left side was the normal default for someone's eyes. Dale had tended to assess that most folks either stayed with the scars or found a spot slightly above his hairline for a focus point when talking with him, except Valerie. She always looked him directly into both eyes.

As they headed toward the exit and then out of the main door to the left of the center revolving door, which Dale had opened for Valerie, Valerie flicked her glance to the right through the folks in line to go through the revolving door. She caught a glance of someone entering the main door to her right. She didn't see him, but she thought that she felt goose bumps.

CHAPTER 9

Earlier that afternoon around four fifteen, Ron arrived. The parking valet asked him before he got out of his car if he was a guest or if he was going to be checking in to the property. Ron told him he was about to check in. The valet told him that if he chose to park in the hotel's garage that the charge would be $45 per night. Ron tried not to show his expression that he thought that this charge was nuts; instead, he smiled and told the parking valet that that rate would be fine. Ron did accept the baggage handling service that was offered. The attendant grabbed a cart, and from Ron's car, he retrieved a garment bag and two other bags that Ron pointed to. The attendant then guided Ron toward one of the main doors and pushed the cart through the door. Ron approached the counter to check in and asked the clerk about the festivities for the ISF. He was told that there was a check-in on the mezzanine level and that he could get all his information there. He thanked her and found the elevators that she had told him about that would get him to his floor. Ron exited the elevator on the fourth floor and found his room 436 right along the wall away from the elevator. He gave no thought at this time about the traffic pattern of guests exiting and continuing in their late-night reveling once they exited the elevator.

Ron had no comparison to the rooms on the twenty-ninth floor to use as a reference, but he was having some difficulty understanding that this room with a queen bed and tight walking area between the foot of the bed and the dresser that had the television sitting on top of it could cost as much as it did on a nightly basis. The bathroom was tight also. He concluded, "Welcome to downtown Chicago to a sold-out hotel hosting several events over the next few days." While settling in, Ron was doing his best to stay mindful that this forum was the right place for him to be to make the next steps in his future. He wanted out of sneaking into homes or cars to plant devices and peeking over the top of newspapers or magazines for the purpose of gathering information. He wanted to get into the corporate world of security and surveillance. And this was the path. *Stop thinking about the expenses for the week. Spend where you got to spend. Buy drinks for who you need to buy drinks for and be available to talk to decision makers,* Ron mused. He had researched many of the companies that would have booths set up and knew the names and companies that were his ideal targets. He also had created his secondary and tertiary lists as well. He was focused to change his standing in life over the next few days and that he was not going to be denied. He washed his face and hands, sniffed his armpits through his shirt, accepted what he smelled, went back into his tight room and grabbed his sports coat off the back of a chair, snatched up his key card off the dresser, and headed toward the door.

Ron took the elevator two floors down to the mezzanine level, and there he searched the check-in booths for last names, beginning with the letter *W.* He found it off to his left where there was a setup for last names that began with the letters *T* through *Z.* While many of the items that were put into the bag that Ron was given at the check-in table were explained to him including the two free drinks at the mixer tonight, tomorrow night, and Wednesday night, he still found a chair that had a table near it to go through everything again. He was satisfied with what he inventoried, which included the location of the booths, the sessions that were available, the schedule of events, the keynote speech, and dinner for tomorrow night and the free drink passes. Feeling ready to remake his future, he headed into the direction of the Wrigley Ballroom, where tonight's mixer was being held and where he could cash in two free drink coupons.

After a couple of hours of mixing with no real success toward his future but with success of lightening him on his feet through the two free coupons and the self-purchase of other drinks, Ron was feeling really fatigued. He was operating on limited sleep. His current life still needed to be executed, and as a result of working his real job all night the previous night and only nodding off for a couple of hours earlier in the day, Ron was feeling the weight of the lack of sleep and fast consumption of alcohol. He left the Wrigley Ballroom and was looking for the elevators. He believed he was walking in the right direction while also looking at his phone to check for any texts and phone or email messages. He focused on the texts and reading and typing as he walked. As he was nearing the elevators, he found himself approaching the mezzanine rail that allowed a person to look down onto the lobby sitting and check-in areas. Still focusing on the text messages and his typing, when he glanced up, he saw a black man leaving the check-in area clerk and headed to the elevators. He lost his breath, his throat dried, and he had no impulse for any action. That glance of the profile of this tall black man then was obscured by plants, banners, and signs before he was covered by the wall where the bank of elevators were. Those were the same six elevators that Ron passed by here on the mezzanine level.

Finally, he was able to breathe and to have a throat that was washed in normal levels of salivation and the reflexive actions to have an impulse to react. The impulse turned into him yelling down to the lobby level at full blast, "Rick Smalls!" There was no response from the man that had now been hidden by the walls that housed the elevators. There was a response to the volume of his yell from folks near him on the mezzanine level and in the lobby check-in and sitting areas. All were looking toward the source of the outdoor yell in the midst of this beautiful indoor setting. Ron didn't realize how loud he was, and his next instinct was to look at the elevators. He quickly realized that the odds could be against him for him to be able to stop the elevator that this man was about to get on, so he turned to the winding stairs and took them as fast as his fatigued, alcohol-filtered body could take two steps at a time. When he got to the bottom, the person that he saw was not there. He turned and went over to check-in and pushed past folks and practically yelled at the clerk, "What room is Rick Smalls in?"

The clerk was caught off guard and, not wanting to embarrass Ron in front of the other folks, asked him if he could step off to the side. The assistant manager saw this unfold and told the clerk that he would attend to this guest's needs. "How can I help you, sir?"

"Rick Smalls, Rick Smalls just checked in. What room is he in?"

"Sir, I'm sorry, I can't share a guest's room number with you. I can call the guest's room and connect you on the phone over there." The assistant manager pointed toward some phones down the corridor. "Can you tell me again the name of the guest that you are looking to speak with?"

"Rick Smalls, his name is Rick Smalls."

"Let me check for you. I'm sorry, I am not finding any guest by that name."

"He just left here. She must have not put him in the system yet."

"Sir, whether he just checked in or if he was scheduled to check in, I would show his name if he were a current or future guest for the property tonight or over the next week or so. I'm sorry."

Ron just mumbled a thank-you and turned and walked toward the elevators. That was the most excited he had been about anything in years, and it was over so quickly. He decided he would go back to his room and regroup for a while.

CHAPTER 10

Michael thought as he settled into his standard suite room on the twenty-fifth floor, a room that was larger than Ron's but smaller than Valerie's. His thought on the oddity of hearing the name Rick Smalls in Gary and now in this downtown Chicago hotel was outside the normal probability. He knew that if he wanted to be precise, how probable it was to hear the name in Gary, to see a four-page, well-researched article in a Gary newspaper, and then—the kicker—hearing the name called in this hotel that he could figure it out. It was part of his great education from MIT that allowed him to think through these things. Hearing the name directly in Gary was one thing that was low in likelihood. If he overheard someone using it, that would be another level of likelihood. But to hear it directly, in the newspaper article and now here, that's very improbable for one day since he had not heard it from another source for seventeen years. He hadn't told his friend in Boston of the name change, and he made certain to stay off the paths where he and his classmates would be together when he was meeting his friend. She still called him Rick then because she didn't know any difference.

He sat on his couch and actually gave thought to doing the calculation on the probability of these events in a single day. Instead, he got up and went over to his backpack and removed a bottled water and drank down about six ounces. That felt good. So he swallowed about another six ounces. He sat back down and began to think about the article in the newspaper again and thought about why there would be questions about an accident that caused his parents' deaths. He tried to think about how he would ask questions without giving up his real identity. He knew he needed to do some preparation for his side meetings for tomorrow. After all, that was why he was here. He was an independent contractor with an expertise that the companies that were in town would pay handsomely to get a part of for their futures. He knew this, and he needed to be prepared. He thought about preparation and also the death of his parents. Again, he went to his backpack. This time he pulled out four laptops, one of which needed to be removed from a cotton bag. He set them all in front of him. The first three to his left were all related to the forum and the contacts that he needed to work with over the next few days. The fourth laptop to his far right was what he called his burner laptop. It was used when he needed to go places so that no one could know that he was in a particular place on the internet or private servers. The MIT education was not only beneficial in the workplace, but it also proved to be resourceful in other places as well.

He stared at the four laptops, and then he decided. He picked up the first and third laptops on his left and stacked them on the laptop second from his left. He carried them back over to the backpack and restored them. He then removed from a side compartment a small black bag. The bag was cinched closed with a drawstring. He loosened the drawstring and pulled out a pack of roll-on fingertips. He applied one to all his fingers and thumbs. He then wiped down the fourth laptop from touching it when he removed it from the cotton bag, and then he logged on. This was his burner laptop that went to places that he needed to keep secret, and he did everything that he could to stay separate of being connected to this laptop. Rapidly he inputted commands, and just as rapidly, he would stop to read the displays. Then he would put more commands in and then read some more. He did this for nearly three hours and stopped. He logged off, wiped down the laptop, returned it to the cotton bag within the backpack, and removed the fingertips. He didn't unpack the other laptops again. He sat down again. After a few minutes, he got off the couch, went over to the backpack, zipped it up, and grabbed it. He checked his pocket for the key card and took the stairs down twenty-five flights to the first floor. He chose to exit the property from one of the side doors and, without hesitation or specific direction, immediately turned left and began walking at a pace that a six foot two, two-hundred-and-twenty-pound mental and physical machine could move at without being noticed.

Chapter 11

"Dale, I will see you in the morning. Tomorrow is a big day. Quite a bit of our future plans depends upon how aware we are over the next few days. Our competitors today are not a threat to us. However, if they were to get the program that we believe is being marketed to select companies here over the course of the forum, then the competitive advantage and future success could be changed."

Dale listened to Valerie carefully, knowing that she was right and that it was another one of his responsibilities to know if the developer of that program truly was going to be searching out companies to sell this program to while the forum was going on. "Valerie, I have many folks from our teams scouting out the forum, the booths, the hallways, and the side rooms to be aware of the potential for small, discreet gatherings around the events here. I have also brought in a few outside contractors to support us if we need to expand to the floors where the guests' rooms are located," Dale responded to Valerie.

Valerie and Dale have reached the bank of elevators back in the hotel now, and this brief conversation was drawing to an end. It only began when they got out of the car. "When you say contractors, are you suggesting anything that I would not authorize, Dale?"

"Valerie, I am preparing the best that I know how to keep the future of International Safety Services protected."

"You didn't answer the question. Good night." Valerie boarded the elevator and left Dale standing outside looking in, and then she pressed the bottom to go to the twenty-ninth floor and turned away from looking at Dale directly in his eyes.

Chapter 12

The call had to be made. There was death. There were taxes. And there was the absolute need to make this call with any potential information regarding Rick Smalls no matter the thinness of the thread that might be attached to Rick Smalls or the course thickness of a rope that could be used to bind him. The phone was answered on one ring. The receiver of this call responded with the word *yes*. Never had the caller known an entire speech of words to carry the weight, power, force, and seriousness of this single word from the receiver of the call. Much of the weight, power, force, and seriousness was even felt when it was known to the caller that the call had to be made. All those things became weightier, more powerful and forceful, and more serious as the number was being dialed. So at the moment when the voice on the other end said yes, the caller had every intention to deliver the message that led to the call, but nothing came out. Then the pressure to breath felt like an elephant putting a foot on one's chest while they were lying down. That's because the voice said yes again. With every effort to remove the elephant from bearing down any further, the caller's body squeezed out the words "I think I saw Rick Smalls tonight."

The caller did not want to feel the weight, power, force, or seriousness from the sound of the Voice anymore, so the caller rushed into telling the Voice the conditions of the evening that planted the notion that Rick Smalls was seen. Once the caller was done speaking, the Voice spoke again by simply but reverently saying, "Thanks. I'll be in touch." With that, the Voice hung up the phone.

CHAPTER 13

The receiver of the call name was not the Voice. It was what the receiver of the call had become known by in certain circles. Those circles would be made up by arcs of the following: people who had had this voice speak to them over a phone, people in a group who would be hearing this voice through a speaker, or people who had had this voice come from behind them in a very close setting. There were some people who had heard the Voice in none of the aforementioned settings; instead, they had seen the face that went with the voice at the same time that they heard the Voice. To these people, that did not make the Voice any less in weight, power, force, or seriousness. The Voice got calls twenty-four hours per day on all types of matters that normal folks would not know where to begin to comprehend, process, and then provide solutions to the matters that were presented. There had been many calls that the Voice had received that left the Voice to wonder throughout a night. The Voice slept, but it seemed as if the Voice did not need sleep. After receiving this call, the Voice did not sleep. The Voice felt excitement and apprehension, stimulation and a dulling of the senses, gratitude for knowing, and fear about where and when this sighting took place.

Now about four hours after the Voice received the call, it was decided what needed to be done. There was a need to bring Rick Smalls back to life in the eyes of the Voice. The available information trail all ended fifteen years ago in Beirut, which was after Paris, which was after Cairo, and which was after London and Brussels. And fifteen years ago, the Voice was not seeing Rick Smalls as Rick Smalls. He was under another name by the time that their contact had broken off in Beirut. The Voice made his call now. The retriever of this call was a lady that gave no indication one way or another if she was in the same time zone as the Voice or if it would even matter. The call was answered by Jill Estridge after one ring. Jill had this phone to be available to one potential caller. So her greeting was not so much a greeting when she answered the phone; instead, it was more of an acknowledgment that she was prepared to serve the needs of her boss, the caller, the Voice. While it was 4:00 a.m. EST where the Voice was making the call from, the Voice's call was answered with the alertness of someone in a place where it might be normal business hours. The Voice didn't think about that at all because it was not a concern where Jill was at any given time. It only mattered that Jill could do what was required. "How can I help you?" greeted Jill.

"Open the file on Rick Smalls, a.k.a. Darrell Hunt. The last verified sighting was in Beirut fifteen years ago. Possible sighting in downtown Chicago earlier tonight at the Chicago Hilton Towers. Find him if he is there. Report back to me only on this one. Check the—"

"Excuse my rudeness for cutting you off. I know how to do what you pay me to do. I get a feeling on the urgency on this, and you will get my best effort. Is there anything else?"

"Report only to me," the Voice repeated.

"Understood." Jill hung up.

Sleep would wait for the Voice. The Voice made another call. "How soon before my plane could be ready to go?" The next thing the Voice said was "Chicago," and he hung up. The Voice headed toward the front door of the estate that he lived in to leave via automobile for his private plane not far away.

CHAPTER 14

After leaving Dale standing in the lobby outside of the elevator, Valerie had much to do and many folks to talk to. She also hadn't forgotten that odd feeling that she had when she was leaving the hotel for dinner with Dale earlier in the evening. Somewhere in her peripheral vision, something alerted her, and she was unusually stuck on it. She thought about it or tried to grasp it as she entered her hotel room, while she tossed her purse onto the chair closest to the door, and even while she sat to remove her shoes. As she stood to head toward the bathroom in the bedroom area and reached around to the back of her dress to unzip, she stopped in front of her suitcase that was not completely unpacked and pulled out a shirt to sleep in. After the zipper was undone, she let the dress fall to the floor and immediately slid the shirt over her head. The shirt came down to the middle of her thighs. The shirt by the retailer probably was not thought to be a sleeping shirt. Nevertheless, that didn't stop Valerie from using it for that purpose exclusively. When she saw it in the Logan Airport in Boston earlier this year, it triggered a singular thought, and she knew that she wanted it; and she knew she wanted it only for the closeness and privacy of her restful periods, which would allow for any intimate thoughts to come to mind. It was a shirt that advertised MIT.

Before heading off to bed, she had work and calls to make. One call stood out as one that she knew she wasn't ready for, but it needed to be made. The sooner the better. She made her call. It wasn't a long call, but it needed to be made. The man on the other end didn't look to have this conversation to go on much longer. So the call came to a quick end. With this done, Valerie sat on the couch and closed her eyes with her arms folded over her chest, as if they were the arms of the MIT shirt holding her, and wished for sleep.

CHAPTER 15

He sat in his tight room, saying the name over and over again to himself and out loud, "Rick, Rick Smalls, Rick Smalls, Rick Smalls, Rick." He moved on from the mumbling and cadence calling of Rick's name to asking questions to himself silently and out loud, "Was that really him? Could that have really been him? Why would he be here? Was that really him?" over and over again until he realized that he had to call him. The call couldn't be delayed any longer. He didn't want to make the call. He paused and eased his face into his hands and closed his eyes to get the confidence to make the call. He knew that a lot of things would get shaken up by making this call. Yet the call had to be made.

He made the call. It was short. It was over. And he was shaken in the moment and very concerned with what was going to happen next.

CHAPTER 16

Michael was on alert from the moment before he started typing on the burner laptop because of the potential trapdoors that he could have triggered in his various searches. His alertness level raised as he was about to leave the hotel room. He pushed through, and he knew that once he left this room, he needed to be on hyperalert. There had been times that he felt the need to go to this self-described level of alertness. It just hadn't been called on as much since the times that he spent overseas in Paris, London, Cairo, Brussels, and especially Beirut. As Michael descended the stairs, he thought about Beirut and then kicked it out of his mind because of the need to be alert for the moment. In times of what would be described as a normal alert level, Michael would have earbuds in and listened to music when he was about to walk a mile. That walk would take him fifteen minutes. It's not in a hurry, and it was not slow. It wouldn't grab attention. Tonight, he knew that he would probably cover two and a half miles to go the targeted one mile away. After all, he was on hyperalert now. He didn't know who could have been triggered by his hacking or if they were already in pursuit. He knew whom he did not want to run across tonight or anytime soon. Some he would know if he saw them. One he would know by only his voice. He had no desire to hear that voice again. He last heard it in Beirut. That was the last time that he was Darrell Hunt also. Since leaving high school and that night in Beirut, he had gone from Rick Smalls to Darrell Hunt with no fewer than seven other names in between. It was his life. While he knew he went to MIT to prepare for his professional life, it was prior to getting into MIT that a path for his career was really launched.

Most high-achieving or achieving kids in high school could recite to anyone willing to listen to them that they were going to this or that university upon completing high school to major in this or that and, once they graduated, that they would either go into grad school at this or that university or that they would go and get some real world experience for two or three years and then go to grad school. They would go on to tell you that upon completion of grad school, they would be working at this firm or that corporation or in this field of medicine or they would be the head of their own business. As a high schooler, Rick Smalls didn't speak in those terms. Through some folks that he met during a college open house at his high school in the spring of his junior year in the small booth setup showing the Massachusetts Institute of Technology was how he formed his future plans. He was walking around from booth to booth with stops in between, enjoying the time with Valerie Benson. Unless he was on a track oval, baseball diamond, basketball court, or football field, it was a good chance that he would be with Valerie. They were inseparable. They simply were. They enjoyed each other, and the only reason that Valerie was there tonight was because Rick hadn't finalized his college plans, like she had. Her mother and father both had completed their undergraduate studies at Harvard, and it was known that their only child would be attending Harvard from the time that she was conceived. She would get to study or take classes in a building that had her last name on it at Harvard after all.

So while the principal of Bishop Noll and the counselors from the school were in their element in talking with the many college recruiters that night, they did find themselves trying to compete with one another in trying to be the one who helped to guide Rick Smalls to a particular university that was represented there tonight. This type of event didn't normally have the support of the high school athletic department, but tonight all the varsity coaches were out as well. Equally unusual was that the universities represented tonight also had folks from their athletic programs on-site as well. Normally, this was not a part of this open house. But from the high school principal, counselors, and coaches who thought that a professional step could be made in their careers if they were linked to getting Rick Smalls to a particular university, it was the same from the represented universities that Rick Smalls was both an academic and athletic winner. He scored perfect scores on both the SAT and ACT as a high school freshman! He was going to enter whatever university he chose with most of the general studies classes or credits already completed. He began college work as a second-semester high school freshman. He could have tested out of high school and went then. Some thought he should have. Some thought he stayed in high school because of the sports. Some thought he was ready for college basketball as a high school sophomore. Some thought he stayed in high school because of the attention from many folks. A very few had pegged it close to accurately. He stayed in high school because of the time it gave him to be with and around Valerie Benson.

He knew on that night as he thought of his future that he could get into and excel at Harvard, but he also knew that he needed to be where he needed to be. So while he and Valerie toyed with the different universities when they approached their booths or played with the principal, the counselors, or coaches and told them that he was leaning toward a university favorable to them, they both seemed to notice the low crowd and lack of push by anyone toward the booth near the baseline of a corner that Rick had made a number of three-point shots from. All the booths were set up over the basketball court. The bleachers had been pushed back from the extended spot that they would be in during a jam-packed game that many had come to see Rick lead the team to another victory. "Let's go over there," Valerie said, pointing toward the low-crowd area around the MIT booth.

Rick shrugged his shoulders and said, "Okay."

There was not a lot of attention paid to the fact that Rick had gone over there initially. It was only after five minutes had turned into fifteen minutes and then fifteen minutes had turned into thirty minutes that principals, counselors, coaches, and other university personnel started to pay some level of attention to the fact that Rick has spent more time in that one spot than probably ten other spots combined. Indiana University didn't get this time nor did the University of Michigan, Stanford, or any of the Ivy league schools. Time suddenly stood still for all the watchers of Rick as a representative from MIT came from behind the table of the booth and motioned for Rick to walk with him. Rick didn't know it, but with that walk, who he was as Michael Dixon was being formed at this very moment. The MIT recruiter guided Rick away from all the booths in the gymnasium and toward a door that would lead to the surge area outside the gym. It was this area where on many nights folks pushed in to get to what would be a standing room-only gym to watch Rick and his teammates play. Once they got outside that area and after having left Valerie inside, Rick was told some things that caused him to think differently than he had ever thought before. Some thoughts were education based. Others were on family. Other thoughts were on career, his future, and financial capabilities; and surprising to Rick, the one area that spoke to him the most was lastly spoken to him by this MIT recruiter: country. He thought about country like he had never done before as a result of the words spoken to him by this recruiter.

As Rick was wrapping up his walk to determine if he was being surveilled on this night, he was left to think about country again in a way that he never thought of it before but different from that night toward the end of his junior year of high school.

CHAPTER 17

As Michael approached his destination on Division Street, he scanned the surrounding areas. Traffic was lighter, but still at ten o'clock at night, traffic was still around. Division Street was a busy east and west boulevard. Years ago, this was not the place or area to be at this time of the night. Two blocks farther west from where Michael stood right now was the original Cooley High School. This was the same Cooley High School that was a title of a move from the midseventies. That school was torn down as gentrification or the financial exploitation of the previous community residents moved through the area. Just one block farther west on the south side of Division Street once stood the Cabrini Green Apartment Complex. When they were originally constructed, they might have been considered an apartment complex due to the original nature of the idea of constructing thirteen buildings, all twenty stories, with as many as forty apartments on each floor. This was the television home for the show *Good Times*, also from the midseventies. Michael knew a little about these apartments as well but not from firsthand memories. His parents were living in one of those one-bedroom, one-bath, three-hundred-square-feet complex apartments. He was told later in his life that these complex apartments had some units that had two bedrooms and some even three bedrooms. But what he was able to learn later when it meant something to him was that the larger units barely exceeded five hundred square feet. He later estimated that the twenty floors of forty apartments would probably house as many as

3,200 to 3,500 people, and for the total of thirteen buildings, this put the potential of 41,000 people in a footprint that he later would learn would be the footprint of one hundred suburban homes.

The Cabrini Green Apartment Complex was later simply called the projects. Leading toward their demolition and the other projects around Chicago was the death of a twelve-year-old kid. He wasn't the first kid killed there. He was one of probably thousands. No, he was the one who was killed by a bullet to the back of his head on the roof of one of the buildings in September of 1994. After suffering the indignity of being killed execution style by a thirteen-year-old kid who was trying to show he deserved to be in a gang, his dead body was thrown off the roof of one of the thirteen twenty-story buildings. This building, like the other twelve, was dilapidated, nearly vacant, and used for drug selling and drug use and for the purpose of the insanity of earning gang membership at this point. The national attention behind that dreadful loss of life led to the decision to demolish all the projects around Chicago.

Where Michael was eyeing to enter tonight was a local favorite sandwich shop. It stayed open late. It stayed open late in the height of the Cabrini Green Projects, and it remained here today, tucked away practically underneath the elevated train track. Michael went there as a kid often. When his family moved out of the Cabrini Green Projects, they moved over on Mohawk a couple of blocks farther west and a few blocks north on Mohawk. Even after his parents moved them to Gary, he would still come over this way because his father's parents lived a few blocks north of here on Sedgewick. They are long deceased now, and their passing occurred before the gentrification that could have affected them greatly. Even with his grandfather owning multiple properties with multiple rental units in the area, he was being hit by phase one of gentrification raising the tax base. This was done to force the property owners to raise the rent on the current dwellers or to sell the property. In most cases, the current dwellers didn't have the financial wherewithal to absorb higher rents.

So when Michael set the sandwich shop meeting, he knew it would bring back memories. He was comfortable with determining that he did not see surveillance that either he or the person that he was meeting attracted, so he went into Sammie's. He went in and ordered a Polish sausage with fries and a large Coke. His memory was that the Polish with grilled onions, mustard, and sport peppers would be really good. He also expected to receive enough fries with the sandwich to feed a family of three, which it did many times with him and his parents. He got what he expected and took a table toward the back of Sammie's, near the rear door. He saw his contact across the aisle from him at a table with two seats. Her back was to him, and her backpack was in the seat opposite of her. She was Tammy. Tammy Spears. She was a contact that Michael had developed over the years for his needs in Chicago when he didn't have the communication and electronic equipment with him upon his arrival into town or firearms and ammunition. She also supported logistics similar to other folks that Michael had developed in other cities around the country and abroad. She was one of the first contacts that Michael had made earlier in the night on his burner laptop.

Tammy only had a pop in front of her. In Chicago, soda was pop. Tammy got up and grabbed her backpack and started for the backdoor. As she headed toward the backdoor, her body swayed as she tried to settle her backpack on her back. During the swaying, she dropped a napkin on Michael's table and then exited. Michael looked up to make sure no one was watching him, and then he looked outside the windows of Sammie's to see if there was any action around Tammy. No one was watching him, and no one appeared to be paying any attention to Tammy. So he looked at the napkin. There was a note on the napkin instructing Michael to head two blocks back east on Division Street to Wells Street. He would then go north on Wells to meet Tammy in fifteen minutes. Michael ate a bit more of the sandwich and fries and drank some of the Coke. He readied himself to exit the same way that Tammy had and travel over to Wells Street. As he began to go north on Wells, he saw Tammy in front of an all-night tattoo shop. He walked up next to her, and they both were looking in through the window like they had some interest in what was going on inside.

For the next three minutes, they talked back and forth while looking in the window, and during the conversation, Tammy eased her backpack off and laid it at Michael's feet. Shortly after that, she told Michael that she was going to hug him. He knew why. When she hugged him, she appeared to be aggressively grabbing Michael's butt. In reality, she slid a car key into his back pant pocket. As they stopped the hug, she told him a location for the car in the multilevel parking garage across the street. Michael told her that he had already forwarded the agreed amount to her designated account, and she said that she knew that. Michael bent over to grab the backpack, and now he had two of them with him. As he began to stand upright after picking up the backpack, Tammy sort of swiped his left arm with the back of her right hand. With that movement, Michael looked at her squarely in the eyes. Tammy said to him, "Be careful, Michael. I don't feel right about this one."

"I will, and thanks. I'll call you soon." And with that, Michael crossed the street toward the parking garage in the middle of Wells Street.

CHAPTER 18

Michael didn't have a problem locating the black Toyota 4Runner. He liked his Toyotas. He liked seating above normal traffic, and he liked the ability to blend in because they were the most popular brand of vehicle on the roads here in the United States. He put his original bag in the footwell of the front passenger seat. The backpack from Tammy he sat on the front passenger seat. He had no reason to think that everything that he asked for wasn't in the backpack. He was looking for the one thing that he wanted before taking any more steps, and he found it inside the main compartment of the backpack in a zipped-up compartment. It was the 9mm handgun that could hold a clip for sixteen bullets with the seventeenth being the bullet in the chamber. He removed the clip while holding the gun low and looking around his surroundings through the windows and the mirrors. He looked at the clip. It showed that it was full, and then he popped the loaded bullet out to check the mechanics of the handgun. This was his handgun of choice now, as it was in London, Paris, Brussels, Cairo, and most fortunately in Beirut.

Comfortable with the mechanics of the weapon, he put every-thing back in place and only to look in the backpack for more clips. He saw all that he requested. He looked in the back seat and saw the jacket that he requested. It was needed for the night air even though the temperature dropped to a nice sixty-six degrees. The jacket would allow him to carry the handgun concealed. He grabbed it and maneuvered in the driver seat to put it on. In the right pocket of the jacket was a sleeve that held a key card. Printed on the sleeve was the name and location of the hotel. Michael might still go back to the hotel that he left earlier this night, but for tonight, he needed another hotel. He could call his contacts tomorrow and reschedule the meetings to another time at the hotel where the forum was being held, or he could even guide them to another location away from that hotel. They wanted him and what he could provide for them, and they would adjust. Michael knew this and would use it to his advantage if necessary.

Michael started the 4Runner, checked his mirrors, and put the car in reverse and headed for the Embassy Suites Hotel on State Street a number of blocks north of the other hotel. The indoor parking facility door opened as he pulled into the lane. At the bottom of the ramp, an attendant stood there waiting for him. Michael was asked if he was a guest of the hotel, and he said that he was. He was asked what room was he in and had looked back at the sleeve and told him that he was in room 1014. The attendant pointed in the direction of the elevator, gave Michael a claim stub, and asked him to call down before he headed down for the car so that he could have it ready for him. Michael said, "Thanks."

CHAPTER 19

After last night, six in the morning came fast, it seemed. Ron didn't sleep well, but he did sleep. He wondered as soon as he gained consciousness if he really did see Rick Smalls last night. As he wondered about this, he saw on the edge of the dresser near his room key card the tickets for the free drinks for today and tomorrow. He decided then that today was not going to be inconclusive because of the possibility of alcohol. He would take them with him. If a prospective employer or employer representative wanted a drink, he would use the coupon for that cause. Other than that, the coupons had no purpose in his employment search or the potential identification of his long-unseen friend, Rick Smalls. Ron decided that it was time to get this important day started.

CHAPTER 20

Her cell phone ringing at 6:00 a.m. was not unusual. She dealt in things around the globe, and she was prepared for the need to speak to someone at what was convenient to them regardless of the time of day. This call was different from the moment that the ring started. It was the only incoming call that was set to a different ringtone. With the sound of the ring, she swung her feet to the floor and grabbed the phone, and before answering, she practiced her voice with a few mi, mi, mis. Now settled as best as she could for the moment, she answered the phone. Valerie said, "Good morning, how are you doing?" She listened and then said, "Okay, I will see you then."

Valerie's call was already disconnected. There was no time to shower and dress, so she grabbed a facecloth and washed her face and then put on the guest robe from the closet. She cinched it close, and by then there was a knock at the door. She went and opened the door without looking through the keyhole. "Hi, Dad, why are you here? I mean, when did you get in?"

"Good morning, sweetie, I just got in. I thought I would come to support you and International Safety Services in any way that I could. Besides, I am very proud of you, and I wouldn't miss your speech tonight for anything."

CHAPTER 21

No alarm was ever set. If Michael was in a continental United States time zone, he awoke at 4:30 a.m. Eastern time. This morning, that was no different except by local time, it was 3:30 a.m. So at 6:00 a.m., Michael had already been up for two and a half hours. He had accomplished plenty already. His body and mind were in overdrive yet under control. He hit the treadmill for forty minutes at an ending average speed of six minute miles. He has laid out, inventoried, and repacked most of what Tammy sent to him. Part of the contents from Tammy were three more burner laptops. He had scorched the keyboard on one of them to identify many of his objectives for the day. He had used the three business laptops to reschedule meetings into the evening and early night. He suggested that all the meetings for other venues away from the Hilton where the forum was being held. Two of those meetings were accepted for the off-site locations. The third was met with some resistance, and Michael acquiesced to a meeting within the Hilton for that contact. He had sent the messages to each of them shortly after getting in his room from the parking garage. By the time that he had finished his run, he saw that he had the two acceptances, and then the third required a couple more emails to settle. He knew he was dealing with some Type A personalities that didn't sleep much neither. At 6:05 a.m., he called down to the garage to have his 4Runner ready. When he arrived down there at 6:15 a.m., the car was ready. He tipped the valet and drove out of the Embassy Suites parking garage.

CHAPTER 22

Howard Benson Jr. moved into his daughter's room and reached out toward both her elbows, gently gripped them, and pulled his daughter in for a hug. He also kissed her on her right cheek. She, in turn, kissed him on his right cheek. As they separated, Valerie looked at her father, as she always had, with a look of marvel. Here he stood in his early sixties, retired from the business that she took over five years ago, looking as fit as ever, and here at six in the morning bright-eyed and bushy-tailed after some early morning travel. He stood every bit of six three even to this date. As a young adult, Valerie would wish that she had got a bit more of that versus the five-foot-two stature of her mom. She was glad that she had passed her mother's height. Her mother had been deceased now for six years, and it was in the year after her passing that her father stepped away from the business to allow her to lead it. He told her then and he maintained today that he would always be there for her if and when she wanted to talk about any aspect of it. Well, she didn't ask for his presence at this time, and yet he was there to watch her keynote speech. She wondered if her father maintained contact with some of the long-term leaderships for something other than card games, golf, and private investments. She wondered if he knew of the program grab that she had in mind as she and her team were at the forum. Quickly her mind turned to think that it was good to see her dad, and boy did he always looked extremely fit. She didn't even know what he did to maintain his physique. She simply acknowledged that whatever it was, it worked.

"Do you mind if I sit out here while you prepare for your day, sweetie?"

"Not at all, Dad. Have you had breakfast? If not, do you want room service? I can call for something. They will be delivering me toast, eggs, and grapefruit at seven along with coffee and juice. I can add something for you if you like."

"That sounds good. Just get me the same as you ordered. Thanks. Make the order and then go on and get ready, and we can discuss your day over breakfast. Also, if you want an audience to practice your speech on, then you can practice on me. I will be an attentive audience for you."

"Dad, now that you are here, there are some things that I could cover with you for your thoughts on. I won't bore you with the speech. It's not a canned speech, but it has the usual warnings about how the industry needs to prepare for our next security challenges. You may or may not be surprised by how many folks in our line of work still won't take what the Russians accomplished on our 2016 elections as truth because of their politics. Dad, you were right. In business, leave your politics at the door."

"So you were listening to me," he said, lightly laughing.

CHAPTER 23

This Hilton Hotel was very large. To accommodate the needs of their guests and convention goers and others, they had many in-house restaurants. Ron thought that by getting down before seven thirty this morning, he might beat the rush in the restaurants so that he could have a quiet breakfast. Seven thirty should have been seven. It's not that he had to wait for a table. Instead, the restaurant that he chose was probably at seventy percent capacity already with a wait staff to support fifty percent capacity. Ron still ordered something not quite on the menu that they said that they could do. He wanted an omelet with salmon, cream cheese, spinach, tomatoes, and capers. He asked for sourdough toast, two strips of bacon, water, and coffee. While waiting on his food, he searched his phone for the contact that he was looking for and hit dial. "Morning, Sarge, how you doing? Long time, how are you doing? Still haven't found any rookies that you liked as much as me?"

Sarge was Sergeant William Reece, now a thirty-year veteran with the Gary Police Department. He no longer had responsibilities of breaking in the rookies, like he did sixteen years ago. But he would acknowledge to everyone other than Ron that he liked Ron more than the others. "Why are you calling me? Are you looking to go through the academy again so that you can drive me even crazier than you did those many years ago? You do know that it is early, or are you about to go to bed after staying up all night peeking on some innocent woman who needs the touch of a man, and she can't help it

DERRICK L. SMITH

that her husband is out of town, so she thought it might be okay to replace him with the kid's math teacher?" Sarge responded.

"Can't I just miss you and reach out to you, Sarge?"

"You could, but you don't unless you want something. So what is it, Rook?"

"I thought I saw somebody last night."

"Was this through high-powered binoculars or a keyhole?"

"Nah, it wasn't like that. I'm downtown Chicago for a convention. And while I was up on the mezzanine level, I saw someone down on the lobby level heading toward the elevators that looked a lot like Rick. Rick Smalls."

"You been reading the *Post-Tribune* online again?"

"Not lately, why?"

"I thought maybe your thoughts would have been clouded by this big spread that they had on him just yesterday. It covered everything, almost from his first poop to after his parents died. The story writers' opening stated that the disappearance of Rick was timely to right about since no one from the area had seen him since he graduated twenty years ago. It also noted that those same rich kids that he went to high school with were having their twentieth reunion this weekend there in downtown Chicago at one of those Hilton Hotels."

"Which one? I'm at one right now for this conference. Maybe that was him that I saw last night."

"Hey, Rook, I got to get going here. You can check the article from the paper. It said which hotel the reunion was going to be at. Did you call me to interrupt my morning walk before I go to work, or did you want something?"

"Yeah, I do. Sorry. Do you have Bobby Ashipa's number?"

Sarge told him that he would forward to him the contact information for Bobby, and they wished each other well and promised to talk again soon.

58

CHAPTER 24

"Are you sure that you have the right inside and outside operatives in place to catch the potential meetings timely? It's one thing to catch the meeting between the parties. It's a totally different thing to stop a merger or buy from happening. I think you are right that there are only three to five players besides you that could meet the potential cost of this program. I think that the noise that you have been hearing is credible. I think that this forum would be ideal for the Programmer to surface and to meet with folks. But what you don't know is still a lot. You don't know how many people are here representing the Programmer. You don't know if they all are moving and involved in the same meetings altogether or if they are dividing up negotiating responsibilities to conduct multiple meetings at once. You don't know what they look like. You can go crashing meetings and actually be interrupting interviews for new executives. How are you going to beat all of that?" Howard Benson Jr. asked his daughter over what would be his last of three cups of coffee.

"Dad, you make some good points. I didn't mention that with three of those identified companies, I have some highly placed people in place that could give us a lead on the potential conversations. I wasn't a big fan of the thought of Dale bringing in some outside contractors to be ready to hit guests' rooms here in the hotel. But after sleeping on it, I believe that your old friend was right for preparing with that move. Dale has been great for a long time now. I hope he never retires. He will be waiting in the lobby for me about thirty minutes from now."

"Sweetie, Dale has always proven to be solid. Just remember to keep him focused by letting him know the importance of his role within the company. If you do that, then Dale will take a bullet for you or do anything else that you need done. Where is he now?"

"I am. Excuse me, I got to take this." Valerie's phone vibrated, and she recognized the number. As she said this to her dad, she stood and wandered back into the bedroom area of the suite.

As she left the living area of the suite, her dad stood and looked into a mirror to adjust the perfectly placed knot on his tie. He really didn't adjust the knot. He merely acknowledged that he needed to be certain to be on his game today. There was plenty at stake. Then his phone vibrated. "Yes?" After a bit of information was conveyed to him, he said, "How long ago?" He followed this up with, "Keep me posted." He then hung up as Valerie came into the room.

Valerie held no prestige over her dad to ask about his calls. He had plenty of interest that were not related to her and the business that he used to run. "Dad, that was one of my contacts on the inside. His boss has rescheduled a meeting to an off-site location for the early evening. This might be one of the Programmer's meetings. I will call Dale and advise him."

"Sweetie, don't call Dale yet. You can tell him in person in a few minutes. Can I join you with your meeting? I don't want to be in the way; but it would be good to see Dale again."

"No problem. Thanks for being here, Dad. Your insight is invaluable. I love you."

"I love you too, sweetie."

CHAPTER 25

Michael knew that even at six fifteen in the morning, Chicago travel would begin to suck anytime soon regardless of the direction of travel or even weather conditions being somewhat normal. For his destination this morning, he had three potential paths to travel. He could get over to Lake Shore Drive and head south there on US Route 12, or he could get on Interstate 90/94 east. If he chose Interstate 90/94 east, then he would need to choose either Interstate 90 or Interstate 94 along the way. Of the three potential paths, US 12 would wind up with many local roads and lights. Taking Interstate 90 was by far the fastest path with normal conditions. Michael chose Interstate 94. The second fastest route in normal conditions. Interstate 90 is a toll road. This led to people at booths or more concerning cameras. Michael moved his meetings to later in the day so that he could make this forty-minute drive over to Gary. He was intrigued by the words from Jerry at Ray's, the *Post-Tribune* article, his research, and the report that he had waiting for him this morning from the additional research that Tammy threw in for him. Even on that note, she asked him to be careful.

Michael knew that he would stop before getting over to Gary. Tammy was thorough. He requested some items to alter his appearance. He knew if he was going over to Gary to snoop around, he needed to change some things about his appearance. One, because he never knew who might be asking questions behind him, and he wanted to distort the descriptions that someone could give, and two, he didn't want to be recognized or questioned by someone wanting to know if he was Rick Smalls. It just wasn't the accident that his parents had had; it was his life. He knew people wanted him, and one of the places that they knew was connected to him was Gary. He rode past the turnoff for Interstate 90 and continued through the south side of Chicago, staying to the left so that he would not get onto Interstate 57 south. He wound around the interstate until the portion of the road carried the name of Bishop Ford. He didn't know where he was, but it was probably the roughest surface portion of Interstate 94, not only in the Chicago area but also from the full length of the interstate from the East Coast to the West Coast of the United States. He exited on 159th and went back east. He wanted to pull into to the Beaubien Woods, a forest preserve that many folks would use for family outings in a wooded setting. He wanted to use this area to put on the items from Tammy to alter his appearance. He started with the false teeth. They were caps that go over his upper incisors. They were longer than his and bit more distorted in stains from what someone might think as tobacco stains if they were trying to describe his features. He also inserted padded rolls against his molars in all four positions. This gave an outward appearance of puffier cheeks.

Michael had been clean-shaven for many years now. And this was the reason why. One could add facial hair a lot easier and then go back to being clean-shaven quick and easy. To go the other way was not ideal for changing one's appearance. From the hair features that Tammy had provided to him, he had chosen the somewhat thick mustache-and-beard combination. This helped to sell the puffier face. Michael finished it off with a pair of black framed glasses. The glass was simply clear glass. With this being all set, Michael felt ready to drive on over to Gary. Before he got back on the interstate, he put on the shoulder harness that Tammy had packed for him in her backpack and then put on his jacket on over the shoulder harness and golf shirt. For this trip, he packed two golf shirts in his original backpack and wore one. They were all black. He had on the same jeans from the day before. Michael said out loud to himself, "Let's go see what's going on in Gary, Indiana."

CHAPTER 26

For this last fifteen minutes of his drive before he got to Cline Avenue, he connected his phone to the car's stereo system and hit playlist three on his iPod. He didn't see getting out of the car for a while, and he wanted to come into his past with music from his past. This music was still a part of his present life because he really liked it, but right now, it was being used to set a frame of mind. It was all Prince. With Michael, it didn't matter when the music from Prince was put out. It was only called Prince. It wasn't Prince and the Revolution, it wasn't Prince and the New Power Generation, and it wasn't called music from the symbol. First in coming through the speakers was "Sign o' the Times" from the album of the same name. If Michael was the guy to participate in the debates of what was the best of this or the best of that, he would confidently tell anyone willing to listen that the *Sign o' the Times* album was Prince's best. And he would say it in a way so matter-of-factly that the most informed person wouldn't even consider to debate him on the subject anymore. That conversation or debate would be led by most folks being lazy in their assessments by going straight to Purple Rain. It was still a phenomenal work, Michael would tell them. He would concede the commercial success. But if he was so inclined to debate with someone, he would really get them excited by telling them that the *Purple Rain* album might be the fourth best album ever put out by Prince. With this thought, he smiled, turned up the volume, and headed toward Gary under the hypnotic beats of "Sign o' the Times."

CHAPTER 27

Michael planned to come into Gary by going north on Cline Avenue until he got to US 20, which was also Fifth Avenue. He would travel east on Fifth Avenue, passing Burr Street, Clark Road, Chase Street, and Bridge Street, all busier roads and roads that he remembered to have stoplights. His memory was intact. However, the light at Burr Street was now a flashing light. As he looked around, he understood. The elementary school on the northwest corner was boarded up, and the storefronts on the northeast and southeast corners were boarded up respectively also. After passing his street, Taft Place, he continued on past the light at Taft Street. Fifth Avenue was a one way going east and was three lanes wide. He got over to the far left lane after traveling about eight blocks so that he could turn left and travel north on Grant Street. He got stopped at the light there on Grant Street, and after a short wait, he made his left turn. He rode up toward the light on Fourth Avenue, and shortly before he got there and crossed Fourth Avenue, he began looking for the address 363. That was his destination this morning, and it was the third house on his right. Before turning off the car and getting out, he listened to the last part of "The Morning Papers." He thought that this was ironic and turned off the car and got out.

CHAPTER 28

There was no answer when Ron called Bobby Ashipa, so he left a message for him. Ron finished his breakfast and started back toward his tight room. He needed to sort out the day against the forum's agenda. It was a bit after eight now. He thought that maybe he ate too much. But then he started to think about how good the breakfast was and said to himself that the meal was just right. He stood waiting for the elevator to take him back upstairs after he pressed the button. He looked at the location of each of the elevators and saw that the one farthest away back to his left showed the number 2 for the second floor, and the *L* for the Lobby was now lit up. Ron tried to be the guy who would not crowd the people that were potentially about to exit an elevator, so he stayed where he was. As the elevator began to open, his phone rang, and he recognized the call coming back from Bobby because he had saved the contact into his phone. He almost dropped his phone as he tried to answer it quickly before he got on the elevator. He gripped his phone and answered it. He quickly said, "How you doing, old buddy? Say, I'm about to get on an elevator. If I lose you, I will call you right back." As Ron began to take his baby steps toward the elevator, he saw an older man and woman probably a bit younger than him get off together. He assumed they were together because they seemed to be interacting with each other. He said to himself, "She is too fine to be with that old man." He kind of laughed to himself. Before getting back to Bobby on the phone, he noticed a wonderful fragrance on the elevator and thought about that woman again, thinking, *She is too fine...*

Once the fragrance in the air was absorbed and Ron put his thoughts of that lady's fineness aside, he turned his attention to his phone and Bobby Ashipa. "Hey, Bobby, how you doing, CC?"

Bobby Ashipa was an eight-year veteran on the Gary police force when Ron was a rookie on the force. They never partnered together. Bobby was a detective when Ron started on the force. They got to know each other in the off hours. The police station was located on Thirteenth and Broadway, and the favorite after-work drinking spot was Rudy's on Fifteenth and Virginia ten minutes away. It didn't matter if it was after first shift or after second shift. Many of the street policemen would find their way over there to Rudy's. Rudy's was owned by Frank Miller, a retired policeman. Rudy's was the name of the bar before Frank bought it. He never changed it. It was a drinking spot for policemen before Frank brought it, and the name was important to him in his memories, so he never changed it. Bobby was known as the corner cop or CC by the policemen. It only had meaning if one went to Rudy's. There was a corner table at the back of Rudy's that seemingly was reserved for Bobby. When Ron first started going there about two months after starting on the force, he didn't pay any attention initially to the corner table. But after going there two or three nights a week, he began to notice the activity around the corner table. He also had picked up on the conversation from other policemen that he hung with at the bar about how CC acted like he owned the place.

One night, about six months into the job and after completing his work hours on second shift and having shown up over at Rudy's, there was a huge roar from the policemen that was already there when Ron came in. They were cheering him for losing his street virginity. What this meant was that during a domestic dispute in which he responded to, he got repeatedly hit in his face by the woman that was being abused. The woman took offense to Ron and his partner being aggressive in their response to her drunken husband. So instead of her being happy that she wasn't the target of her husband's drunken abuse, she was bothered by the policemen physically handling her husband. She responded by attacking the policemen that was nearest to her. She leaped toward Ron and just started swinging wildly at him with open hands across his face and neck area. Before Ron gave his full attention to her, he had to secure the husband. By the time that he had completed securing the husband, he had been slapped, scratched, or pushed in the face or neck fifteen or twenty times by the wife. He was able to secure her, and by the time that Ron and his partner left that home that evening, they had both the husband and wife in handcuffs in the back of their patrol car. Ron's reward for losing his virginity or for shedding blood on the job was evident by the bandage beneath his left eye.

After the crowd of cops settled down their hassling of Ron, Frank called him over for a beer on the house. He settled into a booth with his partner Hamilton Carey. Ham was cool and helped Ron where he could in learning the ins and outs of the job. He had been on the job and street for three years now. They sat alone and talked stuff. Other cops came by, slapped Ron on the back, and left a beer. This seemed like a pattern for the next couple of hours. Ron drank a lot of beer and was feeling it both in consumption levels or drunkenness and also in bladder pressure. Ham announced, "I got to go. My girl's outside ready to pick me up. When you got beat up by that girl, I knew we were going to get drunk tonight, and I called my girl to be ready to pick me up. You are going to need a ride yourself. Don't be trying to drive tonight. I'll see you tomorrow, Rook."

"I'll be all right. I just got to hit the head. See you tomorrow. And she didn't beat me up!"

They shook hands. Ham headed to the front door, and Ron headed toward the restrooms in the back. He staggered and staggered on his way. When he got even with the booth that Bobby was in, he just dropped in the bench seat opposite of Bobby. Further inside the bench seat on the side that Ron dropped in was a woman of some age. Ron couldn't tell. It could have been because he was so wasted. It could have been because there was not much lighting in the area. It could have been because her hair was in front most of her face. Bobby didn't say anything when Ron flopped in his corner booth. Ron had only nodded or said something like "What's up?" in passing this booth previously on his trips to the restroom. He had not been introduced to Bobby before. Tonight was different. Through the courage of lost inhibitions from drinking quite a bit, Ron just began rattling word after word out of his mouth, "What's up, CC? You know the old Parliament song about CC? It was for a chocolate city. You know they mentioned Gary in that song? Is this your city as well as your corner? I'm sorry, I got to go to the bathroom."

"Go ahead, Rook. When you come out, why don't you let me buy you a drink to celebrate you losing your virginity tonight," Bobby said.

"Okay," Bobby replied and pushed himself up from the table to finish the journey to the bathroom. When he came out of the restroom and headed back to Bobby's booth, he noticed the lady was gone, and in front of Bobby on a circular tray was what appeared to be eight shots of some sort of alcohol. As Ron slithered into the booth, this time he instantly began waving his hands and forearms from side to side and saying, "I can't drink no more tonight, I'm sorry."

"Look, Rook, I'm your designated driver for the rest of the night, and I am also the one that will complete the ritual of the lost virginity celebration with you."

"How are you going to drive me after drinking four shots?"

"Those eight shots are all for you, now get going."

"All right, CC."

"Call me Bobby."

CHAPTER 29

"I'm all right, Rook." Bobby came back. "I didn't recognize your number, so I let it go to voice mail. That tells me that I ain't heard from you in a while. What's going on with you that I crossed your mind? You looking for somebody to do shots with again? Hahahahaha. You were so messed up! You talked a bunch that night in between losing every ounce of food that you had ever eaten. I remember it like it was yesterday!"

"Very funny. Do you know that every time that we have spoken since that night, you start with recounting that night? It might have been funny once, but now it seems like old news."

"You know, there never was any completion to the ritual. I got those shots because your rudeness in flopping in my booth ran my lady friend off. You cost me a night with her. So I paid you back with shots!"

"I know. You always remind me of that too! Hey, you still 'PIing'?" The last time they talked, Bobby was retired and was working part time as private investigator for some lawyer in Merrillville.

"Yeah. Why? You need some tips?"

"Nothing at all like that. When I first thought about you last night, I was going to ask you to meet me in downtown Chicago later today to help on something. But now I think I need to come over that way. Can you meet me at the diner on Washington and Ridge Road at eleven?"

"Yeah. If I get there before you, I will have your shots waiting on you!" With a loud laugh being the last thing that Ron heard, Bobby hung up with this parting shot.

CHAPTER 30

Dale was sitting in the atrium of the lobby when he saw Valerie and Mr. Benson turn the corner. Even though he had worked with Howard Benson Jr. in some capacity for over thirty years, he was and would always remain Mr. Benson to Dale. Dale stood to signal to them, and they headed over to where he was now standing. Valerie said good morning to Dale, and he responded in like. Dale turned toward Howard and said, "Good morning, Mr. Benson sir. How have you been? It is good to see you, sir."

"Dale, I'm well. It is good to see you. You look well. How have you been?"

"Sir, I'm also well, thank you."

"Now that you two have caught up, maybe we can discuss some work," Valerie injected. "Dale, I have told my dad all that we discussed last night, and I also have gained some information that one of the purchasers may be having an off-site meeting with the Programmer later today. Before we get into that, why don't we discuss a few other things."

They talked for the next half hour, or more precisely, Valerie talked for the next half hour more in a directive manner toward Dale with her dad simply nodding from time to time.

"Look, I just thought of something that I need to address. Dad, can you cover this afternoon and the off-site with Dale? I will be tied up between now and the speech tonight. Is there anything else that you need from me before the speech is completed tonight, Dale?"

"No, Valerie. I should be fine."

With that, Valerie got up and walked away. She headed back to the elevators and boarded the farthest left one for the twenty-ninth floor.

CHAPTER 31

After getting out of the car and heading toward the door at 363 Grant Street, Michael knew that he had to convince the people that he was about to come into contact with that he was as a different person. He then thought back to becoming a different a person when he went off to MIT. It started two weeks after he met the MIT recruiter at the end of his junior year of high school. The Recruiter asked Michael to call him with any questions that he might have about MIT. Michael had questions because the Recruiter had talked about MIT but stirred him when the conversation got away from MIT and into the country or, better yet, patriotism. It reached Michael someplace that he had never been reached before, and it poked at him over the next few weeks. So Michael called him.

The Recruiter met Michael on a Saturday in Munster, Indiana, just south of Hammond. Hammond and Munster were not quite separated by Interstate 80/94 passing by above Calumet Avenue but a bit farther south at Ridge Road. They met on Ridge Road at the Aurelio's Pizza restaurant just west of Calumet Avenue. The Recruiter was there when Michael or Rick Smalls arrived. He stood and waved Michael over to the table that he was at. "Rick, I am glad that you could make it today. Here, pull up a seat. How are you doing today?" the Recruiter said.

"I'm good. You really got me thinking after we met at the college fair a few weeks back. I never knew that I had the type of desires in me about the importance of our country."

"Rick, very few people realize that it is in them until something stirs it up. It takes different things with different people. And even after it is stirred up in some people, not everyone is capable of doing something with that new feeling. Do you think that you are capable?"

"What do you mean? Sure, I'm interested in knowing that if something is working against the interest of our country that they need to be stopped."

"Can you turn into that person that looks to stop someone from bringing harm to the United States?"

As Michael rang the doorbell at 363 Grant Street, he realized that ever since that meeting at Aurelio's, he was turning into somebody different many times over. The irony of hearing the song "The Morning Papers" was that Michael was now going to become an investigative journalist for the *Indianapolis Star*. Just as the door was opening, Michael thought that it was seventy-six degrees and overcast again this morning.

Chapter 32

Ron boarded the elevator on the fourth floor to go down to the lobby. He had called the valet for his car. He was going to Gary. As the elevator to his far left opened, he got on. It was in his mind now. That smell from that fine woman was in the air again. He thought about the old man that was with her again and thought that she needed a young man. Ron got off the elevator and headed out toward the valet. The car was waiting. The valet took Ron's claim ticket and asked him if he was going to be returning, and Ron said that he would. With that, the valet escorted Ron to the driver's door and opened it for Ron. Ron reached toward the valet's hand and palmed a few dollars to the valet. The valet acknowledged this with a head nod, and then after Ron was comfortably in his seat, the valet closed the car door for Ron.

Ron headed east to get to Lake Shore Drive where he would go south until he saw the exit for Interstate 55 south. He would take Interstate 55 south until he could get on Interstate 90/94 east. Ron did this and then stayed with Interstate 94 to avoid the tolls as he headed toward Gary. He left the radio on The Score sports radio WSCR for the Chicago-based blathering on firing the White Sox manager or the talk about the yuppies who had taken over Wrigley Field and how great it was when the fan base was just your average joe. The volume was low. Ron needed to think. Ron thought on his drive about many things. Ron was going to ask Bobby to come over to surveil the hotel to look for Rick. But after Sarge told him about the article in the *Post-Tribune*, Ron went online and read it, and he had a need to know some different things, some things that he never thought about before. Maybe it was because he was too close to those things to think about them any other way than how he would think about them by being close to them.

Time had passed. The vantage point was different. It was as if Ron had been looking at a portrait up close with his head in a fixed position. But then he eased away from the portrait and began to look at the portrait with his head tilted, instead of looking at it straight on. Ron's vantage point of the portrait would also be different if he were to take steps to his left or right even. It was these changes in vantage points that would allow Ron to see a portrait different than it appeared when he stood close to it. The article caused Ron to step back from his memories and to tilt his head.

CHAPTER 33

Valerie was settled in her room again after removing a different pair of black pumps. These were with two-inch heels that went well with her pantsuit. She removed her jacket, threw it on the couch, and sat down. She was thinking over the plan that she had worked out with Dale over the past few weeks leading up to the forum. She thought about the conversation that she had with Dale the night before. She thought about her thoughts once she got back to her hotel room last night, and she then thought about her dad showing up this morning. She loved her dad. She respected her dad. She loved seeing her dad. She just found it a bit uncanny how Howard Benson Jr.—with all that he had accomplished, all that he had done, all that he had and still oversaw—this morning, similar to many other days in her life, showed up out of the blue. She wondered if he was really some kind of an angel looking out for her, and this made her smile. She believed that he cared for her and loved her dearly. He might even love her more now since his wife, her mother, passed away six years ago. Besides being there for the events, her bat mitzvah, high school graduation, Harvard graduation, Columbia graduation, lunch on her first day at the UN, dinner the night of her first day with the firm, or over her shoulder in the background as he handed over the control of the firm to her, he seemed to be uncannily in other places at other times in her life.

She thought then about high school and how her dad was actually home from his Washington, DC, office for an extended time toward the end of her junior year of high school just before the college fair. He was talking a great deal about the greatness of Harvard but mentioning another East Coast school that was doing some great work on behalf of the country and how some of those students would be making great contributions to the world in the years to come. Or when she was in London on a UN junket, his uncanny timing in arriving kept her from joining her colleagues for dinner. She later learned that three people that had dined in that restaurant that her colleagues went to that night had gotten quite ill and actually died later. Or when she had traveled for the firm to meet with some clients in Paris, and he popped up to join her for the meetings. It was then that he thought that they could meet the clients in a different location to impress them, and he changed the arrangements. It was back at the original location in the same time frame that they would have been arriving that someone was struck by a van as they were crossing the street to go in the same building that her original one had been destined for. She tilted her head and thought that maybe her dad was an angel. She wondered what her angel had in store for her on this pop in. She smiled.

CHAPTER 34

"Dale, Valerie gave me a bit of information on how you planned to cover the activity areas around the forum. She even mentioned your outside support to cover the guest room areas of the hotel. Now with Valerie dropping in the off-site meeting location later today, what are your thoughts on covering that meeting?" Howard Benson Jr. asked.

"Sir, with this being mentioned this morning less than an hour ago, I don't have a plan just yet. But I should have something to share back with you and Valerie within the hour. I am not totally surprised by the idea of an off-site meeting, and I had already given some thought to how to cover this one or any others. To meet away from this hotel would be a smart move."

Dale Langford was a polished professional. Howard hadn't asked the question to think that Dale would lay out the intricacies of this surveillance already. He asked because he wanted to subtly let Dale know that he wanted in more of the works that Dale and Valerie had been working on. Dale knew this from the question. Dale had worked under, directly, indirectly, and in any other form or capacity that could be described for Howard Benson Jr. for the last thirty-four years. Initially, it appeared to the leaders of International Safety Services that this young man that was recruited out of the Marines as a project manager was a person that was eager to please. It turned out that this young recruit out of the Marines was a zealot. He believed. He was given a cause with International Safety Services. He worked every day as if he owed the leadership at International

Safety Services something beyond a fair day's work for the fair day's salary that they were paying him. Some in leadership saw him as the perfect salaried employee because he was tireless. He worked eighteen hours a day. He worked weekends. He wanted more, and he did more. Some others in leadership saw him as a burnout waiting to happen. They were workaholics themselves; they just saw that this Dale Langford didn't have it and that he covered the lack of it with fake zeal.

Howard Benson Sr., who ran things in those days, saw what he saw, the man to protect his company for the future. He didn't see any walls that Dale wouldn't get over. There were no desired results that Dale wouldn't achieve. Howard Benson Sr. knew where the future was for International Safety Services, and he had groomed Howard Benson Jr. for the future of International Safety Services. But most importantly for this point in Howard Benson Jr.'s development, he needed a Dale Langford. Howard Benson Sr. attached Howard Benson Jr. and Dale Langford together at the hip it seemed. He met privately with them. He groomed both of them together. Each knew their roles. Howard Benson Sr. knew then what was still true today. And that was that Dale was the soldier that was needed and that he didn't need to worry about pride or personal want consuming this soldier. He knew then, and he told Howard Benson Jr. then that he must keep this soldier fed, and he would stay loyal to him forever. Being fed meant to keep the country first in front of him and allow him to build his network to protect the country first and also to allow him to correct the things that got in the way of keeping the country first. Now Howard Benson Sr. and Howard Benson Jr. were not patriots first. They were capitalists that needed for their growth patriots. And Dale Langford was the patriot of all patriots.

Howard Benson Jr. said, "Call me when you see how to do this." With that, he got up and headed toward the door to exit onto Michigan Avenue. From Dale's vantage point, it appeared as if a car pulled up at the moment. Before a minute had passed, he saw Howard Benson Jr. climb into the back of that car.

CHAPTER 35

In thinking about her angel and the impromptu times that he showed up in her life, Valerie remembered the one about the college fair with more excitement because of how her dad had gone on and on about the other East Coast university. It wasn't that her dad wanted her to go there. Harvard was the university for her from the womb. It was how her dad spoke on the important programs that were going on there and how they had shown some willingness to work or team with International Safety Services on some projects, how some International Safety Services employees were already working with that university, and in turn how many of the university's employees were working with International Safety Services and how they could someday have curriculums in place that had intentions of outfitting International Safety Services with the best and brightest. So it was not a complete surprise on the night of the college fair that as she was just having fun with Rick at the college fair, when she looked over toward Rick's favorite baseline, she saw a familiar school name. It wasn't Harvard. It was Massachusetts Institute of Technology, the university that her dad had gone on and on about since he had been home from DC. She remembered that when she pointed toward it that Rick only went that way because she pointed toward it. As she and Rick headed toward it, she had her first real thought that maybe they both could be in college in Boston together. Rick had told her on plenty of occasions that he didn't see himself with the pretentious snobs like her. She remembered how she would laugh and come back and say something like she wasn't a pretentious snob and that she was a Jewish princess! And they both would laugh. But Rick was serious about not going there.

Over the next few weeks, she remembered how she kept asking him what he and the Recruiter had talked about. He never told her fully. Her thoughts of him going turned into her asking him if he thought he would want to go there and then into asking him if he would or could seriously consider going there. She remembered that as the summer between the junior and senior year of high school was going by and it seemed that many folks expected Rick to name his college choice at the beginning of the school year, Rick stopped talking about college more and more. His ticket or tickets were already written. He had full scholarships offered from twenty of the perennial top twenty-five programs for Division 1 football. He had been ranked as high as thirtieth on one list of high school senior basketball players and by position in the top five for shooting guards. He even had as many as five colleges telling him that he could play both sports for them. She remembered how this expectation to the start of their senior year seemed to weigh not heavily but differently on Rick's demeanor. She wondered, like others, why he had not announced his plans after their senior year had already been going on for three weeks now in mid-September. She played with him about it, but she was serious in wanting to know why he hadn't decided. She just remembered that this time and most of their senior year was a bit different Rick.

It was during this different Rick period that she not only loved Rick, but she was also in love with Rick. Valerie didn't lack confidence. Valerie didn't need anyone to be a crutch for her. Valerie knew that she was prepared to be a success by any definition of the word *success*. But when she realized that she was in love with Rick, she began to wonder more and more about MIT since he had not made his decision about school known to anyone. She wanted him there really bad. But then a minute later, she might think that she didn't want him there at all because Valerie Benson don't need or want a crutch! As much as Rick was in her heart, he was equally present in her head.

Valerie snapped back to her hotel room and thought it would be nice if somehow he showed up at the reunion. After all, in hopes of the wildest of possibilities, her foundation had put forth a lot money to accommodate her schedule for the prospect of him to show up. Valerie leaned her head back on the couch and wondered, *What will my angel bring with him this time?*

CHAPTER 36

"Good morning, sir. I'm sorry to disturb you. My name is Steve Long. I'm an investigative reporter with the *Indianapolis Star*. I drove up here today hoping to get to talk to you and some other folks in town about the article that the *Post-Tribune* ran yesterday. When my editor saw the story, he thought that there might be some other angles to bring out that hasn't been covered yet."

"Who are you? What do you want? Who are you looking for?" queried the man. Will had opened the door to his house, but he was looking at and talking with Michael through the screened mesh of his security screen door.

"I'm Steve Long. I'm with the *Indianapolis Star*."

"Yeah, yeah. You already said that. Who are you looking for?"

"I'm sorry, are you Will Jackson?"

"Why are you asking who I am?"

"Sir, I am looking to further the story that was in the *Post-Tribune* yesterday. Did you see it? It was around the life of the region's own Rick Smalls. Did you see it?"

"I don't get the paper. I did years ago. The delivery service was not as good as it was years ago, so I stopped getting it. I had no paper in about ten years."

"Sir, do you mind me asking you a few questions about Rick Smalls and his family?"

"Who?"

"Sir, do you remember about twenty years ago, a phenomenal student athlete grew up here in the region?" Northwest Indiana, for decades, had been noted by many simply as the region.

"Hey, we have had plenty of good kids in sports. I've been here long enough to remember when we had six high schools, and they all had someone good. And that was just here in Gary." He stretched out the sound in Gary as if it was spelled "Gayry" when he said it. "What was so special about this Rick, Rick what's-his-name?"

Michael seemed to be catching his footing with Will. Will seemed to like to talk. Michael knew he needed to be careful not to spook him. So he fed into Will's willingness to talk by taking it away from Rick or himself to other athletes from the region, and then if that worked, he would pull it back to the discussion of Rick and his family. "Will, maybe for some background, who are some of the athletes that has stood out in your time around here?"

"Aw, how much time do you got? Hold on. Let me grab something." Will stepped away from the door. When he came back, he opened the screen door and stepped out onto the landing between the stairs and his screen door. "Step down so I can spread this so we can sit on it while we talk. My back doesn't hold up the way that it used to, so I got to sit down." The landing was ready now, and Will stepped down two stairs from the landing, and then while holding the rail that traced the path of the stairs, he settled his backside onto the landing. "You can stand or sit with me. Your choice."

Michael sat, thinking that this would lubricate the memories and tongue of Will more than standing over him.

"Let's see now. I was coming through school in the late seventies. We had some stars. Let me tell you. Between Roosevelt and West Side High Schools, they won almost all of the state titles in track and field in the seventies. West Side had this kid, Duckett. Terrence Duckett he played basketball too, but it was track. When this kid ran the 220—it was yards then, not meters—it seemed like he was leaning on the curves. He was something to see. Roosevelt had their stars too, but the 'Velt played some serious ball. They had this kid, Nadi. Renaldo Thomas. That boy was the best in the area, while he played before him. You had two seven footers over at Emerson, Wallace

Bryant and Frank Smith. They balled. Nadi's cousin was older than him, and he played against those guys. John Hegwood. Left-handed. It must have been something in that family genes. Both John and Nadi could jump out of the gym. We also had that left-handed guy over at Bishop Noll. He was from here in Gary. Thad Garner. That boy was bad. He dunked on everybody! He went to Michigan."

Michael had heard the stories of many of these kids when he was a kid. He saw that he had a chatty guy in front of him, and he had brought up Bishop Noll. This might be a point to interrupt him. "Do you remember the name Rick Smalls from Bishop Noll? This was some years later even after Glen Robinson was at Roosevelt." Michael knew that Glen Robinson had gone onto Purdue and the NBA. He was the first pick in the NBA draft when he left Purdue.

"So you know a little about the region. That boy Glen dunked on more people than Thad ever did. I kind of remember that other name Rick Smalls too. He played everything. I wasn't going out to see the kids play as much at that point. We all used to fill the gyms and support all of the kids. Something changed. The area changed. I don't know. I remember reading about the Smalls kid a little."

"Some of the things that this long story in the *Post-Tribune* pointed out was that he left the area with no known destination and just seemed to fall off the map. It also talked about his parents. They lived not far from here on Taft Place. The story talked about a bad car accident where they lost their lives. Do you remember that?"

This was where Will came into the story. It was not in the story in the *Post-Tribune*. In the *Post-Tribune*, it made mention of a scene with a fire truck, police cars, and ambulances. Through Michael's deep research, he had found out that one of the paramedics on the scene was this Will Jackson. Will's glow from the pride in talking about the region changed. His eyebrows seemed to connect as his brow furrowed. His newly formed unibrow tilted from one side to the other in alignment with a newly tilted head. As he looked to his left, where Michael was seated, the highest portion of his head and his unibrow was to his right. "Why you asking me about some accident? What does that have to do with the region? What kind of story you doing?"

"My research has led me to many parts of this family, including the accident where Rick Smalls's parents lost their lives. My research further tells me that you were on the scene that night. The questions that I have about the accident and the death of Rick's parents seemed appropriate to ask of you. You were a paramedic. You were on-site. You transferred the bodies to the morgue. So what do you remember about the accident that killed them?"

"Look, I ain't trying to talk about something from long ago that wasn't pleasant. I live quietly here at 363 Grant Street. I raised my family. I don't bother nobody. Maybe you should talk to the police or the firemen that were there. That night made me sick. I ain't never tried to talk about it. I was told not to talk about. I don't want to talk about it now. Maybe you should go."

"I'm sorry if I upset you. I'm just trying to get a firsthand description of what was seen by some folks that were there that night."

"I told you. Talk to the police. They talked to my boss, and that was when I was told not to talk about it."

"Why would someone direct someone not to talk about a one car accident that seemed to slide into a utility pole on a wet road and then the car catches on fire? Between the crash crushing the car and not allowing a way for them to get out and then the car bursting into flames, what would require people to need to not to talk about it?" Michael asked with a bit of exasperation.

"Look, I ain't never talked about it. But I'm gon' tell you this one thing, and then you gon' get off of my stoop and never come back. And don't use my name in your newspaper! You hear me?"

"Okay, what's the one thing?"

"By the time the paper was out the next morning, it was said that these people died in a car crash late in the evening the day before."

"Okay. I don't get it. What would make that something not to talk about?"

"Mr. Reporter, you ain't trying to listen. I listened. This voice. The policemen, the firemen, and me and my partner all listened to that voice. We all seemed to get the same message not to talk about that night. I'm old. I ain't got nobody. That voice froze me all these years. I got handed a cell phone right there on that site that night.

That voice chilled me. Until you came around, Mr. Reporter, I ain't said nothing to nobody. I ain't taking this to my grave. One thing that ain't never came out was something really odd about those two bodies that were in that wrecked, burnt car. The next morning, the paper said some things about that accident. But the paper didn't say nothing about how those two dead burnt bodies somehow drove that car into that utility pole with two bullet holes in both of their heads!" Will went into the house, and before he closed the house door, he slammed the screen door and locked it with a violence that probably broke the lock. The slamming of the house door followed quickly thereafter.

Chapter 37

The thing about irony is that when it shows up, you immediately recognize it as irony. When Michael got back into the 4Runner, he was stunned, and through habit, he plugged in his phone for the iPod to continue the song after "The Morning Papers" on his playlist, which was "Sometimes It Snows in April," and Michael put the car into gear and drove off.

CHAPTER 38

Ron exited the interstate in Gary at the Broadway exit and went south toward Ridge Road. Not only had he grown up here, but he also served as a policeman here for four years. There were things that he missed about Gary. And there were things he didn't miss at all. His parents had moved to Florida. His siblings all lived in or near Atlanta with their families. He had tried a family for a short time himself. He had liked the idea of a wife. He didn't like the idea of being married. So his marriage lasted almost as long as a pro football season. This was while he was still a policeman. The combination of working second shift, drinking three nights a week after a shift, hanging out on Saturday and Sunday all day drinking, and coming home drunk with the same reason of being "just out having some fun with the guys" had lasted from the NFL third preseason weekend or the third week of August until the Bears were six and four after week ten in early November. She was gone. He felt bad because he knew that he hadn't tried very hard on the marriage. No, what he really knew was that he didn't try at all. He wanted a wife. He didn't want a marriage.

He was here to get some background. That article or the stepping away from the portrait view had stimulated some things that he didn't even know were there. Bobby might be able to help with some of that. He knew everybody. He had connections. He played both the good cop and the bad cop depending on who he had to be. Some folks had described him as a dirty cop. Others thought he was a good cop who stretched everything to the legal limit. He remembered that after the night of the shots, whenever he saw Bobby at Rudy's, Bobby always bought him a drink and invited him over. It grew into when Bobby came to scenes where Ron had been the patrolman to secure a scene that Bobby helped Ron to understand the type of things that made a good, preserved scene for a detective like himself. Bobby had started to feed some tips to Ron about where some out in the open, midlevel drug transactions would be taking place, and through the normal course of patrolling their area, Ron and his partner would roll into this action, going down and making arrests. This helped Ron a great deal. He remembered preparing to take the detective exam before his police life changed because of the night when he was injured in the line of duty. He had gotten shot.

Ron was about to turn right to go west on Ridge Road and just past the first light, which was Washington. As soon as he crossed the light, the diner was on his left. Just before he went through the light, he passed the now boarded-up small warehouse. This was not the neighborhood that he grew up in, but he remembered the warehouse. When he got his first car just before his junior year of high school, he had found the car wash that was in that warehouse. It was one of those places where you pulled in and got out of your car, and the car wash guy gave you a chit that had the cost of your wash on it. You would go over to the booth and pay. You could pay the amount on the chit, or you could give some total above that as a tip. There was no change ever returned. In the beginning, he remembered tipping $10 for a $10 car wash. He remembered the tips growing to $20, $50, and all the way up to $500 for a $10 car wash. He also remembered that when he would get back into his car, he would check above the sun visor. There was always something inadvertently left in your car depending on the tip amount that you gave. It might be $10 or $20 or $50, and he even remembered it being as much as $500 worth of marijuana. When it was over $20, it was left in the glove compartment. He also remembered that he sold a little marijuana in high school.

He parked across the street from the diner about a hundred or so feet away from the door and on the opposite side of the street. He jaywalked across the street with a light jog. He stepped into the diner, and he saw Bobby in the back. Ron headed that way.

CHAPTER 39

Bobby slid out of the booth and greeted Ron with a big hug. Ron hugged him back, but not quite with the same affection. It didn't take Bobby long before he dug into Ron with Rook this and Rook that. Ron let it go for a while until after they ordered. Ron just got some fries and a Coke. He had had a big breakfast after all. "Listen up, Bobby. I need some help. I'll pay for your time. I need to find some people and talk to them about something from a few years back. Can you help?"

"Depends. Depends on who you want to talk to and what you want to talk to them about. Where did you get my number?"

"Sarge. Why does it matter who I want to talk to and what I want to talk to them about?"

"You know I played in the sandbox a long time. I just need to know that the sand that you need to uncover ain't gon' show nothing that I buried, if you know what I mean."

"Look, I ain't trying to step on your toes. Let me throw out a little bit at you, and if you don't have any problem with the subject matter, then maybe we can work together. Cool?"

"Cool. Shoot. I'm sorry, no offense." Bobby was referencing the gunshot that Ron had taken back in the day.

"Do you remember Rick Smalls?"

"Never knew him. I knew of him. Heck of an athlete."

"Any problems there?"

"Nah. Go on."

"His parents died in a car accident about twelve years ago. Any problems there?"

Just then, the waitress showed up with scrambled eggs, bacon, and toast for Bobby and the fries and Coke for Ron. Bobby already had a drink. While the waitress settled the food in, Ron kept his eyes toward Bobby. In that short time that the waitress was there, Bobby had taken his napkin out of his lap and wiped his dry, unsoiled mouth three times. When he looked and saw Ron's eyes on him, he started shifting his plate around. The waitress asked if they needed anything else. Ron said no, and Bobby shook his head from side to side.

"Why would his parents be in my sandbox?" Bobby jumped back into conversation. "What you got going on? Just spill it all to me, and I will let you know if I got any problems."

Ron picked up the red ketchup tube and squeezed out a pile of ketchup in the corner of his plate. He sat the tube down and then sprinkled some salt over his fries. He picked up two long, fat fries and skimmed them across the top of the pile of ketchup. He held the fries in front of his mouth and blew them three times. And then he bit off half of each fry. He began to talk to Bobby with the remaining two halves of fries still in his right hand, and as he talked, he gestured with them. "Okay, here we go. Yesterday, I thought I saw Rick Smalls in a hotel in downtown Chicago. I haven't seen him since right after high school graduation. We kicked it together then. We didn't go to the same high school. He went to Bishop Noll. We lived on the same street, Taft Place. I saw him leaving the check-in counter at the hotel. I couldn't catch him before he got on the elevator. The manager said that they didn't have any guest by that name. I still think it was him. I want to have some coverage on the hotel, so I thought about you this morning. I didn't act on it last night because I was a bit off-kilter from drinking before I saw him. This morning, I called Sarge with the intent of getting your contact information to see if you would come over to Chicago to watch the lobby of the hotel for me. I have other business in the hotel that requires me to be there. I'm thinking that it was him even more after I talked to Sarge. Sarge thought I had Rick on the brain because of an article that was in the *Post-Tribune* yesterday. I told him I hadn't seen it. Sarge forwarded to me your contact information. We said goodbye.

"I called you and left a message for you to call me. I searched for the article and read it. This article, it seems, was almost a 'Where is Rick Smalls?' sort of story. It tells about how no one ever saw him after he graduated from high school. It had recapped all that he had accomplished in sports and how he could have gone anywhere and done anything. This kid was not only good in all of the sports. He was brilliant. In the article, they talked with his old teachers, classmates, and some of the folks from our old neighborhood. Nothing but good stuff about him. The story finished with his parents' death in a car accident. It talked about the tragic scene, their car having appeared to slide into a utility pole. It recounted how the car was totaled. The front of the car indented by the pole almost turned the front of the car into the shape of the letter *V*. The article talked about some things not being clear about the initial reporting of the accident. It also talked about how the car had caught fire and that the fire spread before the fire department got there and that both of his parents were burned to the point that if they hadn't died from the impact of the crash, they surely had died from being burned to death." Ron paused then picked up again by saying, "I was working that night. My partner and I were outside of our patrol car about to approach some guys over by the Dorie Miller apartments that may have been doing deals on drugs. We were freelancing a bit, and we hadn't called it in. So it wasn't a surprise that we got a call to respond to a car accident. My partner turned faster than I did back toward the car, and then I turned as well.

"We never made it to the car accident. I found out later that it was Rick's parents' accident scene. It wasn't far from where we were over by Dorie Miller. We were over on Twenty-First and Mississippi just past King Drive. Two blocks on the other side of King Drive is Ohio Street. Rick's mom's mom lived on Twenty-Third and Ohio. Again later, it seemed that they must have left by going south on Ohio and turned right on Twenty-Fourth. You remember that area? This turns into a frontage road with trees and bushes on the south side and those funny painted apartments on the north side of the road. It was on this frontage road where they skidded into that pole. We never made it there because that was the night that I got shot. I got shot when I turned to go back to the car with my partner. He had his back turned still as he was getting closer to the car. I got shot and went down. He took cover on the opposite side of the car. There were no more shots. The group of guys that were out there were all gone. To this day, me getting shot was not the worst part of my day. Finding out later what happened to Rick's parents tore me up. His house was my house growing up, and my house was his house. It felt like I lost my parents when I found out. My life changed so much from that night. And then I think I saw him last night, and then I saw that article this morning. The reporters on that story finished with some open-ended questions. Their questions have left me with some questions that you may be able to help me with. Tell me, CC, am I in your sandbox?" Ron ate the two remaining halves of the now cold fries, wiped his hands against each other over the plate of fries, and then pushed the plate of fries away from him.

CHAPTER 40

The Voice had some people that could do things for him. He called Jill Estridge last night, and she immediately had gone to work both on the digital and electronic reconnaissance and the tapping into the security systems of others. She knew Chicago, and she knew people in Chicago. Jill didn't need to be anywhere in particular. She needed to know people that could do the work that needed to be done in a drop of a hat. Her financial resources were not limited. Her financial resources were the resources of the Voice. The Voice's call with her was completed five hours and forty minutes ago, and she had been working on this with techs for five hours and forty minutes. Her running start of information was limited. That was not to say that the limited information was good or bad. It just meant that the information that she had to start with was limited. She had been on the payroll for the Voice for some time. Over the years, she had received assignments that were started and finished in short order. She had had other assignments that had gone longer in duration of time. She had had assignments that required assets on the ground, and she had had assignments that required the magic of hacking. This assignment was a bit different. When she first began to work for the Voice twelve years ago, she was given a photo of Darrell Hunt. She was told that the picture was from a security camera in the Beirut airport two days prior. She was told that this was the last known picture of him. She was told to find him.

Jill's reputation had preceded her to the Voice. His expectations were that it would not be easy to find Darrell Hunt or Rick Smalls, as the Voice first knew him; but he expected him to be found. Jill got other assignments from the Voice shortly after getting the assignment to find Darrell Hunt. Those assignments closed quickly. Darrell Hunt was still open. He was Jill's white whale. In the last twelve years, Jill had rewarded the Voice confidence in her on other assignments with phenomenal results. She hadn't delivered the white whale. When she got the call early in the morning from the Voice in the first two minutes after their call ended, she did nothing. She didn't move, and she really didn't think that she breathed during that two-minute span neither. In the next three minutes, she activated her best operators. She got a ground team activated, she got her hacking team activated, and she got her wet team activated just in case. Her white whale had alluded her long enough. This was going to end.

The early returns of this deep-sea dive into finding her elusive white whale felt like looking for a specific minnow in the Atlantic Ocean so far except she had hoped that her white whale was out there and that the sighting was real. That's because from the limited information that she was given initially about the time that her white whale was thought to be seen, it gave her a window to work in. She had her team to hack into the security system of the Chicago Hilton Towers. While none of her operatives saw any white whale sightings, what they did see was of interest to Jill. There were probably no less than twelve operatives working on the video of the property, and three of them reported back anomalies. Based on the reported time of the sighting from these three operatives, each of them had found that there was some missing video coverage from the hotel's security system that they had hacked into. It wasn't minutes. It was seconds in various areas—the main entrance, the check-in desk, the staging area in front of the elevators, and a side entrance and exit. These were enough by themselves to get the hunter in Jill to get excited for the rare catch. But the area that excited her even more was that there was a missing video from every floor in the hotel. She thought that was an extremely smart move. But it also could have been a tip that her white whale was staying in the hotel.

She surmised her conclusion this way. It wasn't an accident that many of the video cameras in the hotel had some missing footage. It wasn't an accident that all the missing video was somewhere after the reported time of the sighting of the white whale. It would be too obvious to a potential floor where the white whale might be staying to only have footage deleted from a particular floor. It was an exceptional move to delete footage from twenty-seven floors of guest rooms. Without knowing what floor a potential guest or the white whale was on, her operatives were left with over one thousand rooms to consider where the white whale might be staying. Her white whale was out there, and he had help.

Tammy had been busy. Tammy has remained busy. She wanted to help Michael to be very careful.

CHAPTER 41

Seven p.m. was eight hours away. The potential meeting between the Programmer and one of competitors was five hours away. Her information had been good up until now, so she believed that the report of that meeting with the Programmer at four this afternoon was real. She believed what she heard about the Programmer setting up only three meetings. She has had good information up until now. She would like to know about one more meeting so that her team could do something to know more about the Programmer's direction. She was confident that if she was to find out just this one other meeting, her company could be well positioned to swoop in and steal the deal with the Programmer. That's because she had an off-site meeting confirmed with the Programmer tonight at 11:00 p.m., four hours after the start of her keynote address and twelve hours from now.

CHAPTER 42

Valerie led International Safety Services and had led it exceptionally for the last five years. She had expanded the vision of her grandfather and that of her father. She held both of them in high reverence, and she had been proud to continue their visions. But she had a vision of her own that could not be seen by her grandfather and that her father would probably not agree to. So she got in the game of going after the Programmer. As far as she knew, no one knew who the Programmer was. No one knew if the Programmer was one person or ten or twenty. She didn't know what to expect in her meeting tonight. She did want any advance information that she could get. She wanted the diligence of Dale's support to get this advance information. But it was not the best interest of Dale or for her dad to know that she was the third party that had a meeting with the Programmer. She had her own vision. Dale wouldn't understand. So he didn't know.

Valerie executed the mission and vision of International Safety Services flawlessly for her first four and a half years in leading the organization. She found it essential to make every effort to protect all their clients in all phases of security known to the world both domestically and abroad. She was out in front of this mission and vision both internally and externally for International Safety Services. She took the team that she inherited and got even more out of them than her dad had done. The business grew. She needed to expand her leadership team to keep up with things. She even had some of these additions to visit with her dad before making a final determination about bringing them on board. He was the best adviser that she could have, so she used him.

Somewhere along the two and a half years into of leading the company and going through the growth, she thought that maybe one day Dale Langford would eventually step away from the business. She didn't want to insult Dale by asking him how much longer he intended to stay in the business nor did she want to designate someone for his eventual replacement. She feared that designating someone to be Dale's eventual replacement would be even more disrespectful than asking him how much longer he planned to stick around. Valerie hired someone in a role that wasn't quite senior level so that it would not draw a lot of attention. This role was a ruse. This was someone that was her staffer for the molding into the role that Dale had had now for years. About six months ago, this internal plant by Valerie brought something to her attention, and that was when her vision changed from what had been the executed vision of her much revered grandfather and father.

CHAPTER 43

After calling the Voice several hours ago, everything seemed to get bunched together. There was no need to be distracted from the things that normally needed to be done. But all that changed after the thought of Rick Smalls being seen. The Voice wanted Rick Smalls for his own reasons. There were plenty of them. Rick Smalls had cost the Voice plenty. It was crystal clear why the Voice would not be satisfied until he had the opportunity to confront Rick Smalls and to tear Rick Smalls apart piece by piece. The sighting of Rick Smalls the previous day gave this caller reasons to consider the memories of Rick Smalls. The caller knew Rick Smalls when he was Rick Smalls and by every other name up until the last time that they were together, and Rick Smalls was Darrell Hunt. For the time that they were in association with each other, there were times when Rick Smalls seemed like family. They were close until they weren't. There was much to do yet today, and now there was also the possibility of Rick Smalls. Why now or why here? It didn't take much to conclude the "why now" and "why here" because here and now, Rick Smalls could add reasons for the Voice to have problems with him. And here and now, the pain that Rick Smalls had brought to the caller seemed as fresh as that day in Beirut. The caller wanted Rick Smalls to know that same type of pain.

CHAPTER 44

The Voice had always shown patience. That was because he was normally three to four steps ahead of everyone else, and there was no urgency in finding out anything. Right now with no new information on the possibility of Rick Smalls being available, he was steps behind. He wasn't patient right now. He called Jill Estridge again. "What do you know that I need to know?"

"Nothing that confirms or identifies him. But there are some things that stand out to me that gives me some belief that there is a likelihood that someone was on that property that does not want to be seen or for it to be known that this someone was there," Jill responded. She went on to fill the Voice in on the anomalies that her team had turned up.

"Call me when you have more." And with that, the Voice hung up. The Voice couldn't help but think about the here and now and why.

CHAPTER 45

"Sometimes It Snows in April" finished. "Strollin'" played and fin-ished. "Controversy" had played and finished. The same was the case with "7" and even "1999." And as Michael arrived at the doctor's office, "Irony" was playing in his memory background as "Let's Go Crazy," the extended version, was blaring. Michael realized now that the volume was turned all the way up. He knew that usually when this song came on, he normally turned the volume all the way up. He just didn't remember turning the volume all the way up this time. As he pulled in the vacant parking lot to another boarded-up building, he eased the volume level down. He turned the music down to eight on the volume knob. He still wanted to hear it thoroughly, but now his mind went back his senior year of high school. He remembered that he was a bit distant from everyone. Everyone was expecting an announcement about his future plans any day then. He wished that he could make such a commitment, or better yet in some ways, he wished that he could talk about his future commitment and plans. As the summer passed by leading into his senior year, he spent more and more time with the Recruiter from the college fair. The Recruiter seemed to be always available. The Recruiter was looking to meet. He challenged Michael when they met. He would describe scenarios to Michael that would require some very thoughtful solutions. More times than not, Michael responded with very thoughtful answers.

The Recruiter told Michael that the majority of the popula-tion could provide thoughtful responses with nothing at stake. He told Michael it was when something was hinging on the thoughtful response that the majority of the population would then dwindle down to a select few percentage points of the population. Michael doubted the low percentage that the Recruiter spoke of, and the Recruiter said that he could prove it to him. He also asked Michael if he thought that he was a part of the few percentage points of the population that could thrive in an environment when something big was on the line. It was at this point that the Recruiter seemed to mock some of the things that Michael had accomplished by asking him questions like, "What was truly on the line when you made two free throws your sophomore year against Clark High School to give your team a two-point lead with less than a second on the clock? Nothing. Because the game was already tied, and the worse-case scenario was overtime" or "Where was the pressure your freshman year when you scored the perfect scores on both SAT and the ACT? The only pressure was whether or not you would have enough lead in your number 2 pencil. That's because you could only score a perfect score because your mind was wired that way!" The Recruiter threw out other things as well, just random things around the other sports that he was involved in, the debate club, the coding club, and things with his parents.

Michael remembered that as if it was yesterday. He was astonished by this man that was recruiting him and seemingly belittling his accomplishments at the same time, and this man questioned whether or not Michael was just another guy in the population or if he was wired to perform when something was on the line. Michael also remembered that in that moment, his mind asked himself how this recruiter knew those things about him. Michael didn't ask then or at any other time. But he got his answer before the summer was over. Michael told the Recruiter that he wanted to show him that he had the instincts to provide the thoughtful responses under any situation. The Recruiter didn't toy with him or deny him once Michael affirmed what he could do. He simply said "Let's see" and told Michael to get in his car. The Recruiter drove Michael to this parking lot. None of the storefronts seem to be open now. Back then in the summer between his junior and senior year of high school on that day, the parking lot might have been half full. The Recruiter told Michael to follow him into this business. The business was actually shown to be a doctor's office. The window was painted with the words, "Dr. Milton Bergal, MD." On either side of this were other businesses. It was an area where there was an anchor store, which was a grocery store called Wise Way. There were other stores between Wise Way and the doctor's office. At that moment, Michael was only really focused on the doctor's office.

When they got to the door, the Recruiter rang a bell, and there was a buzz. The Recruiter pulled on the door and held it open for Michael, and Michael went in. It was a lobby for a doctor's office. Across the room was a window that showed the area where you would check in. No one was there. Off to Michael's left by the window was the door that you would go through to see the doctor, Michael thought. The Recruiter told Michael that they were going to go through that door and down the hall to room number 2. Michael led the way. When he got to room number 2, he turned the knob to go in. As the sun rose with the new light giving the full indication that a new day had started, the same could be said for Michael. The light that was in room number 2 brought a sudden change to Michael. As if, in that moment a new day began for Michael. He saw everything differently now. What he saw next changed his life. Not only did he see it; he also solved it. In a matter of moments of the door opening wider and the light of the room inviting Michael in, he saw a man with his back to the door, and the man was holding down a nurse with one hand, and raised above the man's head by his right hand was a knife. Michael seemingly glided across the room and grabbed the man's right wrist as it was coming down toward the nurse. It was Michael's right hand that controlled the man's wrist. Michael used his left forearm to get a choke hold on the man from behind him. Michael torqued his own lower body to turn the man to the left and away from the nurse and then used the power of his legs to drive the man into the wall. The momentum of this move caused the knife to fall. It was then that Michael began beating the man in his right kidney area. Michael got out maybe eight to ten blows before he heard what sounded like a gunshot directly behind him. With that sound, Michael instantly turned to understand his circumstances. It was the

Recruiter, and the gun had fired a blank. The Recruiter told the man and the nurse to leave the room, and he told Michael to sit down.

Michael started to say something, and the Recruiter interrupted him and told him to stay focused and to now tell him as much detail as he could about what had just happened. Michael started by pointing toward the door to ask about the nurse. The Recruiter stopped him and told him to stay focused and to tell him what happened. Michael looked directly in the Recruiter's eyes and recounted the events in such a way that you would have thought the events had happened in slow motion. Sure, the big things were that there was a man, a nurse, the nurse being held down, and the knife extended above the man's head, but Michael captured so much more. He told of not only the brightness of the light from the ceiling but also the additional light from the desk lamp. He mentioned the stool that had four wheels on it in the first right corner of the room. He told about the examination table having a tear in the fabric near where the man's right thigh was. He told of the wallpaper lining around the top of the walls near the ceiling with clowns on it, the eye chart that was on the wall to his far left near where the scale was stationed, and the scale that had one of those fixtures to raise to measure someone's height. There were a few other things that he noted as well. The Recruiter stopped Michael from talking and then said to him, "That was your first test, and you were okay."

"Test? Okay? What are talking about?"

"We were looking to see if you were part of the majority that only could generate thoughtful responses when there was no pressure or if you were a part of the three percent or so that could deliver a thoughtful response under pressure. This is my test facility. And on your first test, you did okay. Well, really you did do exceptionally on about ninety-nine percent of the test. In the end, you failed. Sorry."

"This is nuts! Hold it, what do you mean failed? I stopped the slasher-rapist's guy!"

"She would have still been slashed and raped because you didn't stay aware of your surroundings, and the slasher-rapist's buddy came in and would have put two shots in your head from behind. So you did okay until you would have been killed," the Recruiter said casually.

CHAPTER 46

It was in this doctor's office that Michael was run through many tests in the summer between his junior and senior year of high school. Each of the examination rooms had different things going on in them. Through the door marked 7 was an opening to a warehouse. In the warehouse was an obstacle course and shooting range. By the time that the middle of August had come around, Michael was doing exceptionally well on all the tests that he was presented with by the Recruiter and the Recruiter's staff. Michael had never fired a weapon before coming to the doctor's office. That didn't stop him from shooting regularly here in the bull's eye area of the targets. It was over the intercom system in the warehouse of the doctor's office in mid-August that Michael heard that voice. This voice that stirred him like no other voice. It was here in that building that he first heard from the Voice. He thought that it had to be the same voice that kept Will Jackson silent for so many years. It had to be.

CHAPTER 47

"What are you getting at, Rook?" Bobby jumped in with a stare that was not so much looking to engage a tough conversation but with more of a glare of trying to show that he was offended instead of being accused of something.

"I just said a lot. Here, let me simplify some parts of it and maybe even rephrase parts of it. I get to know you, and you begin to feed me tips on outside busts to drug sales, which coincidentally narrowed some of the drug traffickers. I get recognized for being this rising star from busts that you fed me, which you fed to me on a cell phone. So nobody else had a clue why I was where I was. Nobody knew where I was, Bobby, but you on many occasions. On the night of Rick's parents' death, I got one of those calls from you. Me and my partner were heading toward the people when we got a call from dispatch. We never said or did anything at the spot that you told me about. But still, when we had turned to leave, I got shot. My partner not only didn't get shot, but he also didn't even get shot at! I never thought about it. Luck of the draw. The shot that hit me could have never been confused with an attempted kill shot. From the rear, I got hit on the backside of my right shoulder. Yeah, it retired me from being a street cop because I wouldn't be able to consistently raise my arm to the standard shooting position. Getting shot stopped me from going to a site where I would have found folks that I loved dead. But when I read that article this morning, I didn't know what to think, and that's where you come in.

"The reporters suggested that there were unanswered questions. It made me to think about that night, and I got my own unanswered questions. Like, was I going to get shot at that night if I confronted those people over by Dorie Miller? Or why shoot at me and me only? We were leaving without saying anything? My other questions are, Did you set me up? Did you know something about the death of Rick's parents? I was told in the hospital about which patrol team that showed up at the accident site. I talked with them after I got out of the hospital, and in passing, they told me that you were there, a detective at an accident scene. Then two weeks later, you were giving me a ride home from Rudy's in a different car. You told me that your other car got sideswiped and was getting fixed. You might remember that you and I were talking at the station before you were heading out and that Sarge asked were you being careful because the department wasn't going to keep covering the cost of you running the front of your car into things. Do you remember that? These are some of my questions. My life is my life. I made my choices, and I live with them. But I need to know what you know about me getting shot and what made this street-smart detective to be at a simple car accident and also to lie about his car to me. Can you help me with this? Like I said, I can handle what I brought on myself. But I do want to know if you have influenced my life or my friend's parents' lives in any way. So tell me something."

"Rook, I don't like how you playing me, and I ain't going to sit here for no more of it. I'm out." Bobby stood and started toward the door and yelled toward the waitress, "He will pay for the lunch!" No more than twenty-five feet outside the door, Bobby whipped his cell phone out and hit a single button and put the cell phone up to his ear.

CHAPTER 48

Something that Ron kept to himself that had made some of his questions come to the surface was that after he got out of the hospital, he had followed up a bit on the accident. The patrolman's report showed that the Smallses' car had been towed to Ripley's out in the Miller neighborhood part of Gary out east on US Route 20 just before getting to Portage, Indiana. He had gone out there to see the car. He wanted to see the car where his friend's parents had died. When he got out there, he saw the car. While he knew it to be an older gray or silver Mazda 626, he knew if it wasn't pointed out to him, he would not have known that this was the Smallses' car. He saw it then, but it wasn't until he read the article and stepped back from the vantage point of looking at the car in person to the vantage point of something being out of place about the car. He thought about this some more before he left the diner after his mind cleared from the thought of Bobby jumping on the phone so quickly after leaving the diner. He asked himself what was wrong about the car or if there was anything wrong. He remembered the car was charred. He remembered the extreme dent in the front bumper at the point where the bumper met the utility pole. He remembered the driver's door and how it just hung open, and he thought that might have been because of the need to open that door with the jaws of life or, in this case, just the jaws because of how the entire driver's side compacted from the impact with the pole. The windshield cracked in a pattern that would be consistent with the cracking from the force of the collision. Nothing, Ron saw nothing in his mind.

He put some money on the table and took a long sip of the Coke as he was looking to go. He dribbled some of the Coke out of his mouth. He reached toward the napkin canister on the table, and then he thought about the car. That's it. That's what was out of place, and he didn't see it until now when he reached for the napkin in the severely dented canister. The rear of the Smallses' car was smashed! He stood to leave and smacked his hands together in such a hard way that the clap snapped all the heads in the diner to his direction. He headed toward the door. He told the waitress that the money was on the table, and he left. As he was headed toward his car across the street, he wondered about something. When he was in about the same spot that Bobby pulled out his phone moments earlier, he thought about hearing back then that Bobby had damage to the front of his car, not on the side, as Bobby had said.

CHAPTER 49

The Recruiter recruited back then. He traveled to different cities to follow up on potential recruits. There was an established network that his boss had established in cities large or small across the country. They had a vision for what the right recruit looked like. The Recruiter and his staff had offices in many different areas. They targeted the brightest and fittest. They targeted recruits that would be able to break way from the family unit easily. The targeted recruit was not necessarily a loner, but they were ideally someone with very few real friends. The normal process would be that someone in the network would get a lead on a recruit, and the word would get to the Recruiter, and the Recruiter would start some level of covert checking on the potential recruit. This could proceed into a few meetings, like Rick had with the Recruiter. If the potential recruit held up through this, then the potential recruit would get a test similar to what Rick had gotten in room number 2. From that point, the potential recruit, over the summer between the junior and senior year of high school, would be further tested in many ways until the most critical point of the process came into play. The boss got in on the observations of how the recruit was handling the various tests. When the boss was sold on the recruit, regardless of where the office was set up, the boss was introduced the same way: over the intercom. The boss was the Voice.

Getting Rick to this stage was a bit different from most recruits. This time, the Recruiter didn't get to have someone in the network reach out to him. Somehow Rick had gotten on the radar of the Voice. The Voice told the Recruiter directly about Rick. Uncharacteristically, the Voice was there that day on Rick's first test. The Voice was there for other tests for Rick as well, all of which was outside the pattern of handling any previous recruits. The Recruiter recognized that Rick was quite exceptional himself. Rick grew on the Recruiter. Both the Recruiter and the Voice saw the potential in Rick that could allow them to do all sorts of projects in the future. In late August of that summer of testing for Rick, the time had come to finalize the recruitment of Rick Smalls. Rick had realized on his own from his first conversation with the Recruiter that he was very interested in protecting the interests of the United States. So patriotism was checked off the list for this recruit. Instincts, analytical thinking, physical dexterity, physical endurance, physical strength, mental strength through adversity, and so on were all checked off as well. It was time to get Rick to understand what all this was for and to close the deal.

After the Voice had been heard over the intercom, Rick was taken for the first time into room number 1 in the office. In this room, there was a small table and two chairs. From the entry point into the room, one chair was to Rick's right, and the other chair was to his left, and the table split the chairs apart. Rick was guided to the chair on the right to sit. Behind Rick's chair was a wall with a door in the middle of it. The Recruiter sat opposite of Rick, and this was how the final recruitment of Rick Smalls was handled. "Rick, you have shown yourself to be quite adaptable this summer," the Recruiter began.

"What does that mean?" Rick wanted to know.

"Shortly, that door behind you is going to open. The man behind the voice that you heard over the intercom is going to come into the room. Under no circumstance are you to try to turn to see him. He is not seen by anyone with very few exceptions. He is going to make you a onetime offer. This offer is going to come with exceptional benefits and for you, extraordinary sacrifices. The offer has benefits beyond you. Those benefits are for your country and family. There is no way to describe to you everything that will be asked of you at this very moment. The testing that you have undertaken up until now gives all indications that with your compliance in following all of your future training, you will always go into what would be your future assignments prepared for success. You will receive additional weapons training. You will receive further training on hand-to-hand combat methods. You will receive language training, surveillance training, surveillance detection, and so on. I'm not asking what you might have conceived this time was leading up to, but I am telling you that you are at the point where, before you leave here today, you must decide if you are willing to sacrifice yourself to be a part of something much larger, greater, and necessary." As the last part of the word *necessary* was touching Rick's inner ears, his inner ears were also hearing the sound of the door behind him opening.

The Voice started, "Rick Smalls, you didn't even flinch when this door that I just came through opened. From what I am seeing in your recruiter's eyes, your eyes have not left him. You are impressive. I have seen other impressive recruits before, but I believe that there is something unique about you that can serve our country in ways that no other recruit through me has ever done before." The voice of the Voice was calm, confident, strong, encouraging, sincere, and serious. Rick knew that this voice would be embedded in him for the rest of his life.

"Here is your offer," the Voice continued. "Two weeks after your high school graduation next June, you will enroll in MIT. You will not mention any of your future plans to anyone. It is for the safety of others and for yourself. Being the exceptional athlete that you are, we understand that many folks want to know about your plans. You will need to figure out how to keep all things to yourself without setting off alarms about your future. We do understand that you have a very good friend that will be in the Boston area. We are going to give you the exception of telling her at a later date, and we will allow you to continue to be in communication with her. Once you leave your home in Gary for MIT, she will still know you as Rick Smalls. Once you are enrolled in MIT, you will have an entirely new name and history. Rick Smalls will cease to exist with the one exception, and you must keep your friend from finding out about the new persona. You will leave your parents and your neighbor Ron completely behind. As you comply, we will place in your parents' path financial resources that will be helpful to them in your absence from their lives. For their safety, they must not know. Your training will continue while you are at MIT. You will be called on for assignments even while you are at MIT. There will be assignments with risks, and then there will be assignments that are not only risky, but also they will be quite dangerous. There will be assignments where you are only taking on a defensive position for the assignment, and then there will be assignments where you will be the offense. At some point, people will try to eliminate you, and yes, you will be called on to eliminate people and in ways that are an affront to this great country of ours. Are you on board, Rick Smalls?"

CHAPTER 50

Before leaving the parking lot of where the office had been operated from, Michael talked with Tammy. While they talked on one of the burner phones that she had provided to him, she researched a few things for Michael. While she was researching for Michael, he forwarded to her a link from one of the burner laptops that he had gotten from her. He went on tell her that he needed her to deliver three laptops to destinations that he also emailed to her. He explained in the email while they were talking about the need for each laptop to arrive at the designated time that he showed and not much before. Tammy gave him the answer to his first item of research. She wanted to ask why that was necessary because it was really different from the type of things that she had done for him in the past. She didn't ask. Once she had given him this first information, Michael jumped. "Okay, find out those other things and get back to me. I've got to drive. Thanks for everything."

As he hung up, Tammy caught herself telling him to be careful again.

CHAPTER 51

"Mr. Benson, I have Vasily Kuznetsov and his leading operatives all under complete surveillance. As they head for the meeting with the Programmer, we will stay with him and them. I decided to pick up the operatives as well in the event that the Programmer decides to go through one of the them. From the lead that Valerie passed on, we also have the meeting site covered now. I figured it best to cover it now so that in the event that something changes, we wouldn't have to blow all of our surveillance."

"Good work, Dale. Perhaps it will pay off. As you know with any surveillance, it is only a success if you are able to gain what you are looking for. Have you told Valerie yet?"

"No, sir."

"That's okay. I will. You stay after it. Let me know if anything changes."

CHAPTER 52

The Voice was definitely out of character because of this Rick Smalls thing. He called Jill Estridge again.

"I don't have any tangible updates to pass on yet," answered Jill.

"I'm calling to give a few more targets to watch around this Rick Smalls thing." The Voice gave them to her and hung up the phone.

CHAPTER 53

It is quite unusual to see Valerie out in public in any clothing other than business attire during business hours. While she did do plenty to stay fit, she would normally have a suite where the treadmill or StairMaster was in her room for privacy and for convenience. So for Valerie to leave her suite in athletic wear in the early afternoon was not normal at all. She took the elevator down to the lobby level and headed straight for the main exit while adjusting earbuds in each ear. As soon as she cleared the doorway, she took off in a light jog. She approached the corner of Michigan Avenue and Balbo Avenue as she headed north. She wanted to cross Michigan Avenue and to head east on Balbo, but the light was red for that direction. She continued straight on Michigan until she got ahead to Congress Parkway. She turned right with the light to head east unto Congress Parkway and into Grant Park. She now was free of the car traffic to pick up the pace of her jog.

After going in a near circuitous route for thirty minutes, Valerie stopped at a park bench where a man was seated at one end of the bench reading a newspaper and biting into a sandwich roll of some sort. Valerie was near the other end of the bench away from the roll eater, stretching. Her stretch started with her left foot on the end of the bench, and while her foot was mounted, she dropped into a bit of a squat to stretch the left hamstring and quadriceps. After doing this for about a minute, she switched and did the right side as well. After completing those stretches she interlocked her fingers from both hands and then placed both her hands on the back of her head and, with both her elbows, pointed outward. She began to move her torso ninety degrees forward with the right elbow leading and then back to the starting position. She followed that with the left elbow leading the left side of her torso forward and then back to the starting position. She did this also for about a minute.

When Valerie completed the rotating of her torso, she slid her scrunchie off her ponytail and began to draw her hair tighter together. She dropped her scrunchie to the ground as she was about to reset it on her hair. It had fallen near the back leg of the bench. She bent to pick up her scrunchie and a thumb drive. She put the scrunchie back in place. She palmed the thumb drive and began running back toward the hotel by retracing the strides that had brought her to this point.

CHAPTER 54

With that first bit of information from Tammy in hand, Michael began travelling east on Ridge Road from where the office had been in Griffith off Cline Avenue and Ridge Road. It was faster than to backtrack to the interstate to get to where he was going in Merrillville. He needed to get to Broadway and then to turn south. He would travel at fifty miles per hour with long gaps in the traffic lights. He had turned the volume up to about ten for the music coming from his playlist. The beauty of having a collection of Prince music was that it was a deep playlist. Heading out of Griffith, he caught the mellowness of "The Ballad of Dorothy Parker." On another playlist, he had a recording of the same song from a live performance, and he sometimes debated which version he liked the best.

As he crossed Grant Street and headed closer to Broadway with Harrison Street about the midpoint between Grant Street and Broadway, he was thinking about his approach with the retired doctor that he was going to see in Merrillville. Helping him to think about this was "Pheromone" from the album *Come*. The flute was a nice addition by Prince on this song. He crossed Harrison and then Madison, Monroe, Jefferson, and Adams. As he crossed Adams and was heading toward Washington before Broadway, he was stunned. Walking across the street was somebody that looked like an older version of his childhood friend Ron Winston. Instinctually, he tapped the brakes and started for the power control for the window. When he realized that he couldn't do that, he released the brake and took his finger away from the window control. He did allow himself to follow the guy over to a parked car, and he saw the lights flashed, as if the car was unlocked by a key fob. Michael went past Washington Street and then turned right on Broadway to head up to Fifty-Fourth Street to turn left.

CHAPTER 55

"Mr. Benson, I have an update for you, sir. My team has confidence that they have identified another one of the other parties that the Programmer is looking to meet with," Dale said.

"How reliable do you feel this intel to be, Dale?"

"We think it's solid, sir."

"Dale, I talked with Valerie, and she asked me to run point on this with you if you don't mind. What do you say, Dale? Just like old times, huh."

"Mr. Benson, what would you like for me to do?"

"No disrespect to where you and Valerie were going on this, but it seems as if your best intel believed that it might be only three to five potential contacts that the Programmer was going to reach out to. Is that right?"

"Yes, sir."

"Well, you both think that two of them are pretty solid leads, and you are looking at trying to grab intel so that we could know where to inject ourselves into this at a later time. Again, is this right?"

"It is, sir."

"Let's switch it up a bit, Dale. From what you say, you have some strong operatives here with you. What do you think about some of the approaches that we used before? Maybe like we did in the past where we get in the way of folks making it to important meetings. From what I am gathering from both you and Valerie, the Programmer, by staying low, is probably not going to forgive folks that don't make their meetings. Why don't you look at interdicting Vasily and this other person. Who is the other contact?"

"Xi Ping. I believe that you are aware of him, sir."

"I am. Lower the competitors. What time is Xi's meeting?"

"In one hour here in the hotel, sir."

"Can you get these things done?"

"Sir, I prefer this plan over the one that I had previously purposed."

"Good, Dale. Call me later."

CHAPTER 56

Back in her suite and before she got out of her running clothes to get into the shower, Valerie pulled the adapter for a thumb drive from her purse along with her little-known, alternate iPhone. She put the thumb drive into the adapter and then plugged the adapter into the phone port. The folders from the thumb drive showed up on the iPhone. She browsed the ten folders by title. She then clicked on the folder for audio recordings. These audio recordings were intended to provide her some information on some folks that she had been working with that might not have her best interests in mind any longer. While she had taken a number of precautionary steps, she still needed to have plenty of awareness about what was going on around her. She had instructed entomologists or bug guys to forward everything and that she would get through it all. Her entomologists preferred to deal in the manner that she retrieved the information today. It gave him the opportunity to enjoy parts of the day like sitting in the park, reading the paper, and eating a sandwich.

She saw the listed time for the last two days of recordings all to be like other recordings. They were short in duration. She listened to the first twenty recordings and didn't find anything that was of direct concern to her. It wasn't until the call from late last night where she recognized the voice of the call's recipient. This was not the shock of the call. The shock was that caller called the recipient for the sole purpose of alerting the recipient to a possible sighting of Rick Smalls. Valerie stopped the recording, rewound it, and played it again and unknowingly sat down. And even crazier from the description of the sighting's time and the location, it was near the time that she was leaving the hotel last night for dinner when she had a strange feeling.

CHAPTER 57

This sudden drive into the past sparked an adrenaline that Ron hadn't had in a while. Tailing someone to a hotel or planting visual or audio devices only took him so far up the adrenaline pole. Bobby knew more. He was convinced of that. What more was there to know? He wanted to buy into the damage to the front of the car that Bobby had been driving. He never saw the damage. He only heard it mentioned in passing, which was contradicting to what Bobby had told him about being sideswiped. Bobby was defensive. He avoided real eye contact. He wasn't the confident Bobby that he remembered. Why would this shake up Bobby? Something was not right. Something was not matching up. He needed to talk to the sarge. Before pulling out, he called him. Sarge told him to come by to talk because it would be good to see him since he was already in Gary. Ron figured this to be the last thing that he could do in Gary today because he needed to get back to the forum to work on his future. He looked ahead before pulling out and into his left side view mirror and made a U-turn to head back out on Ridge Road. Sarge lived in the Miller area. Ron would go over to King Drive and take it back up to Fifth Avenue and then go east into Miller.

CHAPTER 58

About the same moment that Ron had begun his U-turn, Michael decided that he was going to see if he could catch up with Ron instead. He made a U-turn in the midst of a few cars on the four-lane boulevard of Broadway. As he was heading back toward Ridge Road, he saw Ron in his car go through the light crossing Broadway heading east. He followed.

CHAPTER 59

Dale gathered two of the operatives that he had on-site. He verified their materials, and he laid out a plan for Vasily and Xi.

CHAPTER 60

Valerie couldn't think of a reason why the caller would even have reason to know to speak of Rick Smalls. She would have understood if the recipient of the call, in some vague way, was to bring up Rick's name but not with the caller. What was that about? She knew that she was having thoughts of Rick because of the reunion after the forum. But why would they ever talk about Rick between themselves? It didn't make any sense. She knew what she had going on, and through bugging the caller's phone, she knew what was going on there until this. In another one of the folders from the thumb driver, she had recordings from the home of the recipient of the call. She scanned through listening to some of them. She found the one that matched up with the heard conversation from the caller. On this version, she couldn't hear what was said on the phone to him, but she already knew that from the other recording. She saw that there was another home recording timed pretty quickly after the other recording. She listened to this, and from one side of this conversation, she heard Rick's name again. She heard about an urgent need to find him. *What is going on?* she thought. She wanted to know more about this. This had to tie into her somehow. Rick was her long-lost friend. Rick was her long-lost love. She couldn't help but think that he was in trouble.

CHAPTER 61

Ron rode King Drive all the way until it merged into Tennessee Street at Eighth Avenue. He continued until he got to Fifth Avenue and turned right. He continued on, a bit lost in his thoughts as he pulled up to the light just after going underneath Interstate 90. He pulled up to the light just before the old Holiday Inn Hotel that was not boarded up. Well, it had boards on it. The homeless or drug users had carved out openings around the property for their use. Ron was sitting at the light, messing with his radio. The mindlessness of sports radio had reached his daily limit. Sometimes it took longer; other times, it didn't take much to get his daily fill about how special the guy in Double-A baseball was and that the Cubs or the White Sox wouldn't know talent if it bit them on the hand. He started hitting his presets.

CHAPTER 62

He was slowing down now because he saw the light turn yellow before Ron got there because he didn't want to get too close to Ron. While slowing, he noticed a white utility van beginning to slow as well in the lane to his left. It wasn't going as slow as he was driving, but it was plenty of time for them to slow down before the light. Michael thought that unless they were tailing someone, the van's speed was odd. As the van did ease past him while he was still moving, he saw the driver of the van reach toward his own forehead. Michael saw the driver begin to pull down a portion of a hat. His instincts told him to look over his shoulders, which he quickly did. This instinct was modified over that first day in the office where he never found concern for what could be behind him. As the van got closer toward the light, Michael's instincts made him retrieve his 9mm from between his left arm and chest. He lowered his window. His distance was about fifteen feet behind Ron. The van was straddling Ron's car, but the nose of the van had only reached the dividing point between the front and back doors on Ron's car. It was then that Michael came to life. He noticed the side sliding door on the passenger side of the van started to slide and saw what he recognized as the tip of some type of rifle starting to be extended outside of the van. He slammed on his gas pedal. In less than two seconds, he had rammed Ron's car to knock it forward and out of the line that the rifle had planned to shoot. He found his driver's door with the downed window now even with the open door frame from the sliding door. Before the shooter could train his aim on him, Michael double-tapped him twice just above the bridge of his nose.

The driver, which was now masked, made the mistake of turning to look instead of pulling away. Michael rotated his right arm thirty degrees to the right and left the driver with two fresh, deadly wounds in his forehead where he had initially reached to pull down his hat. Ron was gone when Michael looked up. This wasn't the place for intelligence gathering. This road could have traffic coming any moment. Michael couldn't risk going for phones or the such. He did take the time to back up real quick to see the license plate. He grabbed the burner phone from the console and took a picture. With that, Michael made his second U-turn of the day.

CHAPTER 63

Xi had colleagues and security around him. He was participating in a seminar within the forum. The thesis of this one was "The Existential Threat to International Metropolitan Areas." Xi had interest because his money or his business interest was no different from all the other companies represented here at this international forum where you could convey to the public that they needed to have help to being safe, then you had the opportunity for a thriving business and the opportunity for greater profits. It didn't matter if the threat was real. Perception was what sold, and Xi, like others in this industry, relished the opportunity to learn new angles to sell fear. All around the globe and through the internet, it was becoming easier and easier to plant fear. Fear sold! Fear required security, and Xi was in the security business for the purpose of capitalizing on fear. Xi and his colleagues were eight in total at a round table for eight near the front of the room. The subject matter moderator was positioned in the front of the room with a screen behind her that had been used for her slides. There were twenty tables similar to the table that Xi and his colleagues were sitting around. There were two of the other tables that were occupied like the table that Xi and his team were at. In that all eight seats were people from the same firm. The difference with Xi's table, which was closer to the wall, was that Xi's security detail was aligned along the wall within a few steps of Xi. There was also a door in the panel of the wall that could be accessed to exit down a back stairway in the event of an emergency. That could be an emergency for everyone or an emergency that Xi identified.

Xi's longtime right-hand man was Lee Fong. He had been with Xi for over twenty years. On any given day that Xi dismissed the rest of the team and even the security detail, he could be found still huddling with Lee. Lee was educated in the United States. He got a PhD in business analytics from Stanford, and he was a perfect fit for the burgeoning business that Xi was driving as an upstart in the United States when he expanded from mainland China. Lee was able to articulate a vision to the leadership team with the full support of Xi. Xi embraced him. Xi saw Lee as smart, personable, and a phenomenal visionary. Lee had done his undergraduate work at the Massachusetts Institute of Technology.

CHAPTER 64

Vasily was two hours away from the time of his off-site meeting. Vasily worked hard, and he played hard. It didn't matter that it was the middle of the afternoon. In his suite at the Chicago Hilton Towers on the twenty-eighth floor that had an adjoining door to another full-size suite like Valerie's suite, there was plenty of activity going on. In one suite, it appeared that much work was being done. Vasily's finance team was working on getting the commitment letters that he might need to purchase what the Programmer had available. Vasily knew that he needed some banks other than from his Mother Russia. He needed some banks from the United States. His team was finalizing all that they needed with a German-based bank that had a large presence in the United States. He knew it would be done, and that was why the other suite through the open connecting door was starting to get louder and louder. Vasily played hard. Sometimes, he travelled with an entourage of women that was a third of his sixty years of age. He was also known to have people to find women of that same age range in whatever city in the world that he might find himself in. And there were times like this where he had the travelling entourage and the local women together at the same time. While Vasily bounced from suite to suite for business, then pleasure and then back and forth, his nonfinance team was mingling primarily in the suite that they could play hard in.

Alexandra had been a part of the travel team for about a year now. She was found in the south of France by Vasily. She was poolside on three consecutive days while Vasily was working and playing hard on the French Riviera. He took note of her in passing each day. To Vasily, she had a future, a future in his renowned travel entourage. On the evening of that third day, Vasily was hosting a party in the hotel that he was staying in. Vasily had been in town for a week at this point, and he had reserved the top two floors of his hotel. There were thirty rooms in total. These rooms were for working and playing. Tonight, they were going to be used the same way but with the emphasis on playing. "And that girl, Alexandra, needed to be there," was what Vasily told his assistant. She was at the party and had been with the travel squad ever since. Most of the travel entourage had been models or actresses or cocktail waitresses. Alexandra had been poolside for those three days at that time. She had done a few other things in her life. Those things were sandwiched around those three days and her time at the Massachusetts Institute of Technology.

CHAPTER 65

His heartbeat was still elevated. He was messing with the radio presets. He got rammed from behind. A couple of shots had come into his car through the rear window, which traveled through the car and hit the back of the headrest on the front passenger seat. Then he lowered his head to just above the top of the dashboard and sped away. He changed lanes to his left and saw that there was no oncoming traffic, so he made the choice to go to the left where the road split up ahead. Speed limit was twenty-five. He was going fifty. His head eased back up. He continued east until he got to Lake Street and turned left twice back to back to park in the commuter South Shore Train parking lot. Ron was asking himself, "What just happened? Who's shooting at me? What just happened? Who hit my car? Was that an accident?" Whether it was an accident or not, he knew that it saved his life. He took a few deep breaths. He exhaled slowly. He popped his trunk and got out of the car. As he approached his trunk, he looked around in all directions. He scanned the area by actually rotating his body three hundred and sixty degrees one way and then back the other way and then the third time back the original way. He stepped up to the trunk and grabbed a backpack from the trunk. He unzipped the backpack and pulled an oily towel from the backpack. He rezipped the backpack and slung the backpack over his shoulder. He pulled a lighter from his pocket and lit both ends of the towel and dropped it into the trunk of his car. He then pulled the trunk down to almost closing it and walked toward the platform of the train station. The oily towel was in the backpack with the weapons that it had been used on to clean.

He checked the train schedule and saw the next westbound train was due in ten minutes. He thought about that being a good thing since in about fifteen minutes a car would have an explosion from the fuel tank being ignited. He knew from many trips on the South Shore Train that the end of the line was downtown Chicago at Randolph and Michigan Avenue. It was just ten blocks from his hotel. He bought a ticket with the destination being the end of the line.

CHAPTER 66

"Tammy, I need some cleanup and some intervention over the next couple of hours," Michael started the call with. Michael told her about the area where the shooting had taken place and the direction that he had come from prior to the shooting. The roads were not populated with residences or industry with the exception of the three blocks between Eighth and Fifth Avenues on Tennessee Street, where houses lined both sides of the street. The longer stretch of King Drive was shaded with sparse wooded areas and some closed businesses. The stretch of road that led to the shooting area from Tennessee Street was not populated with either residences or businesses. His need from Tammy was to find out if there were any cameras that could have captured him at any point of that travel because if someone saw a vehicle with that same description leaving the scene, the police might look to see from which direction it might have come from. "Tammy, I'm sending you a picture of the license plate. Let me know what you come up with. I also had to get on Interstate 90 to go westbound. Wipe me from tollbooths and other cameras along the way. Get me another car. Drop it at the hotel that I checked into last night. Find me a spot to walk away from this car near my hotel. Then have it taken care of. Were the first two packages delivered?"

"They were. You should know. There is a lot of bogeys in your first hotel. They're present and hacking. Do you need to go back there?"

"Right now, I do. I am still wearing the facial hair and jaw pads. Will that be enough for someone running facial recognition off of the hotel's system?"

"Don't trust that only. If you are going back in there, let me know, and I will loop the security system prior to you getting there. You will need to give me at least fifteen minutes' notice. Also for the on-site bogeys, you should consider getting smaller and older. Think about it. Anything else?"

"Yeah. Look up a Ron Winston from Gary, Indiana. He's my age. Get me some intel. I appreciate you. I don't know what is going on right now, but my past seems to have a bit of a collision course with my present right now, and I need to know more. Gotta go. I'll talk with you later." And he hung up.

CHAPTER 67

"That's right, around both of them. I need full audio surveillance immediately. Indefinite period of time. Their rooms. Clothing. If they are stationary in public, get some recording devices near. Feed to base immediately. The key word that I need played back right away is the name Rick Smalls. Get it done now," Valerie demanded.

Chapter 68

This time, the call was even more difficult than any of the other calls to the Voice. It had to be done. "Sir, she broke protocol and was well outside of norm. She went jogging in the middle of the day. We were not prepared for that, so we didn't have someone in place in downtown Chicago staged to go jogging. However, we caught a break. We had been following her staffer that seems to be in a lot of odd places. We only picked him up when he came into town this morning. He wasn't supposed to be here. In following him, she came to us. He was sitting in the park. They ran a dead drop on something."

The Voice said more firmly than any other time that could be remembered by the caller, "Don't lose her again!" The Voice called Jill. "Start full surveillance on Valerie Benson until further notice, and FIND ME RICK SMALLS!"

CHAPTER 69

Valerie had gone to only the snootiest prep schools through eighth grade. This was when her family lived outside of Washington, DC, in Northern Virginia. She liked living in the Falls Church area. She didn't like the schools that she had gone to. It wasn't that she was like the other kids who seemed to think that they had accomplished things in life like their parents instead of realizing that they had earned nothing. It was their parents who had accomplished things. Valerie stayed levelheaded above most. She was always an outstanding student, and she cared for people. As she sat in her suite and was thinking about Rick some more, her mind went back to meeting Rick on the first day of school her freshman year of high school. She and her mother, Rachel, had moved rather hastily to Munster, Indiana, just before school had started. Munster was her mother's hometown. Before her mother had gone to Harvard for her undergraduate work and to Princeton Law School, she had attended Bishop Noll in Hammond. Valerie's mother grew up as an only child, just as Valerie had been.

Valerie never knew her maternal grandfather because he had died from cancer before Valerie was born. She had spent a lot of time with her grandmother over the years, between her grandmother coming out to Virginia for extended stays to Valerie spending time in Munster with her during the summer. Valerie had been told that there was a chance that they were going to move to Munster for some period of time because her grandmother was not well. She was in the early stages of Alzheimer's disease. They didn't want to move her to Northern Virginia because a better way of potentially slowing down the advancement of this disease was to keep her in an environment that she would have more things to remember than changing her environment. Valerie loved her grandmother and really couldn't care one way or another about leaving the school back in Virginia. She knew she was going to miss Gabriella. Gabriella was her family's housekeeper Juanita's daughter. She was two years older than Valerie. Every day when Valerie got home from school she would be looking forward to seeing Gabriella. Gabriella would be at Valerie's home before Valerie got home. She would get dropped off there. Gabriella went to a school for the hearing impaired. She had begun to gradually lose her hearing as a small child through a rare infection that she had contracted.

Valerie rarely talked with the kids at her school, but she always looked forward to coming home and talking with Gabriella about everything by signing. She had been signing with Gabriella since Valerie was four. Gabriella was teaching her as she was learning herself. Valerie asked her mom to help her to learn more. Between Valerie's parents, they decided to get a tutor that would be in their home after school for not only Valerie but for Gabriella as well. Valerie was going to miss Gabriella, but she needed to be there with her mom and her grandmother. Her mother, in coming back home, gave up her senior director role with the prominent lobbying firm Wexler and Truman. Her mom loved the work. But her mom was not going to miss this time with her own mom at this point. So the two of them moved. Her dad stayed in Northern Virginia. His father was running International Safety Services, and her dad was in the number two position primed and ready to take over for her grandfather.

It was a last-minute rush getting Valerie enrolled at Bishop Noll. She had missed the orientation and the open bookstore period, where the students would purchase the books, supplies, and even the uniforms that they were required to wear as students. Freshmen girls' base colors were brown and white. There were brown skirts, brown plaid skirts, and brown pants to go with white blouses and brown pullover or button-up sweaters for the girls. The boys were not as restricted in colors as the girls were. Their uniform was no jeans, and dress shoes were to be worn during school hours with collared shirts that buttoned. They were also required to wear ties every day unless the day had some designation that allowed for them to wear their collars open. On Valerie's first day at her new school, she sat in homeroom in her version of the school uniform since she and her mother had missed the orientation and the purchase or ordering of the uniforms. Her brown skirt was not near the shade of brown that the other girls were wearing and was not quite at the length that Sister Anna Pinto's ruler would find acceptable in relationship to the top of the knee. Some of the other girls did find occasion to look at her as she approached the homeroom and even once she was inside the homeroom. Her initial impression of them was still far better than the snooty girls that she had gone to school with in Northern Virginia. Besides, while she got a little of their attention, there was another student that seemed to get quite a bit more of the attention.

It was a boy. He was bigger than all the other boys in this fresh-men homeroom. He wasn't really built like a freshman or that of many high school kids. You could see that from his attempt at meeting the boys' dress code. He had on a collared shirt that might have been a neck size and a half too small. This led to a shoulder seam on the shirt being higher on the shoulder than the material could wish for, and the cuffs of the sleeves would have been well short of resting on his hands if not for being conveniently rolled up. The length of the sleeves was stretched tight over arms that girls of this age had only seen from the young-adult movie idols that they adored. His pants were showing the strength of his legs as they were pulled tight over his legs as he sat at his desk. His tie was around his neck with the appearance of a tie tied by a six-year-old trying to tie a tie next to his dad without any help. They might have noticed all those things, but they also noticed something that was rare to them all. He was a good-looking male black student in their classroom. This was rare at Bishop Noll High School, but for many of the students, the feeder middle schools these freshmen had come from had little to no presence of black students.

As the homeroom period ended fifteen minutes later and the students were all getting their belongings together to head into different directions, Valerie heard a voice coming from behind. "Hey, what's worse, being stared at because I don't have the look of others in here or missing brown as far as you did with your tan skirt?" Rick had said to Valerie.

Valerie turned, smiled, and said, "I don't know, does tan bother you?"

"No, it is fine with me. Maybe because you are wearing it so well, and you are distinctly different as a result. You do good being different. I'm Rick, Rick Smalls, and you are?"

"Valerie Benson. I've got to go somewhere. I didn't do orientation, so I don't know my way around."

"Me neither. What room are you headed to?"

"Two twelve, I've got math."

"All right, then, maybe I'll see you later."

Valerie now remembered that to be her first conversation with the person that became her best friend.

CHAPTER 70

When Valerie got to room 212, she saw Rick sitting in the third seat in the far row by the window. She headed that way to the open third seat in the row next to him. "You could have told me that you were headed this way. Why didn't you?"

"I wanted to see if you would smile or frown. You have a nice smile. I got a feeling about you, Valerie Benson. I liked the way that you told me where your class was and what your subject were, but you left out the part about it being college prep. That tells me that you are simply confident in who you are and that you are not trying to wave your smarts around in front of people."

Valerie smiled in her room right now. Probably quite similarly to the way that she smiled after Rick said that to her back then.

CHAPTER 71

The Voice answered his phone and listened for about thirty seconds. He swiped the vase off the table with his left hand while hanging up on the caller.

CHAPTER 72

While traveling on Interstate 90 out of Gary toward Chicago, Rick passed through East Chicago and then into Hammond. In Hammond, he saw off to the side of the road Bishop Noll High School. He didn't ride by there yesterday on the streets because he had gotten initially distracted with the article that he had read. In passing it and before leaving Hammond to enter Whiting and then Chicago, he thought back to his first day at the school. All his classes were college prep or the accelerated equivalent. It was a homeroom class, and there were three other classes before lunch, and Valerie Benson was in all the classes. That was a quick, hard introduction to her. They decided to have lunch together on that first day, and they had lunch together every day for the entire four years. Sometimes others joined them or joined near them, but most often it was just them. Sometimes they sat side by side, and other times they ate directly across from each other. To say that they hit it off from the beginning was to terribly understate the facts. Within weeks, it seemed like they were finishing each other's sentences. Their backgrounds on race, family economics, or opposite thoughts about sports never seemed to matter.

It wasn't until shortly after their senior year began that they hit a rough patch, with Rick not wanting to talk about his future plans and with her wanting to know about his plans but not willing to push him. They both were on edge. They had made it all the way to the spring of their senior year without Rick sharing his plans. The rumors around the school ranged from Rick must have had some academic problems, which certainly wasn't possible, or that he was staying home to work because his family was poor and he wasn't going to go to school. There were a few of the unfounded rumors that he had gotten a girl pregnant in his neighborhood and that he was going to get married and stay home.

Rick was frustrated with the weight of what he was carrying every day. He knew why he was carrying it, but it still frustrated him. That frustration wasn't there back in the summer when Rick had answered the Voice by saying that he was in. But with all the craziness with the rumors and the school year nearing an end, Rick was given the okay to share his plans with his friend Valerie. He could tell her that he didn't want to disappoint by telling them that he was going to go to MIT and give up sports, and that was why he hadn't said anything. He told her that he was telling her because he thought he was hurting their relationship by not telling her. He told her that she could not tell anyone. She agreed. Rick felt the burden of his secret lifted. But more than anything, he was happy to see that same smile from Valerie that he saw in the freshman math class on the first day that they met.

CHAPTER 73

Dale was ready to execute the new plans, the plans that Mr. Benson had authorized him to carry out. Dale didn't think any worse for the plans that was worked up between himself and Valerie. It's just that those new plans took him more back to his roots. In his current role, he was required to be more strategic for a big picture. Very seldom did the things in his current capacity that he gave directions on showed themselves to be game changers instantly. In his current capacity, he would receive information and get within a conference room, and they would work out plans to solve the customers' needs over time. Through the operatives that he met with earlier, they had alerted their assets to be prepared to act when the signal was given to them. This type of alert to act just excited him. Over the years, he was the operative that was alerted. In years past, he was the asset. He couldn't help but think about when he ran assets. He had some good ones at his hand when needed. The bad thing about how good he had prepared and executed through his assets was that he no longer directly handled assets. He had good ones. They did everything. They hid in plain sight. They got close to targets. They spoke other languages. They learned all types of skills to secure information, to protect the country, and even to help in defeating both rogue nations and rogue companies.

The operatives separately had gotten back to Dale to let him know that their assets were in place. Dale saw these assets today in the role of protecting the country and defeating rogue companies. It didn't matter if this was what actually was going to take place or not. He was authorized to execute with these assets through those operatives. Dale signaled both the operatives to go live with their plans.

CHAPTER 74

The seminar that Xi was attending was scheduled to last another fifteen minutes or so. The hotel staff that was assigned to housekeeping during live events like this seminar was performing their normal duties. Their responsibilities included keeping fresh water at tables, removing coffee cups, and providing more coffee or even stationary for notes and writing materials. At the table where Xi was sitting, his security detail was still standing against the wall. This was about six feet from where Xi was sitting. For the positioning of the round table, Xi's seat was the closest to the wall and his security detail. In the seat immediately to his left was Lee. Directly opposite of Lee standing was a server from the hotel staff. In the course of providing service, she pulled out a blue towel to wipe a spot of water buildup of one of Lee's colleagues. The water buildup was from condensation from a water glass. When Lee saw that the server was cleaning the area with the blue napkin, he knew that the operation was now live. Lee raised his left hand to about shoulder height with his index finger extended. The server, after finishing wiping the area, came toward Lee on his left, still away from Xi and the attention of the security detail. The security detail's attention was heightened just because of the proximity of the server, but they still hovered close to the wall. As the server was standing near Lee while Lee was sitting, Lee asked the server a question, "Can you get me a pad of paper and an ink pen, please?"

The server nodded and also said, "Yes, sir." With that, the server walked toward the back of the room where there were stacks of pads of paper and also sleeves filled with hotel-branded ink pens. The server grabbed two pads of paper from the table and pulled a pen out of her service coat that had the same hotel branding on it, as all the pens in the sleeve. With those items at the ready, she returned to Lee's left side and sat these items on the table next to him.

Lee looked upward at her and thanked her. Lee took one of the pads of paper and centered it in front of him and then picked up the pen that the server left with him. He wrote a note that he intended to share with Xi. After writing the note, he proofed it by going back over each of the words by tapping the pen near each word to show that he was proofreading the note. The note simply said, "Before you go to meet the Programmer, do you want me to verify the financial transactions again?" That was all that the note said. With the proofreading being complete, Lee pushed the pad of paper to Xi's direction with his left hand across his body to his right. With the movement of the notepad, Xi began to lean toward his left. He and Lee had communicated this way in boardrooms, seminars, banquets, you name it, so he leaned toward Lee almost reflexively. And Lee began to lean more to his right. These movements meant nothing to the security detail. Lee was Xi's right-hand man. They had seen this type of motion hundreds of times. It was nothing to alert them at all.

As the pad had passed the midpoint between the two old friends and while Lee was leaning closer to Xi's left hand that was reaching toward the pad of paper, Lee's right hand was growing closer to Xi's left hand. At about the moment that Xi's left hand touched the pad of paper, it appeared as if Lee had accidentally marked Xi's left hand with the tip of the pen from Lee's right hand. The tip slid on the top of Xi's left hand for about a quarter of an inch. Immediately, Lee said, "Excuse me, sir."

"No worries," responded Xi as he noticed the slight smear of ink on his hand. Xi licked his right index finger and wiped away at the ink spot. Most of the ink was gone, and Xi licked the right index finger again and then wiped away the remaining ink. Xi read the note. Xi reached for the pen from Lee and answered, "Yes, why don't you go now, and we will finish up here, and I will meet you in the suite as soon as the seminar ends." Xi set the pen down.

With that response, Lee picked up both the pad of paper and the pen and then nodded in Xi's direction and got up. He turned to leave the room. Once he was outside of the room, he tore off the note and the next four sheets of paper from the pad. As he headed toward the bank of elevators, he tore those sheets of paper up into several pieces. He then dropped the paper and the pen in the trash receptacle near the elevator bank. The server that was in the room came by within seconds with a trash cart and dumped the contents of the trash bin by the elevators into her cart just as the elevator was closing with Lee on board heading back upstairs to Xi's suite.

CHAPTER 75

Vasily was on the play side of the two suites really enjoying himself as the time was approaching that he needed to leave to go to his meeting with the Programmer. There was a knock at the door. From where Vasily was standing and drinking vodka shots with Alexandra, they both were able to see the person outside the door when one of Vasily's guards had opened the door. The woman, who appeared to be part of the housekeeping staff, told the guard that there had been some noise complaints. She didn't ask if they would do anything different. She just relayed that message and left. The guard, after closing the door, came over to Vasily and relayed the message. Vasily looked quizzically at the guard and turned his head to Alexandra, who had heard the message as well. Almost fully synchronized, Vasily and Alexandra fell out laughing. Neither seemed interested in doing anything different with the noise level, and Vasily yelled out for everyone to take another shot of the good vodka from Mother Russia that they were drinking from this afternoon.

CHAPTER 76

After the hotel representative left the room after giving the message about the noise, she headed toward the center of the floor for the trash cart. She was the same hotel server that delivered the pen and paper to Lee moments earlier. Back in the room with the call for more vodka for all, Alexandra took her shot and asked Vasily to excuse her for a moment to freshen up. Vasily liked Alexandra a great deal, but there were five other women in the room at his disposal, so he barely acknowledged the question from Alexandra. Alexandra headed away and removed a cigarette from her clutch and lit up a cigarette in this nonsmoking room. It wasn't the only cigarette lit in the room. Vasily did what he wanted, and an American hotel room was not going to guide him and his guests when it came to noise and cigarettes and around the world for that matter if it was important to him. He would realize that in the last year between his business team, security, and the travelling entourage, his hotel bills were padded by nearly $150,000 for damages, which included evidence of smoking in the rooms. If Vasily knew this, he still wouldn't do anything different. All that matter was that his life wasn't impacted or compromised by what others thought were good rules to put in place.

Alexandra went into the ladies' room and started to run some warm water while sitting the butt edge of the lit cigarette on the countertop of the bathroom sink. She then turned to lock the door. She opened her purse and pulled out some lipstick to freshen up. She then picked up the cigarette and drew a long puff on it. The

159

cigarette was soiled with the fresh mounting of lipstick that she had just applied on her mouth. She held the cigarette in her hand as she looked straightforward into the mirror. She thought about doing something with her hair but then decided not to. She turned and unlocked the door and headed back toward Vasily. Before getting to Vasily, she grabbed four more shots of vodka and put them on a tray. As she eased back near Vasily, she lightly stretched out the tray, and Vasily took it from her. He then grabbed a shot, and she grabbed one. They both drank it down. Vasily grabbed another one from the tray, and so did Alexandra. After the second shot, Alexandra took another long drag from her cigarette, and when he saw her do it, he said, "Where are the cigarettes? Do you have more with you?" Vasily was so comfortable with Alexandra, and he also found himself wanting to drink and smoke whenever they were together that he had gotten her a cigarette case that had slots on one side for her brand of cigarettes and on the other side slots for his.

"I sure do, Vasily. Here, let me get them out of my purse. Alexandra opened her purse with both hands with her cigarette hanging out of the right side of her mouth. After opening the purse with both hands, she held the purse with her right hand and removed the cigarette case from the purse with her left hand. She closed her purse up against her body, and with her right hand, she put the purse between her left bicep and her rib cage. Then with both hands, she opened the cigarette case on Vasily's side and leaned the right end of the case in his direction for him to take one. He did. From the case, Alexandra removed a lighter, and Vasily caught the flame of the lighter on the tip of the tobacco and took a long, hard pull to get as much of the tobacco flavor into his body as possible.

He looked into Valerie's eyes and said, "Spaseeba," or thank you.

The call came from the space in the door opening between the two suites. "Vasily, it is time to go."

Vasily took another long drag on the cigarette and handed it toward Alexandra and said, "Handle this for me. I've got to go to work now for a bit."

Alexandra took the cigarette and headed toward the restroom and threw hers and his into the toilet and flushed.

CHAPTER 77

Ron seemed to have no control over his thought process on his train trip back into Chicago. He was thinking in the moment. He was thinking back to seeing the man in the hotel lobby that looked like Rick. He thought about his call with Sarge, his meeting with Bobby, and the targeting on his life. Was it a drive-by shooting that wasn't really a drive-by? Was he a target? Only one person knew where he was headed, and that was Sarge. If Sarge was for some reason targeting him, then why then and not somehow before then? What about Bobby? Bobby had some questions that he didn't address or answer. Was he connected to the shooting? Why did Bobby get on the phone right after leaving the diner? Did his phone ring, or did he make a call out? If he made a call out, was it related to Ron and the questions that he was asking? What about Rick? Ron knew that him being in Gary and him making calls to both Sarge and Bobby and then meeting with Bobby were all related to Rick or his parents. So what was the connection? Was there a connection? Ron was trying to think about Sarge and Bobby as cops or, even for that matter, himself as a cop. He knew that when he had gotten into the police force, his intentions were to be a good cop, which in and of itself was vague enough to allow for his flexible moral nature or anyone else's to finish every day as a good cop because when a person was flexible morally, then they were able to reconcile their actions to fit what they seemed to be right. Ron had done things illegal prior to becoming a cop, and his thoughts were that those very experiences would actually help him in fighting crime. It was after he met and got to know Bobby that his moral compass started to show itself with a willingness to go in all directions.

He liked the idea of getting more arrests through the calls from Bobby. It put him in a better light with Sarge and with the lieutenant above the sarge. He knew then that nothing was free, and it wasn't until later that some of the pieces came together. It seemed that the street dealers that he was busting were not connected to the one suspected larger distributor in the area. They were street dealers under other distributors. It was rumored that part of Bobby's lifestyle was supported by a drug dealer. Even then Ron thought that it would be foolish of Bobby to have the distributor that he worked for street dealers arrested. So in essence, Ron was working for the same distributor with his reward being a more favorable light with Sarge and others. He was also aware of the rumors surrounding Sarge. Sarge had peaked professionally. He was a sergeant and was always going to be a sergeant. He would have annual pay increases of two to three percent for being average. Even with this, Sarge had either shown a knack for being the prudent financial investor or just lucky in investing because he lived well beyond the pay range that he could have been in. He had gotten a lakefront house on Lake Michigan in the Ogden Dunes area just west of Portage, Indiana. When Ron had been on the force, he overheard Sarge use the task force excuse for the first time.

On one afternoon after the shift had been dismissed from the shift room for the preshift meeting, Ron left and was headed toward the lot with his partner for their car. Ron realized that he had left his notepad back in the meeting room and turned around to go and get it. As he approached the doorway of the meeting room, the door was open, and he heard Sarge berating another officer about getting too close to some of the gambling houses. While there was some legal gambling in the area, the gambling that Sarge was talking about was strictly illegal. Sarge was repeatedly telling the officer that that was beyond their jurisdiction. It was matter of a task force. From that time forward, whether he was told something by Sarge to stay away from or if other officers were just talking about conversations that they had had with Sarge, they would mention how Sarge would bring up task force. The oddity was that there were plenty of times when task force activities were shared with them through other law-enforcement agencies when a task force was going on in the Gary city limits to avoid the potential of bumping heads on raids or investigations. Ron began to believe that whenever Sarge mentioned a task force, what he really was saying was that they needed to stay away from something because that matter was important to him and maybe to his lakefront home.

Even now, he didn't begrudge Bobby and Sarge for what he believed that he knew about them. They all did it, and they all benefitted from whatever they did; and they all, at the end of the night, extended the compass of their own morality to show that the direction that they had gone was still on course. What did matter to Ron was that whether or not something that one or both of them had engaged in was the driving force in him getting shot at today. And if it was driven by Bobby, that would be the second time today that Ron had reason to believe that Bobby might have knowledge of him being a target of a shooting. Well, with the bag that he retrieved from his car just before he set it on fire to explode, he had retrieved his guns from the trunk of the car. He had a couple of guns now and many clips of ammunition. He thought that if people wanted to shoot at him, then he would be prepared to shoot back at them.

CHAPTER 78

Valerie saw that the time for the off-site meeting that she had shared with Dale and her father was nearing, and she hadn't received an update from Dale. She called him.

"What do you mean that after you talked with my father that he updated the plan? Dale, what is this? This is my plan. You and I had talked through the logistics of it. We would get out in front of this and look to intercept the communication between Vasily and the Programmer so that I could leverage any gained information if I could get in front of the Programmer for International Safety Services. Dale, why didn't you call me with this?"

"Mr. Benson told me that he would review things with you and for me to focus on finding the other potential players that were going to meet with the Programmer," Dale answered.

"Dale, why would it matter who else was going to meet with the Programmer if the direction that my father gave to you was to basically stand down and get out of the intel gathering detail, which is one of the tenets of the business that we are in? Don't answer that. I'll call him!" Valerie hung up.

Dale knew what was going on. He liked working in the manner that Mr. Benson had directed him to execute. He had a good idea why Mr. Benson would want to give the impression that they had backed away. Deniability. He also realized that based on Valerie's conversation, she didn't seem to have any knowledge of Xi at this point, which when she heard anything about him later would only seem to be unfortunate and not coincidental.

CHAPTER 79

"Dad, please help me to understand why I am just now finding out about the change in plans from Dale. Why would you change my plans? You and I did not have a conversation about any other type of plan. You are an adviser to me. You advise me! I choose what to accept. You don't run this business. I do! What is the benefit to an intel organization in not having intel? Help me to understand this, can you!"

"Sweetie—"

"No. Not sweetie, tell me as the executive in charge of International Safety Services what you are doing to International Safety Services. You are not talking to your daughter!" a livid Valerie said over the phone through clenched teeth.

"I'm sorry. I had no intentions of undermining your plans. I just thought that this was one time where if you were able to secure a meeting with the Programmer as a vendor, the merits that you have instilled in the values of International Safety Services would bring home the opportunity. Sweetie, I'm sorry. Valerie, you have done a phenomenal job of positioning your company for this type of purchase or any other purchase for that matter. You have positioned International Safety Services as the industry leader. Why do you think that the industry want you to speak tonight as the forum's keynote speaker? I'll tell you. You have something to say. And they all want to hear it! If I have touched something in a way that is not approving to you, please forgive me, and if you think that I have seen my better times and that they are in my past, then I will step away and not get in your way anymore. Let me know what you want from me, but more than anything, please forgive me. Can you do that?"

"Dad, perhaps I am overreacting. I forgive you. I just need to know things, and I would have rather discussed this with you prior to you having Dale to scrap the surveillance plan. Right now, I don't have a meeting, so I still see this as a gamble. I've got to go. I have some things to do prior to the speech tonight." She hung up. Valerie did not accept the explanation. She recognized that her company was the industry leader, but why would they abandon one of the cornerstones of what had gotten them to the top of the industry in intel gathering? Something smelled to her. She needed to talk with Dave Klen, her insider, the man in the park.

CHAPTER 80

Xi was exiting the seminar with the other members of the team while being covered by his security detail. As they all were heading toward the elevator bank there on the mezzanine level, he walked over to the railing area, about where Ron had seen whom he thought was Rick. He was standing there with his waistline about even with the rail top. He had motioned out over the lobby level, pointing out something that seemed to be only clear to him. The attraction of all the lights that illuminated the lobby area at this moment was seemingly fascinating him. He gestured many times in the direction of the lights and then turned with his back to the railing, and looking at his team and the security detail, he said, "I am going into the light." Many of them thought he said something about going into the night. While they were trying to understand this something about going into the night, Xi, with his back resting on the rail, initiated a backward inert movement that caused him to go over the rail and fall from the mezzanine level to the main-floor lobby level. His landing spot was a shiny marble floor. He stuck the landing in the most unwanted landing form of any gymnast. He hit the marble floor horizontally with the front side of his body being led by his face. The sound of splat shattered the common noise of the area, and the common noise of the area was replaced with screams.

Chapter 81

One of Vasily's guards pressed the down button for the elevator. When the elevator arrived, it was empty. Vasily slightly stumbled getting into the elevator on the twenty-eighth floor. He was accompanied by two guards and two finance guys. As the elevator descended to the lobby, there seemed to be a bead of sweat accumulating on Vasily's brow. He felt it and wiped at it. Vasily tried to say something, but only gibberish came out. The people that was with him was not unaccustomed to the lack of clarity in Vasily's words. Vasily didn't handle his alcohol as well as he thought, and often his words would be unclear. So no one really gave it another thought. The elevator stopped for other guests of the hotel on the ninth and sixth floors. There were now one additional man and two women on this elevator. When the ladies got on the elevator on the sixth floor, one of them noticed Vasily in the back of the elevator, and she wondered if he was okay. There was a grin on his face that displayed a lack of awareness because his pupils were both positioned nearly vertically.

The elevator arrived on one. The ladies exited, and the man from nine followed. One of Vasily's guards exited followed by the two finance men and then the other guard. This was the established protocol of his guards that Vasily's front and back could be covered when he got introduced into a new space, like the lobby, as opposed to the second guard following him off the elevator. Everyone was positioned, waiting for Vasily to exit the elevator. He didn't. Vasily was on the floor in the elevator, as if he slid down from a standing position with both pupils locked in a vertical position. Xi had gone splat about seventy-five feet to the left of the elevators just five minutes previously. As people looked into the open elevator looking to go up, they saw Vasily's lifeless body, and then more screams were heard in the lobby of the hotel.

CHAPTER 82

Dave Klen was in the lobby when the awful sound engulfed the lobby. It wasn't long after that that he and the others in the lobby and from the mezzanine were aware that someone had fallen from the mezzanine level. He was near the area. All that he saw was a stream of blood that was gliding away from the body on the floor. He had no idea who it was or what had led to this body being face-down on this hard marble floor. He noticed that the initial rush that brought many people to the body and down the stairs from the mezzanine level were not as active as they were. He assumed the worst, that this person had died from the fall. After a few minutes of not quite gawking, Dave headed over to the elevator bank to go upstairs to see Valerie. While waiting for an elevator to arrive, he was positioned closest to the elevator to his right. He saw the light come on indicating that the elevator the farthest to his left would be arriving and opening soon, and the up arrow was now lit. As he waded that direction away from the door area to allow for any potential riders to have a clear path to exit, he saw that he would also let the three ladies that were there before him to board. They were also aware of the man on the floor. Two of them were crying, and they were all comforting one another.

The elevator opened, and two ladies got off together followed by a man. Then two men that Dave recognized followed by two men that he also recognized as guards without knowing who they were got off. The next thing he knew as he got front and center with the elevator was that he saw Vasily Kuznetsov slumped on the floor. At that same moment, the three women all began to scream.

CHAPTER 83

"I was just about…," Valerie started.

"Listen, are you alone? Are you safe? Say the safe word," Dave interrupted.

"MIT, what is going on, Dave? You're scaring me!"

"Stay in your room and don't open the door until you get a call from me telling you that I am right outside your door." Dave hung up and went to the mezzanine level, where all elevator activity to go upstairs had been redirected to. After waiting for nearly five minutes, he boarded an elevator for the twenty-ninth floor. He exited and went straight to Valerie's room. Once he was outside of her room, he called her. She answered her phone and then opened the door. Dave entered and closed the door behind himself quickly and applied the door latch as well.

CHAPTER 84

"Are you sure that it was Vasily Kuznetsov? What happened? Could you tell? Who was the other man?"

"Valerie, I told you that I didn't know. But wasn't Vasily supposed to be heading to meet with the Programmer about now?" Dave asked.

"Yeah, yeah, he was. That was what I was about to call you about. I was going to ask you to follow him."

"Why? Didn't Dale have that covered?"

"He did until he didn't. My father injected himself into the matter and changed the plan, saying something about International Security Services being able to impress any vendor on its own merits, blah, blah, blah."

"Look, grab an overnight bag with the essentials that you need to continue to prep for tonight, including the shoes that you will wear. Don't worry about your dress. Get your shoes and toiletries along with your business materials. I am getting you to another hotel, and you will get a dress there, and we won't come back this way unless we know more about the overall security here. We are going to take the stairs down. Put on your workout clothes again. I'll carry your bag. While we are going down, you should call Dale to get an understanding of the security for tonight. I don't know what is going on, but I would bet that this hotel haven't had two people die separately in the lobby within five minutes of each other ever before. I don't believe in coincidences. Can you be ready in five minutes?"

"Yes." Valerie began gathering things and closed the door to the sleeping area of the suite to change clothes.

CHAPTER 85

"Where are you?" Tammy began as soon as Michael answered the phone.

Rick answered, "I'm coming into the loop area now." The greater downtown area of Chicago is called the loop because of the elevated train track pattern that covered the downtown area.

"Don't head over to the Hilton. That area has gone crazy, and here's the part that you need to know more than anything. Both Xi Ping and Vasily Kuznetsov have died there within what seems to be five minutes of each other. I am trying to find out more now. I have eyes on your third meeting participant. She is safe for now. She was led from her hotel room down the stairs and out of the hotel with minimal items. It was Dave Klen with her. They got in a cab and went over to a boutique hotel not far from where you are staying. It's called the Palomar. I've got it watched."

"Thanks, Tammy. What's the early information that you have on the deaths?"

"Xi fell from the mezzanine level, and Vasily dropped in an elevator. Other than a terrible coincidence of timing, there is nothing showing either to be foul play right now."

"This was not coincidence, that's for sure. Can you retrieve those two packages that was sent out for them?"

"It will be easy to get Vasily's since his meeting was to be at another location. I will try to get the one for Xi. But it might be harder since it is in the Hilton. Also, there is a lot of chatter about the need to find someone that fits your description in that property. You need to stay clear because the people are not law enforcement. There will be a high presence of law enforcement with these two accidents and that both of them are foreign nationals in town for the forum."

"Anything else?"

First, she told him where he could drop the car. Then she added, "This could be the worst of all the bad news that I am sharing with you today. From the footage that you gave me from that encounter that you had overseas years ago, I got something. It didn't match from facial recognition. I have an eighty-two percent match on a walk. The difference could be for changes due to age. Your man might be here in the hotel."

"Tammy, figure out my paths to the keynote speech tonight or my path into that other hotel later tonight and get back to me. Good work, and I will be careful." Michael thought that it would be prudent to let Tammy know that he would be preceding with caution. She was going to tell him too if he had not said anything.

CHAPTER 86

Michael pulled into the parking garage, and before exiting, from the inside pocket of his jacket he pulled out a small towel. Before opening the car door to get out, he began wiping down the interior of the 4Runner. He never touched anything in the rear seat, so he didn't bother wiping that area. He wiped all that he could from the driver's seat and then opened the door. He finished wiping the steering wheel and the entire door panel. He shut the door with the towel in hand and wiped the exterior of the door. He patted his pant pockets to search for the valet stub from his hotel. He then reached into his left pocket and pulled it out. He put it back in and closed the door on the 4Runner and walked away toward the stairwell next to the elevator on the third level of the parking garage. When he reached the bottom level, he found the exit to the street level. He exited the parking garage on Grand Avenue between Clark and Dearborn about two blocks away from his Embassy Suites Hotel room. While walking back to his hotel, he was thinking about the man whose walk was matched by Tammy. He understood why the walk was a greater hit than the facial recognition. If this was him, it wouldn't surprise Michael that he was an attendee of the forum. He worked within the security industry when Michael knew him years ago, what Michael remembered as an evolving role in the security industry.

The profile that was with Tammy and the other operatives that Michael worked with was footage from another hotel overseas where Michael last saw the man. Michael had secured that footage shortly after the last time that he had seen him. As he developed his own network since then, he always shared that footage with people like Tammy that worked for him. They all had had the responsibility of scanning this video for various recognitions whenever Michael gave them the heads up on where he might be spending some time. Michael would want to know if he was near. Tammy had set a timer to run this footage for recognition on a loop against the various feed that she had tapped into at the Hilton Hotel.

As Michael was walking toward State Street to then turn left at the corner restaurant, he thought on the man. The man had recruited him into the service of the country. He was in charge of his training and assignments. The man worked for the Voice. Once he left for MIT, the assignments began while the training was ongoing. Some of the assignments were done from the comfort of his apartment in Boston. He was hacking into systems. He was never seen on these. Before he even got to MIT, Michael knew more than most about the inner workings of computer engineering. So when he was tasked with getting inside systems of, what was told to him, global financial institutions to set monitors on some specific activity type so that they could monitor the potential influence operations that could be run to set a financial terrorism trap, Michael did it. He did what was asked of him to the fullest, knowing that everything that he was doing was off the books or known as wet work. There was no cover. There was no governmental agency that could provide him with a "get out of jail free" card. So Michael set traps and false paths that if someone was able to determine that someone like him was hacking into their system, it would lead them to places around the globe that couldn't be traced to Michael. Michael also expanded his role on each assignment for his own benefit to be able to get information that could be negotiable for him only if he was to get caught down the road.

The Recruiter was pleased with how fast Michael was able to turn around the assignments. He wanted to get Michael into the game even more, but he couldn't do all that he wanted to do with Michael without blowing the cover of him being a student. He couldn't pull Michael away from Boston to travel the country or to go abroad during the school term. But as soon as that first Christmas break came, he had something for Michael to do in Miami, which also had been the first time that he had to admonish Michael. While Michael was in touch with Valerie, with the Recruiter's permission as Rick Smalls, Michael had made some holiday plans to spend some time with Valerie there in Boston before she was to meet her family in Vail, Colorado. When the Recruiter contacted him the need to be on a plane the first thing the following morning back then, Michael tried to tell the Recruiter about his plans. The Recruiter ripped into Michael. He told him that while he had the flexibility to make plans in his life, he also needed to stay aware that he had no life before any of the needs or assignments that the Recruiter would put in front of him. Properly admonished, Michael canceled the plans with Valerie and proceeded with the assignment. He hurt Valerie but knew that he needed to figure out another way of having time with her without being positioned to cancel on her in the future.

When Michael waved down the taxi in Miami before noon the following day and got into the taxi, he realized that someone had left a package in the back seat of the taxi. "Excuse me, there is a bag on the floor here. Someone must have left it here before I got in."

"It is for you," was all that the taxi driver said then and for the rest of the trip. He pulled up to the hotel destination that Michael had given to him.

Michael's hotel was the Loew's Miami Beach Hotel. He was right on the beach near the ocean. It was mid-December and eighty-two degrees. This beat Boston or Gary if he had a home to go back to. He was not here, however, for the beauty of the beach or the great December weather. He was here for an assignment outside of the four walls of his Boston apartment. His face was about to be in the world when he was about to progress from protecting the country's interest through hacking and breaking and entering another hotel room to grab a memory device and to corrupt it. He would then leave it behind. They could not be sure when the memory device would have been online somewhere to hack it. The Recruiter had intel to suggest that the person with this information was going to be in Miami Beach and perhaps to sell it in its current form as a stored device. The intel also said that the owner of the information would be with it at all times with attached security. So besides breaking and entering and then having to influence a situation with the owner of the information and his security, Michael was told that he might need to get dirty in this situation. Getting dirty could mean anything from getting the folks unconscious somehow to creating a diversion big enough to make the switch. Michael was given the task of getting the assignment done without a trace of his involvement.

Michael checked into his room on the eighth floor. He carried a backpack, and in his hand was the package that he retrieved from the taxi. He set his backpack on the bed and then sat on the bed as he was tearing open the package from the taxi. After he got the top of the package torn open, he squeezed the package to open it up more so that he could look inside. When he looked inside, he paused for a moment and then reached in the package. He then put his hand inside to retrieve the contents of the package. He pulled out the largest item first, a Heckler & Koch SFP9. It had one fifteen-round clip already inserted in it, and he checked the chamber, and there was a round in it as well. He set it on the bed. He reached in again and pulled out two more fifteen-round clips. Michael set the clips on the bed as well. He looked in the package again and did not see anything else. To be sure, he turned the package upside down over the bed, and then it came falling out. He anticipated that this would be available to him. It was a small vial with the top being a screw-off dropper. This was a narcotic that could knock out someone from one drop to a part of a bottled water. Michael was looking at the tools for the assignment that had been given to him. Getting the storage device and corrupting it were his to-do on-site. Michael had been briefed on the potential methods of executing this assignment, and while he had never been outside of his apartment to perform an assignment before, there was something that he knew about this assignment. He didn't like how it was set up. Michael inserted his earbuds and turned on his music. He then laid back on the bed, closed his eyes, and started to visualize what he would do if he could create the execution plan. While he was beginning to visualize an alternate approach, he had the sounds of Prince's "International Lover" playing in his ears.

The advance information that Michael had received about his target, Enrique Ruiz, was that he was a man that had sold programs that would give the buyer the ability to insert his devices into someone else's server to grab, modify, or destroy the contents of the server that it was introduced to. Michael had been told that the server that Enrique's device was going to get attached to was a foreign national firm that advertised as a branch of a law firm based in Madrid, Spain. Michael's advance intel told him that this office did do some legal work; however, the main intent was its cover as a source to disrupt the various Spanish heritage communities in Southern Florida. Enrique's device was to provide them with detailed census and polling data that could help with the dissemination of misleading community activities. This misleading information was intended to divide the community upon what in essence would be tribal lines. Enrique also liked to try out the night life in a town before doing business. Michael thought about this being the approach: follow him, catch him out, and pick his pocket. But Michael was stuck on how to get it back to him once he had taken it from him or even to retrieve it from his pocket.

Ten minutes after lying back on the bed, Michael got a call. It was the Recruiter. "The target has arrived. Besides the security, his sister is with him. They have reservations tonight for dinner at Byblos not far from your hotel. They also are going to a nightclub called The Raven after dinner. We should have an updated plan for you in a bit."

"No. Give me these things, and I can pull it off." With that, Michael rattled off a number of things that he would need to be successful tonight. The Recruiter acknowledged the items and hung up the phone.

Michael put the package contents into his backpack, zipped the backpack, and headed for the door of his hotel room. He had some shopping and grooming to do. In the original dossier on Enrique Ruiz, not only did it mention his proclivity for the night life, it also mentioned that it was taken to another level whenever his twin sister, Cynthia, was with him. When the Recruiter made mention of her being with Enrique, Michael knew how to guide this assignment to a safe landing. He had no reason to think that he would need the weapon or the narcotic. He told the Recruiter to get him the best available suite at whatever five-star hotel was near the nightclub The Raven. He was now on his way to get himself made over in a traveler sort of way. He didn't want the look of a college kid during winter break. He wanted to match the jet-set way of Enrique and, more importantly, Cynthia.

CHAPTER 87

As it turned out, the hotel that met the criteria that Michael had given to the Recruiter was the hotel that he was already in, the Loew's. The Recruiter got Michael moved to the best suite available but then also booked him in another hotel nearby. By 7:00 p.m., Michael had been made over to fit the folks that were in Miami Beach to enjoy the weather, the night, and the local attractions. Promptly at seven, there was a knock at his door. Michael opened the door, and the Recruiter had delivered. Michael said that he needed five beautiful, exotic Spanish- and English-speaking women to be delivered to his new room. The Recruiter knew where this was, and he delivered. They were to be dressed for an evening of dining, partying out, and partying in. Only two of them would go initially with Michael. The other three would bump into their two friends with Michael when they all bumped into Enrique and his party at The Raven. Prior to that, Michael would be seen at Byblos with the first two ladies. This would be the opportunity to begin fishing for Enrique and his sister, Cynthia.

In the time since Michael had spoken with the Recruiter earlier, he had gotten clothes more befitting the two places that he was going to be that evening and night. He had created for himself a new persona that was close to the truth in some regards but far enough away in other regards to never allow this to be traced back to him in any way. He was one of those new millionaires through the internet. The truth was, he probably was already prepared for the next great thing through the "internet"; however, he was going down a different path with the Recruiter. This also gave him and Enrique some discussion areas. He would describe the women as friends from when he lived in Miami. He would also mix in that he had not lived in Miami since he moved to Silicon Valley. He would explain that they were just out getting to know one another when he would get into the company of Enrique and Cynthia. Michael would make certain that he and the women showed themselves to Enrique and Cynthia while they were at dinner by having a wildly good time at dinner while slightly including Enrique, Cynthia, and other patrons of Byblos in the fun between himself and his two new lady friends. The hope would be that if not from Enrique, then more importantly from Cynthia that an invitation would come from one of them for Michael and his friends to join them at The Raven.

The women were professionals. They would meet the requirements of the evening. The amount that the Recruiter had arranged for each of them to get paid would cover a normal week of their time. By title, they were escorts. Their clients would be someone that would like to have the presence of company, whether in public or semipublic settings. Michael explained to them the roles that each of them would be playing for the night. There were the two ladies that would accompany him from the beginning. They would be friends who had just met Michael the night before. The other three would come into The Raven later and see their two friends with Michael. They then looked to join their friends with Michael. Whether they all got to The Raven with or without being a part of Enrique's party didn't matter. Yes, Michael thought that it would be great to have the connection from the restaurant to lead to an invitation to join them with their night plans at The Raven. But he could just as easily show up there with his two new friends. The hook came with two potentials, one that would be influenced by Enrique wanting to move to a more private party environment because of the comfort that he would feel with this crowd at some point. The other, which Michael preferred, would be to play on some of the information that he had ascertained from the dossier. Enrique enjoyed partying with his sister. She brought a real life to things. The dossier also explained that

Cynthia partied hard. It was Michael's hope that his makeover would appeal to Cynthia and that through Cynthia he could actually guide the party back to his suite. He explained to the women that Enrique must get relaxed. They were to extend their kindness toward the entire group. They should show themselves as friends that enjoyed being out together and in meeting new friends and were kind not only to Enrique but to Cynthia and the security as well. Just beautiful people out having a good time.

He showed them in his suite the balcony hot tub and suggested that it could be used to help relax everyone. He showed them the comforts of the suite. It was a three-bedroom suite, and in the kitchenette area, there was plenty of champagne being chilled for later in the night. There was also a fully stocked bar. It was time to execute a multiphase assignment. The ladies just knew that they were playing a role to allow Michael to get close to some other folks. They were not in any way a part of the overall assignment. Michael called downstairs to have a car ready to take them the two blocks over to Byblos. He left with his two new friends.

Chapter 88

Michael and the two ladies walked into Byblos, laughing and talking. The ladies were encouraged by Michael to have some champagne prior to leaving the hotel, and they did. They were relaxed and showing themselves to be naturals for the role of the evening. The maître d' showed them to their table. From their table, Michael had a good view of Enrique and Cynthia and the two guards who all were seated at another table just in front of the sight line that Michael had taken with one other empty table in between them. Michael knew to expect the guards to be seated with Enrique. The dossier explained that Enrique thought that guards in a position of constantly guarding actually brought more attention to a subject being guarded. As a result, Enrique included his guards in his atmosphere. The restaurant was about three quarters of the capacity, and the menu was of Mediterranean fare. The restaurant was well lit in the dining area, and there was a slightly darker area where there was a bar, and the sounds of contemporary Mediterranean music wafted into the dining area from the bar area. After Michael and the ladies received their drinks from the waitress, one of the ladies asked that the wait staff would provide to all the guests a glass of champagne so that they could join them in a toast. Minutes later when there was a bit of a buzz in the dining area as the entire wait staff were serving their customers with glasses of champagne and directing their attention to the table where Michael and the ladies were and letting them know that it was complimentary of that table, all eyes were on Michael's table.

After they were assured that everyone had a glass of champagne, the taller of the two ladies with the darker hair, red dress, and slight Spanish accent stood and tapped her glass and said, "If I may, I ask you all to join us in celebrating the birthday of our friend Carlos Sosa." It was the name that Michael had chosen for the night. "Carlos came to town to celebrate with us, and we want to make this a memorable night for him. I can't think of a better way than to show him how great it is to be in Miami! To Carlos, enjoy your birthday tonight. You can always get back to the e-commerce world tomorrow!"

The toast went off as perfect as Michael had wanted it to be done. The taller lady followed through on the next part of the plan. She ordered another round for everyone in the restaurant. After everyone got that drink, there was not another toast, just lifting of glasses, and everyone drank. The air in the restaurant became a bit festive. When each patron had been inserted with two untimed drinks, the talking got louder, more things became funny, and the laughter got louder, and the patrons started to order drinks at their own tables a bit faster. As Michael and the ladies worked their way through dinner, Michael saw Cynthia leave her table and head to the direction of the ladies' room just past the bar area. After a few minutes, she returned to her table with a tray of shots. Cynthia bent over the shoulder of Enrique and said, "Come with me." Enrique stood and then followed Cynthia over to Michael's table. "This is my brother, Enrique, and I am Cynthia. Thank you for the champagne earlier. It was exceptional. We would like to extend a happy birthday wish to you, Carlos. I have brought over some shots of tequila."

"Well, thank you," Michael said with a bit of a Spanish accent that would be heard from someone that grew up in a home of Spanish speakers but grew up himself speaking English. "Cynthia, Enrique, the toastmaster is Maria, and to my left is Claudia. They are two of my best friends, and they are determined to see that not only do I get drunk tonight but that I also have a night to remember. Thank you for the shots. You didn't have to do that."

"No, I didn't. But who could have a birthday without shots, right?"

They all grabbed a shot glass, and Cynthia said, "To your birthday," and they all turned the shot glasses bottom side up into their mouths.

Enrique put his left arm around the waist of Cynthia and said to Michael's table, "We don't want to intrude any further. We wish you the best in celebrating your birthday. We are going to be leaving now for a spot that my sister is looking forward to going to tonight."

"My friends are taking me to The Raven. Do you know anything about that place?"

"That is where we are going!" Cynthia said excitedly. "You all can join us there!"

"Well, now we wouldn't want to intrude on your plans for the evening. Thanks anyways."

Enrique, seeing some air being taken out of his sister's sail, injected, "No such thing. If we are going to be partying at the same place, why not party together!"

Cynthia smiled directly at Michael.

CHAPTER 89

The two parties of people had become one party group over at The Raven for about an hour when the other ladies showed up and showed surprise to see their friends Maria and Claudia out for the night. They screamed and hugged and turned to give Michael hugs when Maria had told them that they were out celebrating his birthday. They were introduced to Enrique, Cynthia, and the guards and hugged all of them too, just showing themselves to be fun loving people. The group had taken up a nice area of the club. Michael, Enrique, and the guards all drank less than the women. The women all wanted to dance. When they couldn't coax any of the men to keep dancing to every song that played, they just danced with one another sometimes on the dance floor and other times near the tables where they were seated. It seemed that Cynthia, along with the support of different waitresses, kept shots in front of the group every twenty minutes or so for a couple of hours. The night had grown into the morning.

On cue, Maria and Claudia started to speak on going back to the hotel where "Carlos" was staying. Michael didn't want to seem to be very anxious to suggest to Enrique or Cynthia that this was the move to make, so he didn't voice any support for this move. It wasn't until Cynthia seemed to be taking more and more of an interest into Carlos or Michael that he felt comfortable in trying to move the party in that direction. On one side of the three tables that the group occupied was a bench seat along the wall in the club. On the bench seat against the wall behind the middle of the three tables was Michael, and Cynthia sat after taking another round of shots that she had initiated. After the shots, she leaned toward Michael's left ear and said, "I know that we just met, but I have a birthday gift for you."

"You don't need to worry about giving me anything," was how Michael replied.

"Oh, you're going to get this gift! Even if I have to make you take it, birthday boy!"

"Well, do I get it here, or should we take the party back to my suite?"

"How big is your suite? If we can't have privacy, then we don't need the rest of the group."

"There is enough room for everyone."

With that, Cynthia stood on the bench seat and announced to the group, "It's time for the next stop on the birthday parade route."

With a separate further explanation to her brother, the party was ready to move. Michael had previously arranged with the hotel for them to send their courtesy van over to The Raven when they got the call. He called, and by the time that they all had gotten outside of The Raven, the van was pulling up.

CHAPTER 90

The noise from this group of ten in the van was ridiculous. The noise from the group of ten through the lobby of the Loew's Hotel was worse. It kept up in waiting for the elevator, on the ride up, and through the hall to Michael's room. Once Michael got the door open, Cynthia was heading toward the bar area to see what was there to keep the party going. She found multiple bottles of tequila. She called Maria over to help with the champagne. Between the two of them, they had things flowing. Claudia went out on the private deck and started up the jets on the hot tub. The hot tub was lined with marble counters around most areas on all four sides. Claudia came back in and grabbed one of the friends that came in later to The Raven and pulled her out toward the hot tub. Their shoes were gone before they got back on the deck. Their dresses were removed, and they got in the hot tub in their underwear and sat their drinks on the marble countertops. One of the guards eyed Enrique, as if asking if he could join the ladies in the hot tub. Enrique smiled and nodded, and he began to slip out of his suit coat. The one guard was out of his shoes, socks, pants, shirt, and jacket faster than anyone that Michael had seen. He saw things moving in a favorable direction.

The favorable direction was enhanced when he saw Enrique slip out of his jacket. On cue with the earlier plan, the other two women sat in the cubed area around Enrique and the other guard. With champagne bottles on ice, they were responsible for keeping drinks fresh. It was time for Maria to assume her role of keeping things orderly. While dancing around the area that everyone was seated in, she began picking up the clothes of the women and the one guard that were in the hot tub. She completed the scene by talking about the need to avoid trip hazards and to take care of their clothes and so on. After placing all the items that she had picked up in an open area, she moved to the back of the couch that Enrique was sitting on and, as Michael had told her earlier to do if given the opportunity, asked him if he minded if she hung up his jacket while she was already lifting it up so that she could sit next to him. It worked perfectly. She went toward the hall closet and checked inside the left side of his jacket, and there it was, as Michael said that it would be, the storage device. She removed it and palmed it. When she came back toward the room, Michael was headed toward the bar where Cynthia was still fulfilling the role of bartender for shots. With Enrique's sightline obscured by Michael and the one-inch lip of the bar countertop, she simply set the storage device on the bar behind a couple of already empty champagne bottles. Michael saw it. Maria headed over and sat next to Enrique. Michael grabbed the device and put it in his pocket. He then looked at Cynthia and said, "Excuse me for a moment. I will be right back." Michael headed toward the master bedroom suite of the three-bedroom suite. He went in and closed the door behind him. His laptop was already open. He plugged the device into the laptop, and the screen just went wild scrolling through the program.

As he was looking at the screen, he heard the door open and close behind him. He froze until he heard, "It's time for your birthday present!" Cynthia said this as she began to disrobe while holding a fresh bottle of tequila in her hand.

Michael lowered the screen on the laptop and asked, "Where are the shot glasses?"

"We can share the bottle. We are about to share quite a bit." She was dressed, as the folks in the hot tub, in just her underwear now.

Wow was the word that Michael chose to feign excitement about her appearance. There were no flaws that Michael could determine about the woman that was in front of him, but he knew that he was here for business. He knew he didn't need or want to shoot her, but he realized that he needed the narcotic. He began wandering toward the counter before the private bathroom, where there were some glasses. He intentionally let one fall on the carpeted floor, and he clumsily kicked it into the open closet. He quickly unzipped his backpack, removed the narcotic, unscrewed it, and squeezed off a drop into the empty glass that he had dropped on the floor. He didn't bother to rezip the backpack after he put the drops back into the backpack. Instead, he stood with the glass and grabbed the other one and headed back toward one side of the bed. He sat both the glasses on the nightstand and asked Cynthia for the bottle of Tequila. He opened it and poured them both what would be at least a double shot. He toasted before the shots were drank. "To my birthday present!"

Cynthia had her drink down so quickly and lunged toward Michael. Michael hadn't drunk his shot. While he was still standing on the floor near the bed with her knees on the bed and squeezing right up on him, he held her up against him with his right hand and arm around her waist. With his left hand, he found the nightstand and sat down the drink. Cynthia was working the buttons on his shirt, and before she got to the third one, she faded onto the bed to her right. The narcotic appeared to work. Michael checked her pulse. She was fine. Michael went to work on corrupting the file.

CHAPTER 91

Michael had been working on the file for about twenty minutes when he heard a knock and then a voice at the door, "Cynthia, we should be leaving soon."

Michael turned to make sure that she wasn't about to snap out of her induced sleep. She was still out but probably for only another ten minutes from the narcotic. Michael spoke in the direction of the door, "One minute. Coming." He typed out the last commands, removed the device, and closed his laptop. He put the device in his pocket and took off his shirt and threw it on the floor on the other side of the room. He had laid the blanket from the foot of the bed over the barely clothed Cynthia before he had started on the device. He went to the door and opened it slightly and guided Enrique in. "Hey, man, I didn't take advantage of your sister. We may have gotten involved, but once we took the last shots that she poured, she was out. I covered her and just laid near her. Maybe we should let her sleep just a bit longer. What do you think?"

"Well, I see her clothes here on the floor. I can't dress her. If she wakes in a few minutes, she can dress herself. If not, we will wake her and figure it out. Hey, Cynthia parties hard. She seemed to like you. How long are you in town? Maybe we can all get together again."

"I would like that. Give me your number, and I will call you when I free up from my meetings tomorrow."

Enrique patted his shirt pocket for his ink pen. And then said, "It's in my jacket pocket. One second, let me grab my pen." And he headed toward where his jacket had been hung up by Maria.

"Hey, just say the number. I don't forget numbers."

Enrique stopped and turned back toward Michael and recited the number. Maria then showed up near Enrique with a bottle of water. "Here, I think the night is winding down."

Enrique started toward the couch with Maria and said to Michael, "Give her ten minutes and we should wake her."

"Okay. Maria, can you come here for a moment?" Maria came over to Michael, and he gave her the device and told her to put it back in Enrique's jacket and to take him the jacket.

As Michael was about to wake Cynthia, she was struggling to wake on her own. She sat up in bed and looked at herself under the blanket and said to Michael, "Sorry. Maybe we can get together for my birthday."

"I would like that. I got your brother's phone number. I will call you tomorrow."

Michael's first assignment outside the four walls of his apartment proved to be a success. The Recruiter was astonished in the debriefing with the ad-libbing that Michael had pulled off with non-trained personnel. He was special indeed. As Michael was now near his floor in his Embassy Suites Hotel and his mind back in the present, he realized that his life was still not his own.

CHAPTER 92

Ron came up the stairs from the train station to the corner of Randolph Street and Michigan Avenue. This was the end of the line for the South Shore train service. Ron didn't like that expression at this time, the end of the line. There was much more to be done and to be found out. On top of the urgency of those matters was that he would need to keep his heightened feelings of anger at bay while he worked the known things in front of him. He knew that with someone trying to kill him, his focus needed to be not only on doing more and finding out more but also on staying alive. Ron had dismissed the events as him being a random target. He knew that he would need to contact both Sarge and Bobby again. Getting closer to them would be the path of finding out which one or if both of them were somehow involved not only in the failed hit on him but also in the information around Rick's parents. After coming up the stairs, Ron moved over toward the curb to hail a taxi. He needed to go ten blocks south to get back to the hotel. As he was eyeing Randolph Street's one-way, eastbound traffic, he thought about when he and Rick would come to Chicago when they were teens on the same South Shore train and come up at this same point to, in his mind, be welcomed by the city. It was always the same thing at the center point of their trips, to go to a movie in downtown Chicago. They would eat somewhere, of course, and they would go in and out of the many stores. Most of the time the financing of the trip was done by

Ron. It was in the high school years when he already was selling small amounts of marijuana. He never smoked it, and Rick didn't either.

The taxi arrived, and after Ron got in, the taxi took the first corner at Michigan and turned right. He was heading south toward his hotel with his bag from the trunk of his now burned and exploded car. When the taxi got to be two blocks away, both the driver and Ron saw that traffic was moving very slowly. In fact, to cover the last block of travel, it had taken them fifteen minutes. What they saw at a distance was the strobe lights of many emergency vehicles up ahead. Ron looked at the meter of the taxi and reached into his pocket. He pulled out twenty-five dollars and tapped on the glass divider between him and the driver. The driver turned, and Ron said, "I'll get out here. Thanks." The driver slid back the safety glass and took the money from Ron. Ron continued on foot toward his hotel. He saw that the main entrance with the drive-up lanes were all taken up with the presence of policemen and many of their cars, a fire engine, and some of the associated firemen and multiple ambulances. There was also a car labeled Coroner and a van labeled Chicago Crime Scene Unit. When Ron crossed Balbo Street, he turned right to head toward a side entrance of the hotel. After entering there, Ron saw an atmosphere of controlled chaos with a hint of voyeurism in the air. There was the tent over a spot below the railing where he thought he saw Rick, and there was a shielded barrier outside of the fourth elevator to his left from the spot that he was standing on right now. There were many more Chicago police officers in the lobby than there were outside by the main entrance. There were the windbreakers on a few people indicating that they were EMTs or the CCSU, the Chicago Crime Scene Unit. The firemen were not nearly engaged as the other first responders. Ron had not identified anyone as the coroner just yet. He wandered over toward the check-in desk, and he saw the young man that he talked to last night after he thought that he saw Rick.

"What's going on? What happened?"

"There were two events that happened in short order within the last hour. Sir, if you need to get access to your room, you would be best served to take the stairs to the mezzanine level and to board the elevator there," the assistant manager said to Ron.

"Okay, but what happened? Were you here?"

"Sir, all that I can tell you is that over below the mezzanine rail, it appears that an unfortunate accident occurred where a gentleman fell over the rail. In the shielded elevator, another man may have had some sort of health situation."

"I saw the coroner and crime scene unit vehicles outside. Why would that be?"

"I'm sorry, sir, there is nothing else that I could add at this time."

"Okay, change of subject, this weekend here in this hotel is a high school reunion. Do you have any information on it? I know the high school, and the time frame fits an era when I may have known some people from the school."

"Sure, hold on a second. Let me grab something for you." The assistant manager stepped away and went in the office area in back of the check-in desk. When he returned, he already had his right hand and arm extended toward Ron while holding a brochure. "These have already arrived. They are for the attendees. They seem to have more than enough, so you can take this one."

"Thanks." Ron headed toward the stairs going to the mezzanine level.

CHAPTER 93

"Thanks, I owe you." With that, Dave hung up his phone and turned to Valerie in her new room at the Palomar Hotel. "This is crazy, Valerie. The other person has been identified. It is Xi Ping. They both are dead. While Vasily was known to have a meeting set with the Programmer, Xi and his company would seem to be the same type of players that would be in line for a meeting also. I don't know that for a fact, but it could be likely. Now while both of their interests are different from what you have in mind for the uses and benefits of what the Programmer has available, maybe the Programmer doesn't realize that. and the potential buyers like Vasily and Xi are targets for the Programmer instead of buyers."

"So you're thinking that the Programmer is behind these deaths and that I am a target as well."

"Think about it. It may be far-fetched, but think about it. Besides the two of us, if someone was to think about the product that the Programmer is peddling, wouldn't everyone assume that International Safety Services would want the program for similar reasons as Vasily's and Xi's companies? Everyone knows what the driving force behind our company's interests has been for years. So if these accidents happened to one known bidder and someone else who could be in line as a bidder, why not you if your interest would be in line with theirs?"

"This can't be the case. I know that our business is in a tough industry with some hardened personnel, but killing executives?"

"Don't be naive. There are people losing their lives all the time in this industry, some closer to us than others. You know this. Change of subject. The committee that is running the forum has postponed tonight's dinner and your keynote speech and rescheduled them for tomorrow night in response to the deaths of Vasily and Xi. So now the only thing in front of you is the scheduled meeting with the Programmer tonight at eleven. What are you going to do?"

"I don't know. I don't want to think that I could be a target. Your points are close enough to make me to want to reconsider. I don't know. I got to get out. I need to think. I'm going for a walk."

"Do you think that would be wise?"

"We are far enough away that I should not need to be worried."

"We could have been followed here. I don't think that you should go out."

"I've got to. Let's meet back here in my room in two hours."

CHAPTER 94

"It's pretty hectic over here. There will be some investigations, nothing that will turn up. Even if something was to turn up, there is no path leading in our direction. We're clear. With all that has happened, the dinner and speech by Valerie has been postponed tonight until tomorrow night. With this happening to two of the contacts that we know have meetings scheduled with the Programmer, we should be contacted soon to meet. I just tried calling Valerie and went by her room. I didn't make contact under either attempt. Has she reached out to you, sir?"

"I haven't talked with her, Dale. I'll try to reach her. Keep your ears open. There still may be others that have meetings planned with the Programmer," said Howard.

"I will, sir. I will call you later with any updates."

CHAPTER 95

It didn't bother Howard Benson Jr. that in order to get closer to a deal, the competition had to be impacted in some way. It was nothing against Vasily or Xi as individuals that Howard saw as obstacles. It was what they represented. They represented their companies and a competing worldview. Howard Jr.'s worldview had been carefully cultivated from his father, Howard Sr. Simply stated, his dad's worldview was to win at all costs. Howard had done well to mask the worldview behind a facade of being a loving husband and father, standing up for various causes by supporting them, being charitable, and such. In the end, those things had their place. If it was true that the Programmer had developed what was rumored to be on the market, Howard Jr. knew that it belonged to him. Oh, he would verbalize it as something important for the future of International Safety Services. But when the dust settled, it was for him and his desire to leave a fingerprint on the world through surveillance. While International Safety Services was run by Valerie, it was still his. He was the majority owner of the privately held entity. He had no problem in submitting the day-to-day to Valerie and the team that she had in place. He still had enough tentacles reaching back into the business that he could steer the business in his direction if necessary. That was where Dale had shown a great deal of value. Dale served Valerie without fail unless it was not something that Howard Jr. needed. He would then figure out how to accomplish Howard Jr.'s needs without disrupting his relationship with Valerie. In the case of the Programmer, Howard Jr. knew that he might be headed on a collision path with his daughter. He didn't mind a collision. He was just hoping that when it was over and done, his daughter wouldn't be totaled from the experience.

CHAPTER 96

"Jill, where is she? I understand that she is not to be found nor is she in touch with anyone. What do you know?" asked but more so stated the Voice.

"She and Dave Klen left the hotel shortly after the two lobby incidents. I'm sorry, there were two incidents in the hotel's lobby that has drawn a great deal of presence from first responders. I'll get back to this, but she and Dave Klen boarded a taxi and went north on State Street until just before Illinois Street. They then crossed State Street and began walking west on Illinois. They went into a Hampton Inn. My folks couldn't turn onto Illinois because it is a one way in the opposite direction. One of the team members jumped out of the car after they passed Illinois and headed in the direction that they had gone on foot. The driver had to navigate a few blocks to get to the Hampton Inn. The one on foot went into the lobby and didn't see them. He checked with the clerk, and they said that they didn't have any guest by that name. They're searching the area."

"Get back to the first responders now."

"Well, I had to back my digital and electronic teams out of the hotel's system. The police team went into the system, and I couldn't risk any chances of being discovered. So from a digital and electronic perspective, we have been blind for about an hour. We do still have our physical presence on-site."

"Got to go. Find her and find Rick Smalls!"

Jill had heard the Voice agitated before, but not quite like this. She took on the two names together to see what their connection might be to each other since both of them were going through the same hotel and had triggered this unprecedented urgency and annoyance alike from the Voice. Jill's trail on this research had a strange pattern. The known relationship between the two ended twenty years ago; however, at the very site of this hotel was scheduled an affair that was connected to them both: their high school reunion. While there was absolutely nothing else available about Rick Smalls anywhere in the internet universe, there was plenty more on Valerie Benson. Jill began with the limited high school information, but she was able to find out some things about Valerie's parents. She got some information from her time at both Harvard and Columbia. She followed her into her time at the UN and then into and up through her father's company. She understood clearly why she had been pegged as the keynote speaker in the event at the hotel. She wondered about the high school reunion following this forum and if it connected still back to Rick Smalls. Jill knew that she needed to find Valerie, and she figured that while they were introduced separately to her, Valerie was maybe the key in getting her to Rick Smalls as well. Jill kept digging.

CHAPTER 97

He called Tammy. "Anything new?"

"Plenty. From my surveillance on the hotel, I discovered something. Once the policemen began to go through the footage of the area from where Xi had fallen, I noticed that there was some activity showing others getting off of the system. I was able to track a couple of them. They are freelancers, no different from the type of people that I would or do use. But I got inside of them away from what they were doing, and they both were traced back to a very talented source. This source is a Jill Estridge. If you didn't have me working for you, then you would want her. Her reputation is outstanding. If she has people on a project, then something really important to somebody is going on. She's not as nice as I am, meaning, she doesn't give any discounted rates. She demands the highest fees. It has been rumored that she also became exclusive to this recluse. Recluse in description actually. This recluse is described as a recluse because he is not known by appearance. He is only known by his voice," Tammy concluded.

Michael now had a potential link to both the Recruiter and the Voice. He surmised that one or both the links had to lead to the presence of one or both of them. "What could you determine that had the interests of the freelancers?"

"Only one of them seemed to have a definitive target area. The recipient of the other package that I sent out for your eleven p.m. meeting is under surveillance. I don't know if they were able to track her to her new hotel. I have been able to determine that there is surveillance rotating around the building that may be related to her or someone else. But some of their paths had crossed with the people that were clearly looking over her."

"All right. Call me later. Oh, hold on, did you get some recent background on Ron Winston?"

"I had forgot with everything else going on. He is a guest currently at the same hotel where all of the fun and games are going on right now."

"Thanks. I need to work through some things. There is more for you to do. I'm going to send you some other things in a little while. Gotta go."

The news that Valerie was being potentially watched by the Voice was not good. Her current connection to anything besides him was that she had a scheduled meeting with him tonight. The others that he had meetings scheduled with were now dead. He was not going to let Valerie die because of him.

Chapter 98

Ron got back to his tight room and figured that he needed to work a few things at once. He recognized the danger in some of the things that he needed to work. He just couldn't see any other way right now. He called Sarge. "Sorry I didn't call you before now. I should have called you sooner. There is a lot going on. I had some car trouble on my way over to see you. I had to leave my car. I took the good old South Shore back over here to Chicago."

"You should've called me, Rook. I would've come and got you. What happened to your car?" asked Sarge.

"Not quite sure. It's not drivable. It was getting quite hot," deadpanned Ron. "Hey, now that I got you, can you come over here to help me with something else? If you can, you shouldn't leave from over there until about six or so. No need in leaving now and just getting caught up in traffic."

"Yeah. Maybe. What's going on, Rook? Didn't you get Bobby's contact info from me to help you with something? Did you talk or meet with him? Is he also helping you?"

"That's another matter. Suddenly, I got a few things cooking at the same time. Can you help me or not?"

"All right. Where are you gonna be?"

Ron gave him the address where they would meet and told him that he would meet him at seven tonight. As soon as that call was finished, Ron made the next call. "Hey, man, that went wide right earlier today. I didn't mean to come off like that. Now that I've pissed you off, can I buy some help from you?"

"You got a lot of freaking nerve, Rook! How you gonna play me? You accuse me of something, and now you want me to work for you! Rook, what's going on with you? Why should I help you? All I know is, you can get me into something and then turn around and accuse me of something else. I don't know. Somethings off with you, Rook."

Ron would have been terribly surprised not to hear some of this negative feedback from Bobby, but he also wondered if some of it was staged. "Hey, Bobby, my bad. I was out on a limb with the stuff that I was saying to you earlier. Can you come over to Chicago tonight and help me or not? I really need some help. What do you say?"

"What you got going?"

"Well, it would be better explained if I could show you something first. I can't show you unless you were here. You coming?"

"This better be good, Rook. Where and when?"

Ron filled him in. Ron knew he was playing with some potential danger, and he couldn't think of no other way to bring it all together. As he was about to head downstairs to the forum's exposition room, he picked up the high school reunion brochure with him, and he put his bag over his shoulder. The exposition room or expo room was filled with booths that represented the companies at the forum and vendors who solicited them. Ron was looking for some tools of the trade.

The expo floor was not overly busy, which normally would be surprising. In lieu of the activity in the lobby earlier, Ron understood the smaller crowd size that were in the expo room. The room was every bit of twenty to twenty-five thousand square feet of displays, bars, and other distractions. He walked the rows of displays. He stayed focused. He had every reason to be in this environment. It was this environment that brought him into the city to begin with yesterday. He wanted this environment, and through this environment, he was going to find his next career opportunity. So even now with all the other things on his mind, he looked around for the next opportunity. He stopped and talked with folks about the companies that they represented, he mixed with the various vendors, he grabbed business cards, and he searched for what interested him the most. Yes, he had grabbed ink pens, doodads, and gadgets that were give-aways. He needed some working products. He saw a brand name that he was familiar with: Thurl Products. For years, he had used many of the electronic devices that Thurl Products had to offer. He needed transmitters, receivers, and recording devices. One type of transmitter that he needed had to be small enough to hide in a room that he didn't have total control over. He needed another transmitter type that he could plant on someone. The receivers had to come in different forms also. He needed wireless earbud receivers, and he needed wireless receivers that he could plug into a recording device because he would not be able to listen to all the potential conversations at the same time.

Thurl Products displayed all the goods that he needed. They were products that he was familiar with, so he knew how to set the frequencies on all of them. He would do that back up in his room. Before heading back upstairs, he sought out for some information on the larger firms that were represented. He got some information. There was a large crowd around the International Safety Services display. Since the crowd was so large, he didn't spend the time to wade to the front of the booth. Ron went back upstairs to set up the equipment. He knew the products, but he still tested them. He had some supplies in his bag with his weapons. He needed gum, not chewing gum but a sticking substance that he could plant a transmitter in and then stick to a surface to work for him. Many times that would be under a chair, under a table, or attached to another type of fixture. Now Ron set out to the meeting location. There was a restaurant in the atrium area called Vic's. He went into the restaurant to make the reservation for three. The young lady recorded the reservation for the time that he gave to her. Ron asked her if he could walk the restaurant quickly since they were not busy to see if one table area stood out more to him than another one that he would like. The hostess said to him, "No problem."

After a quick walk, Ron returned and pointed to the hostess which table he would like for his reservation. She said, "No problem," and updated his reservation. Ron thanked her while handing her a $20 bill and headed out the side entrance of the hotel. While Ron walked the restaurant, the hostess was busy with other things. She didn't notice that he quickly sat at the table that he requested for his reservation and grabbed the centerpiece and pulled it toward him. The centerpiece was a ceramic vase that had the stems of some flowers extending out of it. Ron squeezed all the flowers to one side of the vase and stuck his gum and transmitter inside the vase above the waterline. He then rearranged the flowers so that the gum was concealed.

CHAPTER 99

She knew who the recipient of the video was to be. She knew how her own mind worked. She was asked to forward a video to someone's phone. If that request was to be carried out, the phone number that was to send the video would be unknown to the recipient of the video. She knew if she was to receive video or any type of file from an unknown source, whether via text or email, that she would be quite reluctant to open the video or file. She knew where the target was because the planned recipient had been under her surveillance already. The recipient was moving now, but the surveillance was in a good position. She called the surveillance operative on the phone line that they would use to talk. She told her the plan that needed to be executed.

After going south for a number of blocks, the recipient had crossed the street and then headed back north. Getting closer to the original location that the planned recipient had left, the planned recipient entered into Public House. Public House was a corner restaurant that had both a lunch and dinner menu. The dinner menu was, in most cases, just a larger version of the lunch menu. The planned recipient was seated at a table for two. The kitchen was to the rear of the recipient but still about twenty feet away. The recipient's sight lines gave a view of the back of the hostess stand. After the recipient was seated and had ordered water and a small house salad, the recipient just sat there thinking through the things yet to be done and the potential for real-life threats. The operator told her director what was going on before going into the Public House. The director told her to execute boldly. The operator went into the restaurant and was met by the hostess. She told the hostess that she saw a friend and wanted to go over and to speak with her friend. The hostess gave no resistance. The operator headed directly over to the table. Once she got there, she said, "Ms. Benson, I have a phone for you. Here, you should be getting a call shortly. Enjoy your day." The operator turned and left after setting the phone on the table.

By the time that the operator was exiting Public House, the phone rang. Valerie picked up the phone as her eyes were still on the back of the operator leaving through the door. She answered the phone after the third ring. "Hello, who is this? What's going on?"

"I am about to text a video to this phone. I have not seen this video. I was told to get it to you as soon as possible. Don't call me back. I don't know anything else. If I have a need to talk with you again, then I will call you. Good bye." With that, Tammy hung up.

CHAPTER 100

The line went dead, and Valerie sat there with this newly received phone in her hand and seemed to be numb to all things around her. Even with hearing what the caller had said, Valerie was shocked from her numbness by the phone vibrating in her hand with the notification that a text had just come in. She continued to look at the phone. She didn't move to open the text. She didn't think about setting the phone down. Instead, she started scanning the room to see what was going on around her. She didn't see anything out of place. She thought that she better be careful with the phone and the video. She decided to go into the ladies' room to look at it. As she was about to stand, the waitress arrived with her salad. "Just set it there, please. I will be right back." Valerie then went toward the ladies' room to watch the video. Valerie went into a stall and tapped the text message and hit the directional sign indicating to play the video. She saw movement but no sound. She tried the volume, and then she froze. The video stopped, and she played it again. She couldn't believe what she just saw. Fully clothed and without looking, she just sat down on the toilet seat. There was no way that she could have been prepared to see what she just saw. She started crying and held the phone from the stranger close to her heart and cried louder.

After nearly five minutes, she left the stall, put the phone in her purse, removed $20 from her purse, washed her hands, and sprinkled water on her face. She patted her face and hands dry with two paper towels and left the ladies' room. She went back to her table and dropped the $20 bill and left the Public House restaurant.

CHAPTER 101

"Tammy, I am nearly at the side entrance of the Hilton. I need you to locate somebody for me. You told me that you had identified physical surveillance earlier that was connected to this Jill Estridge. I need you to identify one that I can get up on and exfiltrate from the property the easiest. I walked over here. The car that you left me earlier is back at my hotel. I need human intel, and this is my best thought right now."

"Michael, are you sure that you don't want me to tap into the hotel's intercom system and to announce your presence? Come on. Is this move worth the risk or potential reward?" Tammy wanted to know.

"Tammy, how long do you need? I'm going in when you tell me you have identified my point of interest. I have on my normal jeans and black golf shirt. I've added a sports jacket and a black Chicago White Sox cap. I have also refreshed the jaw padding and facial hair. To lower my height, I am going in on crutches so I can hunch over a bit. How long?"

"Give me ten minutes. I will text you with your best approach."

Tammy might not like all the plans presented to her, but she knew how to execute and strategize. She had become a part of Michael's brain in many ways. She texted him the plan and gave some potential risks to two different targets. Michael looked as the second target as the best target. He texted her back to let her know which cameras needed to go to a loop so that he could avoid being picked up on them. Michael chose to enter from the main entrance while slightly hunched over the two crutches. After getting through, there were still some presence of first-responder activity at the front door. The ambulances, fire engine, and coroner car were gone. There were still police cars and the crime scene van out front. Michael made his way toward the main elevator bank after clearing the doors. The elevator that Vasily had been on was cordoned off from use, but the other three elevators were still open to use. Michael waited with a few other folks to board the next available elevator to go up. Michael, being in the perpetual hunched position because of the crutches and with the brim of the ball cap pulled down, was doing a good job of obstructing any in-house security camera views from his face. The elevator arrived, and a few people exited. Michael and three other people got on the elevator. Michael let them press their floors first, and then he asked someone to punch five for him. His stop was first.

Upon exiting the previously communicated floor that Tammy was aware of, Michael was less concerned about the cameras, and his head was raised a bit more. He knew from what Tammy had told him that his first point of interest was to his right as he exited the elevator. He used his crutches to go in that direction until he reached the double doors of the floor's laundry room for the hotel's staff. This was where all the linens were cleaned and prepared along with storage supplies for cleaning. There would be a number of canvas-sided carts that dirty linens would be loaded in throughout the floor when the rooms were being cleaned. This door, like the guest rooms, required a coded key card to be waved in front of the scanner. Michael didn't have the key card for this door, so he went with a sturdy hip into the lock area of the door to bust the door open. This approach, while not the first choice, still limited the overall appearance of damage. Michael was in the laundry and pressed the two doors as best as he could to give the appearance that nothing was wrong with the doors that could draw attention to him.

Once the door was handled, Michael began looking around for the things that he needed. He knew he wanted a cart, a number of sheets, and towels. He knew that the likelihood of finding an employee housekeeping shirt in his size was not likely, but he looked anyways. He didn't find one that was near his size. He took off his jacket, ball cap, and black golf shirt and put them in the laundry cart. He was left with a white T-shirt on. He just needed an appearance that wouldn't stand out as being out of place. He figured that in pushing the cart, he could look like he could be responsible for that with the white shirt. He had a distance of about one hundred twenty feet to cover with the cart once he got back in the hallway that his target could see him in, and he needed to look like he belonged for whatever amount of time that his target might have a clear view of him. He knew that the target was just outside of the stairs at the end of the hall and that he had been opening the door and coming into the hall and heading to room 540. It was a smart move to set them up with rooms so that they could prove that they belonged.

It was Michael's plan to be near the target when he would be looking to go into his room. Michael was about ready to enter the hall with the cart, and then he grabbed one of the midsize towels from the cart. He then laced about half of the towel between his belt and pants. One side was now secured by the belt, and the other half just hung on the belt at about waist level. When Michael entered the hall, he was blind to the timing. He didn't know if the target would be coming back into the hall right then or if he had just made it back to the stairwell or if he had just got into his room or was about to come out of his room or anywhere in the midst of any of those cycles. He started pushing the cart in the direction that he needed to go. Michael had covered about fifty feet of the distance between himself and the end of the hall, and room 540 was the next room on his right. He passed the room and continued toward the end of the hall. When Michael got to the end of the hall, he initially dropped to one knee and played with his shoestring, and then he switched out his knees and feet and played with the other one. He didn't want to look through the safety glass of the door for the stairwell for his target because of the advantage that a closed door and a sighting of himself could get to the target.

Michael rose after playing with the second shoe and shoestring and started to push the cart back toward the laundry room. He figured that he would create his own cycle, and eventually, he would be in the hall at the same time as the target. On his way back to the laundry room just after he and his cart passed room 540, he heard the movement of the door's handle from the inside the room. Michael stopped. The opening side of the door was the side that was closest to Michael, and this provided good cover for him. Once Michael heard enough to let him know that the door was open, he moved fast to get into the doorway and then rammed the door. In doing this, the door smashed into the body and head of his target. Through this surprise, Michael was in the room and closed the door.

Michael, still in what seemed like one motion, punched the target in the solar plexus to drive all the air from his body and to take away the ability to make noise. With the target doubled over, Michael took the towel from his belt and looped it around the target's neck, and Michael had moved to the back of the target, and he squeezed both ends of the towel together to choke off the air in another way to the target. Michael rocked the target toward the floor and then put his right knee in the target's back. With his knee pinning the target down and now with one hand holding the towel around his neck, Michael reached into his left back pocket and pulled out all the strips of a sheet that he had cut up from his pocket. These two-foot strips he used to tie the wrist of the target to the other. And the rest he stuffed in the mouth of the target, and then he released the towel from his neck. He gained the target's full attention by placing the nose of his Heckler & Koch 9mm right on the bridge of the target's nose.

CHAPTER 102

While extending his gun into the face of the man that he had just surprised, Michael pulled out his phone and called Tammy. "I just altered my plan. I am in room 540, and I have this guy with me. I would imagine that he will be looked for at some point. Keep me posted on what's going on around me."

"Will do. You probably have at least ten or fifteen minutes. I'll reach out to you as soon as possible. Take his phone or just the SIM card. I can get something done off of it later. Do your work." And Tammy was gone.

With his gun still trained on the man, Michael patted him down—gun, key card, phone, receiving and transmitting device, wallet with over $200 in it, and a bank card drawing on what appeared to be a corporate account of some type. Michael couldn't do a thorough search of the room with this man being conscious or without being restrained better. He didn't bother with a more thorough search the way that he knew that he should. He figured he'd better work this guy on the three- to five-minute plan. He needed his full attention and cooperation from the start. He knew this was a soldier or better described as a locally hired operative. Just like he had Tammy here in town, perhaps that Jill Estridge had resources like this man in the Chicago area. He wouldn't have a lot of information other than probably an old picture of Michael on his phone. He was probably given some level of caution as to how to approach Michael. He probably was told to call it in first before approaching him. He even might not know who hired him. The gun that he had could produce finger-prints later to identify him better, the phone could help a little, and the bank card had some potential benefit. It was time to find out if this man had any use to Michael in the first part of his plan.

Michael knew of different ways to get someone's attention, but he couldn't think of a better way than what he was about to do. He had given himself just three to five minutes after all. He switched his gun from his right hand to his left hand, and then without any warn-ing from the position of standing over the seated man, he jabbed him in the face. Michael's large, muscular hand covered the man's left eye and the left half of his nose. The portion of the nose that was hit was broken instantly. The strips of the torn sheet came out of the man's mouth as blood gushed out of his nose. "Each question is asked once. No hesitation from you. Any hesitation brings a consequence. How many people are on-site with you here?"

"Man, what are you—"

Michael grabbed the man by his crop-cut blond hair on top and then slammed the back of his head into the wall behind him. "No hesitation."

"There is at least ten of us here scouting the floors of the hotel and others around the forum areas."

"When did you begin looking for me?"

"Who are you?"

Michael slammed his head again but not with the same fervor. His answer was not an answer that fit Michael's question, but his answer gave Michael a bit of a pause. "What are you working on here?"

"My group is to keep a watch on the guest floors. If someone is identified by our contact, then we are to pick them up if they come into our zone."

"Who's your contact?"

"A man named Langford."

It made sense to Michael at some level, but not entirely. He understood that Langford could be interested in finding someone. He didn't understand that he wasn't the specific target. Langford was searching from the beginning. It made sense now. Langford was responsible for Xi and Vasily. "What's your name?" Michael wanted to know because of the potential fingerprints and also maybe some connection to the bank card.

"Donaldson. Hank Donaldson."

"Hank, you are not going to die for others today, but you will hurt for others." Michael slugged him again and knocked him out. Michael stowed the man's gun, bank card, and key card in the bag from the bathroom that the hotel's hairdryer was kept in. He had put his gun back into his waistband in back of his pants. He called Tammy to tell her he was leaving the room and that he wanted to get to the parking garage. She would turn off or loop cameras again. He called down to the garage to have his Sequoia ready. When he left the room, he went to the cart and got his shirt, cap, and jacket out and started walking toward the stairs while slipping the shirt on over his head. When he was about to hit the bar on the door to open it to the stairs, he put his hat on. At the moment that he cleared the door to the stairs, a man that was coming up the stairs bull-rushed him on the landing. Michael's back crashed against the wall. The man got off a couple of close-range shots into Michael's body. They were nothing substantive, but more of a nuisance because Michael had to pay attention to the potential of a blow that could slow him down. Michael had not gained any control on the man yet. Above him, he heard the sounds of what seemed to be more than one person running down the stairs. Time was limited.

Michael hated the maneuver, but it was the one needed right now. He headbutted the man that had a hold of him. The man was stunned from the contact. The man was now standing bent over a bit. Michael reached across his own body toward the man. With Michael's right hand, he grabbed the back of the man's head, and with his left hand, he grabbed behind the man's right shoulder. With these two points of contact with the man, Michael pulled the man headfirst into the cinder block wall of the stairway on the fifth-floor landing, where they were. The man crumpled to the floor. Michael looked up and saw that people were getting near him from above and that one person from maybe a flight and a half higher was aiming a gun in his direction. Michael jumped away from the center of the stairs and started running down the outside portion of the stairs. A couple of shots landed near where Michael had been. He knew that he had to hurry and that the chasers would only be slowed a bit in clearing the man on the landing. Michael got through the stairs, into the lobby, and through the main entrance and saw his car out front. He handed the ticket to the valet. He got into his car and pulled out as normal as he could. Two men caught sight of Michael getting into the car and eyed the license plate as he left. They didn't give chase in any way. They lost their opportunity on the stairs. One of them made a call to Langford and told them about the alert that they got from Hank Donaldson and that they lost the guy. They gave Langford the license plate number.

CHAPTER 103

The message on the phone still had Valerie in disbelief. She knew from the message that the warning from Dave Klen was real. The message also told her that she was not to share the message with any-one. The message also told her that she should not go to the meeting with the Programmer tonight. She had gotten back to her room. She knew that Dave would be coming by in about thirty minutes. She needed to get herself together. She was trying to figure it out. The message was delivered in a very personal way to her. And while that had her completely out of sorts, it was a minor detail in the message that stood out the most. It was something that she saw in the video that her mind stayed on.

CHAPTER 104

Ron needed to see both Sarge and Bobby when they arrived at the hotel. Michigan Avenue was three lanes wide in both directions, and this was where they both would be coming in at most likely. On the outskirts of Grant Park across Michigan Avenue, he might not be able to see them as well as he would hope to. He took up a perch just outside the hotel's car lane outside the main entrance to the hotel. There was a bus stop just north of the entrance. Ron sat on the bench inside the covered area. He had a good view of the cars as they arrived. It was riskier being in that spot than it would be across the street, but there was no advantage for viewpoint across the street. It wasn't that he was concerned with either Sarge or Bobby seeing him when they showed up. He didn't trust either of them right now, and he needed to see if anyone arrived with either one of them.

Six forty and he saw a car cross the path of the bus shelter right in front of him with two people in the car, one of whom he recognized. The car turned into the drive lane of the hotel and was greeted by a valet. Both men got out of the car. The valet said some things to the driver and handed the driver a valet stub. Both men from the car stood outside and talked for a minute or so. They went into the hotel separately. The man that Ron knew went in first. The other man went in about a minute later after standing off to the side, smoking. Nearly ten minutes later from the same bus shelter, Ron recognized another driver crossing in front of the bus shelter. This driver was alone. He was greeted by another valet. The same type of exchange happened with the valet leaving a stub to the man. The man didn't go straight into the hotel; instead, he went off to the side of the main entrance. After a couple of minutes of watching the man, Ron saw another man approach the man. They talked with the new man appearing to be getting into the other man's space directly in front of him while gripping his shoulder with one hand in a way to keep the man's attention. This exchange ended with the first man going into the hotel. The man that came out to join him stayed behind, and another man walked up to him, and they started to talk. Ron kept his focus on them until they parted.

Ron never intended to meet with Sarge and Bobby in the hotel. He wanted them both to get seated at the table that he had reserved and to talk. He was interested in knowing if they talked about him beyond just conversation about knowing him. He wanted to know if the conversation went to Rick and Rick's parents and what specifically they might talk about those matters. They might be clean of everything on those subjects or might not be. But what interested Ron also was that the first one didn't come alone, and the other one immediately met another person after getting here, and that person then met with someone else out here. There was no way that Ron was going back in the hotel right now.

CHAPTER 105

Michael now had two vehicles at the Embassy Suites. The one that Tammy arranged was to replace the 4Runner and his Sequoia. He texted Tammy to send him a courier for the gun, bank card, and key card. Michael took pictures of the front and back of the bank card. He would go to work on them himself while he thought of his next steps. The courier would have a destination to try to run the gun for prints. The serial number was not visible, probably scorched away with acid. Michael got on one of the burner laptops that he had and went to work while thinking about Langford. They knew each other. Langford was a guy that worked hard to please his boss. Langford's boss could be interested in what was being peddled by the Programmer. Langford's boss could believe that an approach to the Programmer would be to eliminate potential competitors or known competitors. This would fit into the deaths of Vasily and Xi.

The bank card showed, on the card itself, International Guardians. Through that name and from getting inside of the servicing bank on the card, it didn't take long for Michael to realize that he was about to go through a string of shell companies that would bounce him around the Cayman Islands and Cyprus. The exercise itself then had tentacles that would reveal other shell companies off one another. He called Tammy. "I gave the courier the items, which included a bank card. The card shows the name of International Guardians. It's a shell. That shell leads to others. I am interested in all the paths and the last month's transaction history of the shells involved. I can't stay with this right now myself. Can you take over this for me?"

"Sure. Are you safe now? You know, getting shot at in a stairwell is a big deal."

"How did you know?"

"While I looped the path of travel that you would take getting out of there, I still maintained the only live feed. The two men that chased you down the stairs followed you out to your car. After they went back into the hotel, they met with the man with the walking match on the mezzanine level. He later went down and met with a man outside of the main entrance. After that meeting was over, he was approached by another man. I never got a view of that man's face."

"That's good work. I believe that I am okay for now. I need something else from you right now if you can help me with it. There is a man that works with International Safety Services named Dale Langford. Get him a message on that company's email, asking him if International Safety Services would be interested in meeting with the Programmer tomorrow morning at ten. Let me know as soon as he responds, routing it as carefully as you have routed anything ever before."

"Understood. Jill Estridge's team is back into the security system of the hotel. I thought that you should now. The filed report from interviews on Xi said that he was behaving in a way that was not consistent with his personality before he fell over the railing. It is too early for reports on causes of death for either him or Vasily."

"Okay, are we current? Have you handled those other things?"

"Yes, we are current. You're playing close to the sun."

"Sometimes it's the only way. Talk to you later."

Tammy knew that he was gone already, but she still said, "Be careful."

CHAPTER 106

Valerie knew that Dave would jump into the safety aspect of moving forward, and she decided to head off any long discussions on it. "I'm not going to that meeting tonight." What she didn't tell Dave was that she was warned of the meeting from the video that she had received. She didn't want him to know about it, and she was also instructed not to share the information from the video with anyone. "What has my dad and Dale been up to?"

"Dale has been visibly busy around the hotel. He has been in places that you would expect him to be on behalf of the business. He also had a quick meeting with someone out in front of the hotel, which was followed by your father meeting him out front for a few minutes."

"Who did he meet out front, and where did my dad come from? Was he already in the hotel?"

"We don't know who the man was that he met, but we followed him after he met with Dale. Your dad came from inside the hotel, almost as if he was waiting for the meeting that Dale was involved in to finish before he came outside. I'm not sure if it was staged because of Dale or if he was watching Dale himself. I just don't know."

"Where did the man that Dale met go to? Was he there for the forum?"

"I don't think that he was there for the forum. He went inside the hotel to the restaurant, Vic's, and sat down with another man. Not sure what that was about. In the time that we watched him, he didn't give any indication that he was there for the forum one way or another."

"Who was the other man that he met?"

"Still trying to find out."

"Dave, anything on Xi or Vasily?"

"Nothing new."

Chapter 107

While Ron was sitting under the bus shelter and looking to make himself less conspicuous, he was flipping through the pages of the brochure for the Bishop Noll High School reunion that would be there in the same hotel. It started with a number of ads that undoubtedly were placed by some of the graduates or the companies that they worked for or that they owned themselves. Those pages were followed by the planned activities, which also showed daytime contacts to be reached on the day of the activities. There were some welcoming events on Thursday night, Friday morning, and Friday afternoon and then larger events on Friday night. There was a scheduled picnic across the street in Grant Park on Saturday afternoon. Saturday night was the scheduled big finish. The last three pages of the brochure were dedicated to the largest benefactor for the reunion committee. It talked about a foundation that had contributed generously and that the head of that foundation was the head person with an organization called International Safety Services. Her name was Valerie Benson. The name didn't mean anything to Ron. It was not until he turned to the last page of the brochure that the name meant something to him. On the last page was a picture of the generous benefactor. He recognized the picture to be Valerie Benson. He thought that this really could be that girl that went to high school with Rick and was the girl that was around a lot with Rick. He knew of International Safety Services and remembered seeing their booth when he was walking around and also remembered seeing the name Valerie Benson associated with the now postponed keynote speech.

This tickled him to want to know more. Right now, he needed to get going on Sarge and Bobby. He was curious about the passenger of the first car and also about the man that had come outside to meet the second driver that arrived. Ron got up from the bench in the bus shelter and headed toward the corner of Balbo and Michigan Avenue on foot. He crossed Balbo and continued north on Michigan Avenue. He used his phone to tap into a website that he used to store electronic information. He had programmed the transmitter at the table to feed to this website. He would listen to any conversation that Sarge and Bobby might have from the website. He would be tracking about one minute behind any conversation that they engaged in. He figured the second driver should have made it to the table by now. He started the playback. "Why are you here?" was how the second driver greeted the first driver.

"I could ask you the same. What are you and Rook into? What's going on? What am I caught up into?"

"You? What are you caught up into? I could ask you the same about what am I caught up in. Where's Rook?"

"I don't know. I was going to ask you the same thing."

"Look, something messed up is going down, and I'm sitting here feeling like a duck on the pond. I ain't involved in none of this history lesson that is going on here. Rick Smalls, where is this coming from?"

"He was talking to you about him too?"

"Yeah. I don't know why this is a big thing right now. But I ain't up to no games."

"Why did he bring you here?"

"He said he needed some help with something. You?"

"Same thing. Where is he?"

"I don't know. Something's not right about this. He didn't say anything about you being here. I'm going to give this five minutes. I'm gonna hit the can. If he ain't here when I get back, then I'm out."

The first driver got up to go to the restroom, and the second driver nodded toward the man sitting alone at the table near him. That man got up and went toward the restroom. The second driver stood to leave and said to himself out loud, "Sorry, Sarge."

CHAPTER 108

When Ron heard, "Sorry, Sarge," he was more than three blocks away from the hotel. What had he done? Did he put Sarge in a position of harm? He disconnected the recording, and he called Sarge's phone while turning and running back toward the hotel. He knew that from the time that he tapped into the recording, it had already showed that the recording was already ten minutes long. That could have been because of the first interaction between the waitress and Sarge or for some other reason. He didn't know how close to live he really was on this matter, but he ran. There was no answer on the phone. It went to voice mail, and while he was running, he was yelling into the phone, "Call me, Sarge! Call me!"

When he got back to the corner of Balbo and Michigan Avenue, his phone rang. It was from Sarge's phone. He answered it, "Why are you trying to kill me, Rook? You better look out. I'm gonna get you!"

"What are you talking about?"

"That man you sent into the bathroom came in to kill me! He had his knife out almost as soon as he came in there. If my boy wasn't with me, then you would have gotten away with it. Watch your back, Rook! I wasn't your enemy. Now I am!"

"I don't know what you are talking about. What man with a knife? What boy with you? Where's Bobby?"

"Bobby was gone when I came out. I'm about to get out of here."

"I didn't do nothing against you. I can prove it. I have a recording from your table. You'll hear it and know I didn't try nothing against you. Bobby did though."

CHAPTER 109

"Sir, I have just received an email from the Programmer wanting to meet with me tomorrow morning. In the email, it does not suggest that this meeting is for the leadership of International Safety Services. Instead, it asks for me as a key representative of the company. I don't know why the Programmer would look to bypass Valerie. I have not responded back to the meeting request yet. What do you think, sir?"

"Dale, perhaps the Programmer believes that you are more flexible than Valerie. You know, the Programmer may be thinking that International Safety Services is the right place for the program to land and that it may need to be sold internally. The Programmer may think that you are the right person to get the company on board. Now the counter to that is that we know that the Programmer was looking to meet with the company heads of the other companies. So what does the Programmer know or believe in wanting to meet with you instead of Valerie? No disrespect to you, Dale, but if the Programmer needed an in to a company and saw that a person in your position was needed in the negotiation, then why not just invite you both to the meeting? Let's see what we can find out. Answer the email with interest in meeting but ask where or how will you and Valerie be guided to the meeting. I want to know if the Programmer is clearly looking to remove Valerie from the meeting."

"Sir, I will do that, and I will get back to you as soon as possible. What about Valerie? Should I tell her about the meeting request and the omission of her name from the meeting requests?"

"Yes. Let Valerie know that you got the requests and that you didn't feel comfortable with the way that the invite came to you. Tell her that you sent a note back to the Programmer for clarification. Ask her for her thoughts on you taking the meeting. Even suggest that it might be the safer approach with what has happened to both Xi and Vasily. There is no need to concern her with whether or not you have talked with me on this just yet."

"I will get on this right away, sir."

CHAPTER 110

With the email sent back to the Programmer, Dale called Valerie. "Valerie, where are you? Are you okay? I have been trying to reach you? We haven't talked, so are you aware of the deaths of both Vasily and Xi? You are not preparing for the dinner and keynote speech for tonight still, are you? That was postponed until tomorrow."

"Slow down, Dale. I'm okay. I just wanted to get away. I did hear about Xi and Vasily. I am also aware about the postponement of the speech. What are your people telling you? Is there anything to be concerned about with two major global security leaders dying within minutes of each other so close to one another? Have you already backed away from Vasily? Do you have any information on his last moments? I want you to know that I still believe that backing away was the wrong decision, and we will deal with that at another time. Do we know if anyone else may be in contact with the Programmer?"

"That was another reason why I am calling you right now. I got an email from the Programmer that is an invite for a meeting as the representative of our company. The meeting would be tomorrow. The email does not make specific mention of you or for the International Safety Services team. Did you get an invite from the Programmer?"

"No, I didn't," Valerie said hesitantly. "Dale, how sure are you that this communication really is from the Programmer? It could be a setup of some sort. If I was to tell you to take the meeting, would you be able to put a perimeter around you to know that you are safe?"

"Valerie, it would not be easy, but it is possible to put the safety requirements in place."

"Dale, if the rumors of what the Programmer has as a product are lined up with reality, we don't want to miss out on this opportunity. Answer the email with interest in meeting, but try your best to make it in an open area. What time tomorrow?"

Dale thought. "One in the afternoon."

"Have you discussed this with my dad? If the meeting gets set for tomorrow, then let's meet early tomorrow with my dad at seven in the hotel's atrium. Let me know if you get the meeting set. Be careful, Dale."

CHAPTER 111

Miami Beach was not the normal assignment outside of the four walls of Michael's apartment when he was a student at MIT nor were the hacking assignments that he completed within his apartment. He was given many assignments where he assumed roles or identities as a representative of different companies. The work that he did truly was, by appearance, all on the up and up for these assignments. He went in and performed system security work for different firms. He saw this work as important. The Recruiter cautioned him not to get soft because all the work would not go this way. That cautionary warning was evident when he went to London for the first time after he had finished at MIT. He wasn't there to work directly with a client. The intel told the Recruiter that the buyers were looking to get weapons and munitions that would then be available to lower-level jihadists in Great Britain. The mission was to stop the buyer and the arms dealer. The assignment was to eliminate all of them at the same time. The Recruiter passed information to Michael that there was going to be a meeting between the buyers and sellers that night at the Côte Brasserie French restaurant on St. Katherine's Way. They were to arrive separate of one another and, by all indications, leave separately as well.

Michael only had pictures of the arms dealer to work off from the advance intel. He had no idea what time the dinner would be taking place or under what name a reservation could have been made. He thought that while they might be leaving in separate vehicles after the dinner, there might be a chance that they would still go in the same direction to view the proposed material for sale. That assumption was risky. To allow the dinner to finish without making a move could prove to be a miss. He couldn't miss. For planning purposes, Michael had gotten into London on the afternoon of the day before the meeting was scheduled to take place. This would give him the opportunity to scout out the restaurant the night before the targets were going to be in the restaurant. Before going to Côte Brasserie, he would go to a pub about the time that people would get off from work in the financial district.

Michael had purchased two suits before going to the pub. He wore the gray suit this evening. His shirt was white, and he wore a patterned gray tie. He wore the tie a little loosened under the collar and had unbuttoned the collar. He wanted to look like the other financial folks in the pub, like it had been a hard day. The pub was around the corner from Côte Brasserie. He was here for a specific reason. Michael had physical characteristics and personality traits that had an appeal to women. The women that would be coming into the pub would have had hard days at work, and they would be looking to relax no different from the men and women from their jobs in the United States. Michael needed someone to walk with him into Côte Brasserie tonight so that he could do some level of surveillance without standing out by being alone and then back in there the next night. He had already communicated with the Recruiter that he needed an escort for the next night to accompany him to the restaurant.

Michael talked with a few different women in the pub. He laughed; they laughed. He bought pints and glasses of wine. Around seven thirty, he noticed a table of three women finishing off burgers and drinks, and they were giving the appearance that their nights were over. Michael had been eyeing the table from the time that the women had arrived while he was at the bar. One of the women seemed to be paying attention to him as well. As she was saying good night to the other ladies that she had been with, she came to the bar where Michael was sitting. "How are you this evening? I'm Daphne.

Who are you waiting on this evening?" was how she approached Michael.

"I'm Greg Sutton. I'm here from the US for a few more days until I complete some work at one of the banks in town. I'm not waiting on anyone, but I am interested in some company. Would you like to join me?"

Daphne pulled up to the bar, and they drank a few glasses of wine together.

"I saw that you had some dinner with the other ladies that you were with earlier. Would you like to have some dessert with me? I am told that there are some wonderful desserts at this French restaurant around the corner."

"Greg Sutton, that sounds delightful. I would truly enjoy having dessert with you. Let's go."

Michael and Daphne went to Côte Brasserie for dessert and cognac. In the hour that they were there, Michael went to the restroom once, caught the names of five of the servers, and learned of the pastry chef's name. He wasn't sure what he was going to do with this information at that time nor was he sure with what to do with the lovely and kind Daphne tonight.

CHAPTER 112

About noon the next day, Michael was talking with the Recruiter. He told the Recruiter to have the escort arrive at the restaurant at seven that evening. The average meal in a French restaurant could last at least two hours and, depending on the reason behind dining out, maybe three hours. He needed to frame a window that the targets would be in the restaurant. Without knowing the time that the targets would be in place, he could be prepared to join the escort right around seven, or he would be able to enter sometime after that if the targets were not there under the cover that he was running late. He told the Recruiter that he would need him to call the restaurant at some point to deliver an urgent message for a server. It was Michael's hope that of the five servers' names that he got the night before, one of them would be serving the targets on this night. Michael would be around the restaurant before seven. In the event that he saw the arms dealer on-site right away, then he would enter with his escort. If not, the escort would go in, and Michael wouldn't enter until the target was on-site. He would enter sooner than the arrival of the target if it got to be seven thirty. The appearance of anyone's date sitting alone for thirty minutes was not the right move to play.

Michael's second suit was a shadow-striped dark-blue two-button suit. His shirt tonight was light blue, and he didn't wear a tie. His escort met him in his hotel's lobby at six fifteen. Michael chatted with her a bit and told her that they would be going to Côte Brasserie. He told her that she should get a ride over to the restaurant because he needed to remain back for a call. She was an escort. This was no problem. Michael needed this lobby time to gain some understanding of who she was and, more importantly, what she looked like. He couldn't have the awkwardness of never seeing her when he was about to walk into the restaurant. She left for the restaurant around twenty minutes after she had arrived at the hotel. Shortly after she left, Michael left to get outside of the restaurant to see if he could identify the arms dealer. Michael couldn't see clearly into the restaurant, so he had made up his mind that he would just go in at seven thirty, the limit to leaving a date alone. His plan in gaining the names of the servers was to potentially know the name of the server of the table that he would be interested in. With that information, he would call the restaurant from his table and to request to speak to that server. This would lead to the distraction that he would need to get toward his targets.

It was seven thirty now. Whether the targets were in the restaurant or not, it was time to go in. Michael crossed the street to head toward Côte Brasserie, and the worst possible scenario came into view. The door of the restaurant was opening, and the first person heading out matched the photos from the dossier on the arms dealer. This man was followed by two other men closely behind. As the men all hit the sidewalk outside of the restaurant, the arms dealer stopped and turned toward the other two men. He could have been telling them to follow him or no deal or good night or many other things. There was a car starting to pull up directly in front of the restaurant. That "room number 2" instinct kicked in like it did at the doctor's office years earlier. Michael grabbed inside his jacket while closing in on the sidewalk from the street to remove his 9mm. His removal of the weapon was smooth, and unobstructed, he put two rounds into the arms dealer's head. This was followed by one shot to the head of one of the buyers and two shots to the back of the other buyer who turned to run. The driver was getting out of his car and beginning to raise his weapon. Michael turned and leveled the driver with two more shots. Michael went to the car and pulled the body away from blocking his ability to get into the car, and then he got into the car and sped away.

London had more cameras mounted within the city than any other city on the planet. And without knowing that this was the way this was going to go down tonight, there was no preemptive plan to get control of the cameras. He had to get out of this car and out of sight. and back to the United States. Michael got rid of the car. He got out of sight, and he got back to the United States. What Michael had come to realize was that Miami Beach wasn't normal, London wasn't normal, and hacking in the comfort of his own apartment or going into what appeared to be normal businesses under the cover of legitimate security business was not normal if you were doing it under the influence of someone like the Recruiter.

CHAPTER 113

Michael told Tammy to tell Langford that the meeting should not include Valerie. He wanted to get near Langford, and he also wanted to see how Langford would prepare for the meeting. He didn't like the idea of getting civilians involved, but he needed to go back to Northwest Indiana. He was going to wake somebody up because it would be late when he got there. He called the valet and gave them the ticket number for the car that Tammy had left for him. He checked the ammunition in his weapon and the spare clips. He left the room to get the car. He needed to see the face of the doctor when he asked the questions that he had for him.

CHAPTER 114

Sarge was not quick to accept meeting with Ron. Ron convinced him to meet him on the corner of Michigan and Congress Parkway. When Sarge was in the restroom, the man with the knife came in and instantly headed toward Sarge while Sarge was in the urinal. The man didn't know that there was someone watching out for Sarge. This was the man that had gotten out of the car with him when he arrived at the hotel. This man was here just for this reason. After Sarge had gone into the restroom, Sarge's spotter saw someone else head into the restroom from a somewhat staged position. He wasted no time on closing the gap. When he entered the restroom behind the man with the knife, he had already pulled his own knife. When he saw the man on the path toward Sarge, he did not wait. He put his knife in the left side of that man's back. The man dropped toward his knees. Sarge and his spotter friend left the restroom then. The spotter was already in place for this meeting with Ron.

"Thanks for coming, Sarge."

"Rook, tell me why I should trust you."

"Listen to this." Ron gave him an earplug and let him listen through the conversation that had taken place between Sarge and Bobby. Sarge heard the end of the conversation with Bobby saying, "Sorry, Sarge."

"How do I know that you were not in on this with Bobby?"

"I didn't know which one of you to trust. I was hoping by bugging the table that I could get some information that would give me some real understanding of some events from earlier today. I didn't get that, but it seems to me that Bobby knows something. He also met with a man before going into the hotel. I was concerned about you having a guy with you, but I understand it now. I'm glad that you had him with you."

"What is going on with you? Give me the whole story."

CHAPTER 115

"Who's out there ringing my doorbell this time of night?" asked Dr. Stovall.

"Sir, I am terribly sorry for coming to your home this time of night and to be disturbing you. I have recently come to know about an accident that you were the coroner on from several years ago. It was on a couple that died together in a car crash where their bodies were burned. Can I speak with you for a moment? If I could have come in the daytime, then I would have."

"How did you find me? How did you know to come to my home?"

"Can we speak in person instead of through this door? I would rather not be speaking in a way that the entire neighborhood could hear our conversation."

"You're going to need to give me a very good reason why I should open my door to a stranger at night. Who are you?"

"My name? My name is Rick Smalls." Michael hadn't told anyone his name was Rick Smalls since he left Gary for MIT twenty years ago. This was an odd feeling to him, but he was seeking some connection to his parents at this time. "They were my parents."

Dr. Stovall opened the door but not the screen door, just like Will Jackson had done before he opened his screen door. "The two bodies? I'm sorry, the two people that were brought before me that night was a long time ago. It was just before I retired. Probably the only reason that I do remember anything about it. You say that you are the son of those people?"

"I am."

"There was a big deal around those bodies not being claimed. There was talk about their son then. The son was a sports legend in the area years before. All the stories that came out at that time were all over the board about the son, from him being dead all the way to how he could have been responsible for his parents' death in some way. Are you the son or a son? There was never much distinction if it was only one son being talked about."

"I am the son. The only son. The only child of Caeser and Elizabeth Smalls. Can you tell me about your examination of my parents? I would sincerely appreciate if you can help me to fill in a couple of blanks about their deaths. Can you help me?"

"I'll try. What is it that you want to know from me that if you were to go to the county office and show yourself as the son of the descendants that you couldn't find out from the report that was on file?"

"I have read the report. There are things that may not be in the report that I am interested in. Was there anything that stood out about that night or those examinations that you can tell me about?"

"Go through the side gate to the back of the house. I will meet you on the patio. We can sit down there. You want something to drink?"

"Water would be fine."

Michael took the walkway toward the side of the house and raised the latch on the gate. He pushed the gate inward and then entered. Once he cleared the space, he closed the gate. He walked along the side of the house until he came into the backyard area where, near the house, there was a concrete patio and bricked-in grill for outdoor cooking. Grass covered the rest of the yard until he saw the detached garage, which was a feature that he remembered throughout Gary and here in Merrillville. Dr. Stovall was coming through his back screen door, leading with his back because he had two glasses of water in his hands and he was protecting from spilling them by walking backward. Dr. Stovall was about five nine with a small frame and the settling of a small paunch outside of the rest of his physical appearance. He was bald, and he wore glasses. The glasses that he had on now had the frames of many of the reader glasses that one could buy off the shelf in a local drugstore.

"I like how you have divided your yard here," Michael said as he took one of the glasses from Dr. Stovall.

"Thank you. I sit out here most days now and many nights. You want to know about those examinations? Here, grab a seat. Let me try to help you. I can tell you that was about twelve years ago. They were not the last autopsies that I performed, but they were near the end for me. I know because I retired a couple of months later. I'm an old man now. My wife has passed on, and my children and their children live all over the country, and I have plenty of time to myself. Rick, I always tried to know as little as possible about the circumstances of the events that brought bodies to me. I approached it that way to lessen the likelihood of being influenced in my recordings of the findings. Of course, there are things that no one would need to tell you either. I mean, if the presented body had body parts missing, you might conclude or speculate that a dismemberment might have played a role in the death. On your parents' bodies, there was the smell that arrived before I saw their bodies. As you may know when any living thing is burned, it has a different smell to it. Skin, when it is burned, takes on a charcoal-like smell. Hair produces a sulfurous odor. Once I saw the bodies, they carried the characteristics of a burned body. The firemen have their own term for the condition of a burned body. You would hear them describe them as bloaters. The body does take on a swelling or bloating after burning. This is because of the body swelling. It is from gases building up from the burning, and this produces an even fouler smell. It was this smell that arrived in presence before the bodies." Dr. Stovall paused and drank a little water. "I began to prep for the examination when a policeman came into the examination room and pulled me to the side. I knew him. We all knew each other. Gary is a small place. He told me a government employee wanted to speak with me before I got started. This had never happened in doing autopsies in forty years, where someone would speak with me before I began my work. I was caught off guard, but I said okay. I told the policeman that we could go into the office. I headed that way, and he backed out and got this other man from the outer office and then brought him into my office. The policeman left."

"If this had never happened before, why would you change up the way that you did things that time?"

"Perhaps since it never happened, my guard or defenses were down. I don't know."

"This man, what government agency was he with?"

"Hmm, I don't know."

"What do you mean? You said that the policeman told you that it was a government employee who wanted to speak with you. Don't you remember what agency?"

"That's just it. Now that I am thinking about it, I don't think I was ever told what agency it was or even given a name from the man."

"No identification was shown?" Michael asked in a way that could be described as incredulous.

"I'm not remembering any name, agency, or identification. I guess I just took the policeman at face value. I had known him from over the years."

"What did this government man want?"

"He began telling me that these bodies were part of something much larger, that an ongoing investigation would be jeopardized if all of the findings were on record or made available to the public. He told me that I could jeopardize the lives of many undercover agents by revealing too much on my report. He went on to tell me that there was no hiding that their deaths would be related to a car accident, and a fire from the accident had caused burning to their bodies. He said that there was a large scene of people that had gathered at the scene of the accident. So that would not be surprising or revealing things that shouldn't be known. He then leaned forward while we were sitting in my office to talk closer to me. I guessed it was to emphasize that the conversation between us was private and important. While he was leaning toward me, he said that these two people were more than they showed themselves to be. He told me that any local reporting on them and their lives would not come close to describing who they really were. I couldn't imagine that people in Gary, Indiana, could be involved in much of a government investigation unless it was drug related. It's not like a more prosperous city where money or other types of crimes other than drugs could be of interest to government people. He never said drugs, but I guess I made it as drugs in my own mind because that was and is something that is prevalent in Gary."

"What did you keep out of the report?"

"I haven't discussed that with anyone. Ever. I am telling you things that I never told anyone else ever before. Hey, I'm doing the same thing with you that I did with the policeman and the government man. Do you have some identification to show that you are those folks' kid?"

"I don't. My story is far longer than what you have started to share with me as to why I don't have identification to show you." After Michael said this, Dr. Stovall began to get up. Michael extended his left hand and rested it on Dr. Stovall's right wrist. "Okay, okay. Wait. I am not going to be able to show you any identification, and there is not a way that I can prove to you who I am tonight. I do appreciate what you have told me up until now. There are two things that you can tell me, and then I will be on my way." Dr. Stovall didn't say anything, and Michael stood to get closer to looking the doctor directly in the eyes. "Who was the policeman that came into your examination room, and did my parents' bodies both have two gunshot entry wounds?"

CHAPTER 116

"Ron, that is a pretty fantastic tale of events. You expect me to believe that in all this time that you've been going around peeking into bedrooms and hotel rooms that nobody has been shooting at you before? But now that you are asking a few questions about Rick Smalls and his parents that Bobby is dirtier than we ever knew, that he was involved in the deaths of those people directly, that he had you shot back then, that you got your car shot up when you were coming to see me, that you burned your car up as you walked away from it, and then that Bobby had someone to try and to kill me tonight? Either you think that I am crazy or you are as crazy as all getup! You got some more convincing of me to do!"

"Look, I don't know what else to tell you right now. None of it is making sense to me. I don't think the questions about Rick are the driver of this thing with me. I think it is my questions around his parents that has set something off. I mean, it is not anything unusual about me, Rick's childhood friend, bringing him up. For that matter, there is nothing out of the ordinary with me bringing up his parents. They treated me well. But what somebody or Bobby may find unusual is that I am asking questions around their deaths. Maybe if these questions, in some form, had been asked when the accident happened, they would have not drawn much attention. It might be if something is not on the level that the questions are being asked all of these years later. Did you have any connections to the accident or anything around it?"

"Oh, so now you are back to thinking that this has something to do with me? How messed up are you?"

"No. It's not that. I'm just grabbing at straws here. I need something. Look, we can't stay on this corner all night. I got a tight room. You and your boy are welcome to squeeze in. But then again, somebody might be looking for you in the hotel. What do you want to do?"

"I'm going back down the street to give the valet the stub for my car, and I'm getting out of here. You can let me know how it turns out. And for your information, I don't know anything else. The newspaper article stoked my memory embers about the kid and a little about his parents. But I don't know anything that is going to help you to figure anything out probably because there is nothing to figure out. I don't know why all of these things have happened today, but you need to keep me out of your stuff. If I'm going to get killed by a knife in a bathroom, I would rather it be at my house with one of the crazy women that I bring through there. Good luck, Rook! No more calls for a while would be fine with me!"

Sarge and the guy that he called his boy headed south down Michigan back in the direction of the hotel. Ron headed off walking west on Congress Parkway to think.

CHAPTER 117

"Valerie, I heard back from the Programmer. The message is that I should come as the representative of the company or not have a meeting at all. What do you want me to do?"

Dale never had reached back out to the Programmer. He did call her dad. Howard liked how Dale had told Valerie that the meeting was at one tomorrow afternoon. If he had told her that the meeting was at ten in the morning, then he would need to have some story for where he was at ten when he was meeting with the Programmer. He also liked how Dale had mixed in the part about him alone or no meeting. This put Valerie in a spot as the head of the company. Did she check her pride as being needed for the meeting, or did she tell him to cancel the meeting?"

"Dale, you should take the meeting. I'm concerned about you. We need to talk about your protection detail. Let's still meet at seven in the morning. I'll call my dad. You're still close to the hotel. Anything on Xi and Vasily?"

"Still nothing."

They both hung up, and Valerie called her dad. She told him things that he was already aware of from his conversation with Dale prior to Dale calling Valerie. He was pleased to hear that she had put the movement of the company forward over her need to be in a meeting.

"Dad, I need something from you. Can you help me?"

"Sweetie, what is it? Anything that I can do for you? You know that I will."

"Don't ask me why. Just say that you will do it. Okay?"

"Valerie, this is sounding quite unlike you. It…it is rather ominous. Are you in trouble, sweetie? What's going on?"

"Can you, through your sources, which we both know that you have plenty of, tail Dale starting as soon as you can tonight and until I ask you to take it off of him?"

"What…"

"My question to you was preceded by saying you can't ask me any questions. I will tell you that part of it is concern for Dale's safety. So they would need to be prepared to help if he needs help. But that is not my only or primary need in this request."

"All right, no questions, but I must say that Dale is almost like family. I know that I am not as close to the business these days, but I can't imagine that you have anyone more committed to you than Dale at this time. I'll do it. I'll send you a text when it is in place."

"Thanks, Dad. I'll see you in the morning when we meet with Dale."

Valerie had set a bit of a trap. She hadn't gotten much from surveillance, but she would want to know his movements tomorrow. She needed to find out where her dad was on some things, and starting with Dale was the right place. Dale had always been and would always be loyal to the man that he called sir first and foremost. Howard Benson Jr. wondered what was going on with Valerie. If she had reason to watch Dale beyond safety, it wasn't Howard who would facilitate this information back to Valerie. Valerie's dad never made a call to support Valerie's request. He did send Valerie a text an hour later letting her know that everything was in place.

CHAPTER 118

One thing verified, and another thing found out. To Michael, this was progress to additional knowledge. He needed this knowledge because the circumstances around his parents' deaths were not as they were reported, and all had indications that others were involved in the falsification of the reporting besides Will Jackson and Dr. Stovall. There was this policeman. That didn't seem like the landing spot to start this conspiracy. There was the government man that never showed or declared his agency, let alone his name. When Michael left Dr. Stovall, he didn't believe there was anything additional to retrieve from him, nor did he think that Dr. Stovall's involvement was any greater. He didn't believe that the doctor would be reaching out to someone to let them know that Rick Smalls had visited him. Michael did not seem overly concerned that he had revealed his original identity to Dr. Stovall. It was in pursuit of information about his parents that he had revealed this information. The circumstances didn't lend themselves to him that there was another way to get the information that he got from the doctor. The doctor seemed shocked with the question about the gunshot wounds. He did confirm this to Michael before Michael left. In the end, it seemed as if the doctor had compromised his professionalism in this matter but did not benefit from his lack of honesty on the report. So he must have bought in to the idea that this was needed for some greater cause in an investigation that Michael knew to be made up. What about the policeman? What was his role? How did he get to be the point person on that night?

Michael called Tammy. "Tammy, is there a confirmed meeting with Langford?"

"Yes. Are you sure that you want to do this?"

"I am. He is going to be in the hotel's atrium in the morning. Get some sound coverage on him. I will need that sound before the scheduled meet. I'm leaving Merrillville, and I will be in Gary in a couple of minutes. I need a location for somebody. The report that you got into around the accident, what is a known current address for the policeman that was on the report?"

"One second." She gave him the address. "What are you doing now? Why are you after this former cop William Reece?"

"What did you say his name is?"

"Sergeant William Reece."

"Are you sure? Are there any other named policemen on the report?"

"No."

"Give me what you have on this William Reece. Here is another name that I need some background and current known address on. Call me as soon as you get it. I am going to hit these addresses before I leave from here tonight. I'm going to head toward the lakefront to the address for this William Reece."

"There was another death in the hotel tonight." Tammy inserted into the conversation. "In a restroom near the atrium area. What I was able to pull off of the security feed is the potential of three-men show in this scenario right now. Man number one is shown leaving a restaurant and going up a corridor to a restroom. Not long after man number one enters the restroom, man number two goes into the restroom. Pretty quickly after man number two enters the restroom, I see a third man go into the restroom. Not long after, I see man number one and number three come out and exit the hotel. They didn't wait for a car. They headed out walking north on Michigan Avenue, and then I lost coverage of them."

"How did you come to get up on this?"

"I didn't catch it live. It wasn't until emergency vehicles started showing up, and I was able to see where the first responders went that I got clued on the bathroom. That is when I started going backwards on the video for that area. I am still trying to back up the video to see where any of these three men come from and other contacts that they may have had prior to the encounter that led to the death of man number two."

"Tammy, were you able to get those two packages back that was sent out of Xi and Vasily?"

"Got them both. Had to steal the one for Xi."

"All right, have one of those packages at the hotel tomorrow morning just before ten for Langford. It doesn't matter which one."

"Are you going back in there again?"

"I am. I will need your help. Find out the address on that other policeman's name that I gave to you and supporting background information on him. Call me as soon as you get it. Then you better get some sleep. I'm going to need you tomorrow, I suspect, through-out the day. Talk to you soon."

CHAPTER 119

Ron knew that he couldn't be out there all night. He also knew that he couldn't get very far both literally and figuratively without a car. He searched for rental car locations near downtown Chicago, and he came up with several choices, none of which opened before 7:00 a.m. *Fine,* he thought. He didn't like it with the possibility of Bobby still being in the hotel. What about the people that he was talking to outside of the hotel when he arrived? Ron was still looking at the possibility that Bobby had been involved in him getting shot twelve years ago. Now he had to consider that Bobby was involved in the attempt on Sarge. This added the question of why it would be important to take Sarge out when Bobby had come to Chicago to meet with Ron. What was the connection? If there was some previous beef between them, wouldn't it had showed up when he had called Sarge yesterday morning or when he met Bobby at the diner? Or wouldn't their conversation at the table in the restaurant showed more of a problem between them? Too many questions and far too few answers were what Ron had come to determine. He decided he needed to get ready for tomorrow. He turned to head back toward the hotel, and he called the twenty-four-hour reservation line for the rental car. He would get up early enough to walk to the rental car location about ten blocks north of his hotel.

CHAPTER 120

"Dave, keep that coverage on both Dale and my dad. There seems to be too many moving parts right now. Let me know if you are seeing anyone else tailing either of them." Valerie only expected Dale to be covered since her dad told her that coverage was in place. "I'm going to try to get some rest right now, and I will talk with you after I meet with them in the morning."

"Valerie, the coverage that I have in place hasn't yielded anything yet. I'll stay after it. Do you want me to go with you in the morning?" Dave asked.

"No, but you can make sure that we are covered. I am meeting them in the Hilton's atrium. Try to get some sound coverage in the area before the meeting. I will leave them at some point, and they will be alone. I want to know what they are talking about."

"Got it. Get some sleep."

CHAPTER 121

When Michael left Dr. Stovall's house and was talking with Tammy, he was driving toward Ogden Dunes. After getting off the phone with Tammy, it was back to the Prince music to think with as he drove. He went away from the playlist and put on the music from the *Around the World in a Day* album. It was said that this was not good music from Prince. It had the place in the history of music from Prince to be the first full album to be released after *Purple Rain*. It was Prince going different in his sound again without a movie to draw you in as well. He remembered his dad saying that he first heard the *Purple Rain* album before seeing the movie and how he and his friends were all sitting around wondering about the music. His dad told him that he and his friends must have listened to the entire album at least six times between the album coming out and the movie opening. While the album started to grow on them before seeing the movie, it was the movie that locked in the greatness of the album *Purple Rain*. The lakefront area where Sarge was living was about thirty minutes away, and the psychedelic funk of *Around the World in a Day* would be just the right thing for the trip.

He didn't ever spend much time out that way as a kid, with the exception being one summer. There was a summer camp that he went to during the summer between seventh and eighth grades. He would take the bus from Fifth Avenue and Taft Place to Fifth Avenue and Broadway to then take the bus from the day camp out to the Indiana Dunes National Park. He couldn't help but remember that when he got off the city bus to wait for the camp bus, there was a bakery near the corner of Fifth and Broadway that lured him in for a doughnut that was called a bow tie. It was a glazed doughnut that had two overlapping twists on it. He remembered getting that and a carton of milk almost every day for the four weeks of the day camp that he was going to.

Going from Merrillville to Ogden Dunes had a couple of options on how to get there. The fastest way would be to continue north on Broadway until the entrance to get on Interstate 80/94 and go east on it. He went this way and stayed on the highway until it intersected with US Route 12. After getting on there, he traveled through some wooded areas to get toward the house that Sarge lived in. Once he got to Sarge's house, he passed it in his car and scoped out the area. He didn't want to park on Sarge's property. He found a path where he was able to pull his car over, and then he started to walk back toward Sarge's house. Even with the lateness of the night, the house seemed to be too still. Michael wasn't interested in ringing a doorbell there. It was time to get more assertive on some things. He had decided to go in. If he was found out or if an alarm would go off, he would be prepared for whatever came behind either of those events. Michael followed the property around to the beachfront side. There were still only the lights on the outside of the house showing along with what appeared to be the illumination from what could be a night-light from a hall or bathroom. Michael saw the stairs leading to the top where there was a sliding glass door. Michael's experiences with sliding doors was that while they oftentimes were locked, they really were not much of a security to someone who really wanted to get into a place. He had known many people that would add a bar of some sort to prevent sliding the door. Michael went up the stairs and checked to see if the door would slide. Maybe it would be unlocked. It wasn't. He took out his phone and turned on the light. He shined it to see if there was anything to impede the door from sliding. There wasn't.

Michael retrieved from his wallet a lockpick set. He went to work on the patio door loop lock. In less than a minute, Michael had the door unlocked. He froze so that he could listen very carefully as he begun to open the door. He was listening for low- or high-decibel alarms as well as movement within. There were no signs around the outside of the property that a dog or any other pet was on the premises, but he needed to be alert to that possibility as much as the possibility of a person. He also had to consider that this man William Reece might not be there and that someone else could be there. He was not looking to involve anyone who might not have any link to what he was after, but he needed to be aware. The last possibility was that this could be someone else's home entirely. Maybe ownership was in the name of William Reece. Michael listened closely.

Michael entered the house and then closed the door back. While it would be convenient to leave the door open in the event that he had to leave quickly, he could not run the risk of outside noise sounding louder inside because the door was open. With the door now closed, Michael pulled his weapon out. There was the protect-yourself element of having the gun out, and there was the element of surprise to someone seeing a gun to freeze them that came into play also. The level of the house that Michael was on had what looked like three rooms in front of him and then an archway that led to another area, which could be two or three bedrooms and two baths maybe, one in the hall and another in the master bedroom. Somewhere there had to be some internal stairs to lead down to the one car-attached garage that Michael saw first when he came up from the road. He needed to clear all the spaces. Michael moved through the space that he entered in, which had a couch, two chairs, and three tables in it. The next space was set with a six-chair dining table and a wooden dining hutch with glass doors that allowed him to see the emptiness of the shelves. This told Michael that there might have been a couple or family here at one time, but not now. The dishes that could have been in there were more important to the person leaving than the dining hutch itself, and that was why the dishes were gone and the hutch was there. Or it could be that a dining hutch was put in place without ever adding dishes. Michael cleared this area and kept going straight to the rear.

He entered the kitchen space. There was a door to his left off the side of the refrigerator and another door just to the right of that door that led outside. It could be stairs that led to the garage, or it could be a closet or pantry. Michael leaned toward the idea of a pantry. He needed to open the door. The door handle was on Michael's left side as he faced the door. He decided to squat in front of the door while holding his gun in his left hand and to open it fast with his right hand. Michael was positioned to do this, and then he did it. The darkness of the kitchen was met by the darkness of the pantry. Michael squinted while trying to focus on the space, and there was no one inside the pantry. He closed the door while he began to raise. The next part of this house was between the archway that could lead to the bedrooms. He backtracked through the kitchen to get back into the dining room and walked toward the archway. When he stepped under the archway, there were two doors to his right and one to his left. He figured that the door closest to his right would be the bathroom. It made sense in this construction's manner to make what would be the guest bathroom closer to where the guests might come from out of the living or dining rooms or even the kitchen. He figured that the other door to his right would be the smaller of the two bedrooms. The first bathroom was what Michael decided upon. This doorknob was on Michael's right. He would use the method for clearing the entry there as he did in the kitchen with reversing the hand with the gun and the hand opening the door. Michael reached out for the doorknob and began the clockwise twist. It opened, and Michael pushed it in. Vanity and commode were to his right. A tub with a shower curtain was to his left, and some shelving was behind the now open door. He needed to clear the tub. He went into the bathroom, and he was able to see into the tub because the shower curtain was not fully drawn. He looked at the vanity, and he couldn't help but think, like he always did, that it needed to be checked. He had no clue about the size of William Reece or anyone else that might be in that home, and under the vanity could be a spot for the right-sized person. His thought went back to the report of Charles Manson hiding under a vanity with a small portion of his hair sticking out of the vanity door as the only clue for the police to even search the space. He always doubted the possibility, but he would, more times than not, check when he didn't know the physical makeup of some-one. He opened it, and it was clear.

The presumed smaller bedroom was next. Back into the hall, Michael saw another "doorknob on the left" scenario. He repeated his kitchen stance and hand use. He swung the door open from left to right into the bedroom. It looked more like it was being used as a storage or an office. *Dishes are gone most likely,* Michael thought. There was no one in here. There was another door on the right wall, most likely a closet in structure alongside the pantry. This door opened outward, and the doorknob was on the left. It was the same thing again, exactly like the pantry with the outward swing of the door. No one was inside. There was a gun locker in this closet and some file cabinets. The gun locker heightened Michael's awareness even more than it was already heightened by being in someone's home at this hour of the night without permission.

The master bedroom was next. The doorknob was on right with inward movement going from right to left. The depth of the hall sug-gested that the master bathroom would be right in back of the hall bathroom. Michael swung the door open. The bed was not made. The blinds were split open to see out to Lake Michigan. There were two windows on that wall and one window to Michael's right. The bed was a queen size. There was a television mounted on the wall to Michael's right to the left of the window. There was a path that probably led to a closet and bathroom farther to the right. Michael dropped to clear the potential of someone under the bed. He rose and went toward what he believed to be the space for the closet and master bathroom. He was right, and he cleared both those spaces. He thought about the garage again. Should he go and check that space now or check the living spaces for something to identify the resident? He decided to do that, and from a stack of mail sitting on the dining hutch, he saw enough mail with the name of William Reece on it to feel comfortable in concluding that this was his residence. He had been in the house for less than ten minutes now. He decided to go to check on the garage. He would go down the lakefront stairs instead of the stairs that left him exposed to any cars pulling up. There was the possibility that while he was going down, someone could be coming up the other stairs, and all the clearing of the space would be lost. Michael placed by the door in the kitchen one of the chairs from the dining room table to block it from opening.

He went down, and at the base of the stairs from the kitchen was a door leading into the garage. It was locked. Michael was restless at this point and probably could have picked it in a minute or less. He didn't bother. He shouldered the flimsy door and was in the garage. It was empty. Michael stepped back out and pulled the door closed. He called Tammy while standing outside the garage. "Tammy, no sign of life here. It appears to be Reece's home. Nothing of great interest on the surface. I didn't search it thoroughly. Not unexpected, there is a gun locker in the house. You find anything on that other policeman?"

"I did. Actually, he retired as a detective. Detective Robert Ashipa. Bobby, also CC. This man has a trail that is not well covered. In his file are many questionable arrests over the years that put him in front of the local police department's ethics board. Only once did he lose. Part of the trail is money. He currently is on a pension from twenty-five years on the police force. However, his savings are not commensurate with his earnings. I checked his taxes. Never showed as a big investor. No IRA nor 401(k) with the department. Too much money for him not to be having a source of other income. Before becoming a detective, he was partnered with the guy Reece, whose house you are at right now. They partnered for two years together. He shows a residence in Gary in the Miller area. Let me give you the address." Tammy gave Michael the address. Michael recognized it as a lakefront in that part of town, about ten to fifteen minutes from where he was right now. "Michael, I've got more. I kept following the video backwards from the hotel's main entrance for the time frame before the bathroom attack. The first and third men into the bathroom had arrived together not long before the attack in the bathroom. I was able to zoom in on the license plate on the car that they arrived in. It was an Indiana plate that is registered to William Reece. I then followed different cameras that showed him going into a restaurant called Vic's in the hotel. In going backwards, I saw another man that I recognized through the video around the valet area, the area where I was able to see William Reece and his car. After seeing this other man enter the restaurant, I went back to see his arrival again. Another Indiana plate. This was registered to—"

Michael cut her off. "Let me finish for you, retired detective Robert Ashipa, known as Bobby, known as CC. Am I right?"

"Yes, you are. There is one more piece to this. Michael, before he went into the hotel, he was met by someone outside of the hotel. I caught that man coming up to him. It was our man that matched the walk that I couldn't get the facial match on. What is going on, Michael? Why are these things showing connections?"

Michael was short of breath. His thoughts all seemed to explode, and on the outskirts was a vision of the man who had met Bobby Ashipa pressing down on a plunger to explode everything that Michael knew in life. "Tammy, I'm heading to Ashipa's house. Check for city or other surveillance."

"What are you going to do, Michael?"

"Tammy, check for me and call me back with any concerns. I will be there soon."

CHAPTER 122

It was back to the playlist. It really didn't matter. Michael wasn't hearing the sounds of "Something in the Water" from the *1999* album. He was only hearing the voice of what he thought was a deranged plan being told to him to execute. It was there in Lebanon. Being in Beirut changed him then and looked to have some impact on him at that very moment. He knew that Beirut was never going to be over until it was over. Over as in somebody was dead. Michael had operated well for the Recruiter. He hacked. He consulted. He interfered where necessary. He killed when necessary. It was for the good of the country. It had started to take on the appearance that it might have more of a corporate leaning to it than for patriotic purposes. Michael recognized the shades of gray. He knew that money was being made somewhere. Heck, he was making money, far more than most midtwenty-year-olds would or should be making. He had the ability to rationalize it all. It was for the good of the country. It was dangerous. He was risking his life. He was taking lives and risking his freedom. He had no real identity. For these reasons and any others that he could persuade himself to accept, he thought that he earned the money. He was even told that he earned the money by the Recruiter and the Voice. He believed them because he wanted to believe them. The promise of caring for his parents by guiding things into their paths had held true.

Beirut was another assignment, another assignment that could be justified, another assignment that he could execute until he couldn't. It wasn't that he couldn't do the assignment. He had set up the assignment to meet the targets for the purpose that was given to him. He was told one thing, and not long before it was time to execute, Michael found out that what he was about to do was not helpful to the United States or to its allies. If money was what the truth of that assignment was about, then that was Michael's moral standing ground that he was not willing to cross. That assignment was multilayered. Based on the given profile of the assignment, Michael thought he was alone, as in most cases, with some limited support for things that he might need. He could get those things from locals that had been recruited, but they didn't work with him. He worked alone. This plan needed about four weeks to properly influence the players. Michael would gain the confidence of some people to stop a planned attack on Israel from a terrorist organization. The Middle East always had something going on, and as a country, the United States stood with Israel even above other Middle East allies, at least in the minds of the ones who stated policy positions. Actual policy positions could be described as not matching the stated policy positions.

Nevertheless there were terrorists coming, and they were going to get to Israel from Lebanon, not an uncommon approach point but one that Michael was not only to stop but in turn was also to redirect the attack to a stronghold of the terrorist organization. In the end, it was described as an in-and-out procedure. It was what needed to be accomplished before he got in, what he needed to accomplish once in, and how to accomplish the getting out alive that needed some defining. Michael took suggestions, but he only trusted himself to get him out safely after assignments, like in Miami and London. He was told there was a large part of that assignment that he would need to trust someone or others to execute. He didn't like it, but he did get some benefit in giving this part of the assignment to some of the locals to handle. They fit the area where they could get through the neighborhoods without turning heads. While the clothing choices for men and women were modern wear, there were pockets of the metropolitan area of Beirut where one would find the women dressed in traditional, colorful skirts and the men in *sherwal* or baggy pants. Those styles of clothing were from the Ottoman influences of the region. Michael would be fine in his modern wear while in the region. His skin complexion did not betray him in any way in this area neither. His skin tone could be described as caramel, which would match many in the region. The suggestion for using locals was that they were not as likely to be watched for any reason. Michael understood.

Michael was given intel from the Recruiter that led him to a location in one of the business districts in Beirut that he would have the opportunity to execute the plan in. The objective of the assignment was clear and concise. Michael would be placed in a position where he needed to set the coordinates on what was described as a suitcase dirty bomb. Michael's role also required him to tap into what was told to him to be a Turkish satellite. It would be through the satellite that the set coordinates on the dirty bomb would be able to be detonated. Michael could do the satellite from anywhere in the world. The dirty bomb would require him to open a panel on the bomb itself. Again, it was why Michael had no problem with the money aspect of his work. It was his life on the line here. The Recruiter told Michael that the coordinates needed to be changed to reflect where the bomb was actually going to be versus where it was originally intended to go to in Israel. This was not something that could be projected from a fixed position in Lebanon. It needed to be delivered to its destination, and then the tapping into the Turkish satellite would be necessary for the detonation, which gave Michael the impression that the dirty bomb had some origin in Turkey since it would be their satellite that acted as the detonation switch for the bomb. He was told that intel had led the Recruiter to understand that the terror group was an offshoot of Hamas with Turkish ties that led up and through the Turkish military. The plan, then, would be to reset the coordinates and have the bomb delivered to some proximity within the stronghold of this group and through the satellite detonate it.

The reason for the time involved was that the bomb would show up to the person capable of making the settings correct. It wasn't just a matter of turning a few dials and setting the latitude and longitude. The bomb had a need to have the programming completed through the built-in software on the bomb itself. Michael would plug a laptop into the system of the bomb and write or overwrite the program to change the detonation position to what he would be given. If the original plan was to follow through from there, it would have been smuggled into Israel and detonated there. To smuggle something into Israel was a big deal, and there could be some opportunities as soon as it was ready from being programmed to get to the Israeli destination, or it could take reworking the part of the plan over and over again to get it to the Israeli location. The position of the satellite would be good for a month. After that time, the satellite would be moved out of position.

Michael remembered when he arrived in Beirut. He had come into Beirut via Berlin. His arrival into Beirut was to be for some work at the American University of Beirut. He was set to do some work for the university on a real project that could enable the university to provide secure access to designated scholars around the globe. The university saw this as a necessary step for future expansion of think tanks on Middle East commerce, security, and education. His work at the university was to last up to two weeks. The bomb was to arrive somewhere between his fourth day in town and the eighth day. He would turn his priority to that once it arrived. Michael got his call from the Recruiter with a time and location where he would be picked up the following morning. The following morning was his fifth day in the city of Beirut. In the time that he had been there, Michael enjoyed the vantage point of viewing the Mediterranean Sea from the coastal town of Beirut. He was on the balcony of his hotel room when he got the call about the meeting for the next day. He was told to be at the Starbucks off General De Gaulle Street at nine in the morning with his equipment to do the programming. This was about fifteen minutes from his seaside hotel. He was told that the coordinates would be delivered to him tomorrow once he was at the location of the package.

That evening, Michael went out to scout the area that he would be going to be picked up tomorrow. He had already been spending each evening and some of the midday time frame going around to get familiar with the streets and traffic patterns. It was all part of his prep work to make an exit. After the events in London, Michael found and developed his own sources for identification and passports that he could have at his disposal. Knowing now that his work on the assignment could be complete tomorrow and that he had gotten the on-site work completed at the university, he knew that he could leave Beirut as soon as he was done with this portion of the work tomorrow. The satellite programming would be completed right after he finished the package programming. He made plans to leave by car going south to the port city of Tripoli to leave from there via boat to Cyprus. He also had a flight from Beirut to Ankara, Turkey, and another flight from Beirut to Athens. These plans were under different names. And no one knew of them. Michael thought that this would be best.

Michael was called at seven the next morning by the Recruiter, and he was told what to look for to know that the contact person that he was meeting at the Starbucks was his contact person and how he was to respond to what would be said to him. Michael got to Starbucks thirty minutes early. He had everything that he needed with him to leave the country. He didn't worry about the spare shirts and jeans that he had brought with him except one of each. He wanted to still have that international student look about him if he had to get out of the country fast. He waited for the contact to show. He showed right at nine. Michael was careful in watching for things to be as normal as possible from his perspective in this foreign land. This was part of his training, to know when he was being surveilled. He was comfortable with things up until now. The contact went to the counter and ordered. He stepped away from the counter to wait on his order. After a couple of minutes, his order was called. His name on his order was the first signal for Michael. Instead of a name common to the area, he had given the name of Jeff. Once he got his drink, he went over to the bar to add cinnamon to his drink. Jeff then walked toward the outer tables inside the Starbucks and stopped near Michael and asked if he knew the way to the Lebanese American University. Michael responded accordingly with, "I'm afraid not." With that, Jeff walked out of the Starbucks and got into a Toyota

Corolla. Michael followed out behind him and got in on the passenger side.

Jeff did not go into any further introductions. He started the car and drove away. Jeff turned right out of Starbucks and got back on General De Gaulle Street, mixing in with traffic at forty-three miles per hour or seventy kilometers per hour. They headed east for a short time and then headed south. Michael was looking to keep up with the street names as best as he could. GPS was fine, but he always found comfort in knowing something about where he was. They had rode south on Salim Salam Street for a number of minutes when Jeff turned left to get off Salim Salam Street and unto Saeb Salam Street. They turned right from there into a building with many dock doors, and the car was parked in a car parking lot. "You go inside. Someone waiting for you," was all that Jeff said. Michael got out and walked up some stairs through a door.

Once inside, Michael saw two men in the distance on what would be the back side of the building. The inside of this space was not the length of the building. The space had a demising Sheetrock wall. This space was probably only about twenty thousand square feet. There were racks and various packages of materials in the rack. Near where Michael came in, there was a small office. Maybe this was a check-in space. One of the men in the distance yelled something while waving Michael over. Michael headed in that direction. There was a crate that had one panel removed by the two men, and there was a forklift in the area as well. As Michael got near the men, his phone rang. It was the Recruiter. "Darrell,"—Michael was Darrell Hunt at that time—"you are about to meet with Ben and Gabriel. Those are the only names that they are offering up to communicate with at this time. You don't have a name to tell them. You are there for work. Ben should be the one that speaks the most to you. Good luck." The Recruiter hung up with that.

"Sir, I understand that you are a friend that can help us with our programming issue that we have for our box. Is this correct?" said the taller of the men.

"I'm sorry, you are?" Michael said.

"I am Ben. My friend is Gabriel. If I am correct that you are here to help us, then Gabriel has some programming information for you to use."

"Can I see the information, Gabriel?" Michael asked as he turned toward the man identified as Gabriel. Gabriel picked up a briefcase from the floor and set it on the seat of the forklift to open it. Once it was opened, he pulled a folder out, walked toward Michael, and extended his arm and hand with the folder toward Michael. Michael accepted the folder. He saw roughly fifty pages of materials. He started to scan the first few pages and then the last few pages. He recognized this program and what stopped anyone from executing the program. It required some interpretation of some math sequences that Michael was familiar with from a theory that he had postulated in his work back at MIT. That this was written for him specifically was what he concluded from the program in front of him. "Ben, is there a chair and small table that I can work on that can be set up near the box?" Michael wanted to get Ben away for a moment if possible since he was supposed to be the leader of the two men there.

"Yes. I will be right back," was how Ben responded to Michael. In walking away, Ben said, "U bilan ko'p gaplashmang," to Gabriel and kept walking toward the office that Michael passed on his way to meet with the two of them. Ben was telling Gabriel to "don't talk much to him," referring to Michael.

As Ben was walking away after his last words for Gabriel, Michael recognized the language but didn't say anything about the language. Instead, he asked Gabriel when the package arrived.

"I'm not sure. It was here when I got here today."

"We will be here for a while today. You should tell your friend that. We may need some coffee. Is there a coffee maker in the office?"

"I don't know. We can ask Ben when he gets back," Gabriel said.

From Gabriel's response, Michael got the impression that they were not to leave him alone. Where Ben had gone was only one hundred fifty feet or so away, but Gabriel was not willing to go in that direction away from Michael to leave Michael alone with the program notes or the box. Michael was trying to fit what could be their native language into the context of the assignment. He turned his attention away from Gabriel to start looking at the program closer. Within minutes, he heard Ben coming back. Ben had two folding chairs lying on top of a small, lightweight table that he was sliding across the floor. "Friend, here you go," Ben announced when he was about twenty feet away.

"Thank you. Can I set the table and one of the chairs near the box so that I can get to work?"

"Yes. By all means."

"Is there coffee here? I think this is going to take some time."

"We can get coffee."

"Good. I don't need it right now. I still have this one to finish." He held up the cup that he had gotten from Starbucks before Jeff came in.

Michael closed the folder and grabbed one of the chairs off the top of the table that Ben had pushed over toward them. He walked with it directly toward the box. He didn't touch the box or its contents. He unfolded the chair and continued to read. While Michael read, Ben and Gabriel were talking near the forklift. Gabriel was leaning on the forklift, and Ben had unfolded the other chair. They began speaking in English, and at some point, they were mixing English with the language that Ben had spoken when he was walking away before. Michael continued to read. He didn't want to touch anything until he had read everything. Michael was nearly done with the pages, and he realized that Ben and Gabriel's conversation was solely in the language that Ben had spoken earlier. Michael was glad that he knew the language because it revealed quite a bit to him from the parts of their conversation that he was able to pick up on. Michael had finished his reading of the program, and he also skimmed through some parts a second time.

"Gabriel, I am ready to get inside the box now. Do you have the tools to remove the covering so that I can get to the control panel and plug in my laptop?" Michael hadn't forgotten that Ben was the leader on this project between the two of them. He was looking to see more from each of their personalities with this slight disrespect toward Ben by calling on Gabriel.

"Sure, sure, I can help with that," Gabriel answered while the front of his face and eyes swiveled between Michael and Ben. "Ben, can you help me with this?"

This request from Gabriel infuriated Ben, and it showed in his answer, "Hozir mas'ulmisiz? Sizga bu yigit yoqadi, chunki u sizni tan oladi. Men uni o'ldirganimda seni o'ldriishim kerak."

Michael knew that he had touched a nerve with Ben, and he found out even more about the plans of the day when Ben had replied to Gabriel with, "Are you in charge now? You like this guy because he acknowledges you. I should kill you when I kill him." Michael had no reason to trust Ben or Gabriel, but the reason was solidified now even more. His trust was already shaky from what he overheard them talking about earlier while he was reading the program. He needed to figure out his advantages. Michael had settled on his plan. He couldn't trust that he was the only person that could do the satellite programming portion of this job, so he had to stall the completion of the work on the bomb itself. Part of what he learned in reading through the program that was given to him was that he could prevent the detonation of the device through a point in the program and that the command would need to come from another source after the signal from the satellite was given. He knew now that he would set the trapdoor on this program with that redirection. There was something that still troubled him from what he heard the two of them had talked about earlier that he hadn't figured out because they referenced it metaphorically, and Michael wasn't aware of the metaphor that they used when talking. He needed coffee, and he needed Gabriel alone.

"Guys, I don't know how much you know about this device, but there will be a point during the programming that the potential for it to be live occurs in the programming that I will be doing on it. I'll let you both know when I am approaching that time. You may want to go and get the coffee then. For your own safety."

Ben and Gabriel looked at each other. "That's not possible. We were never told that. You just keep working, and we will stay here," Ben said as his voice went from shaky to a false confidence as much as he could to reassure himself.

"Look, I'm just telling you what happens. Would you have come here today if you knew that there was a point that this could become live?" Ben and Gabriel looked at each other again. Michael had them. "Maybe that is why you were not told that it would become live. So that you wouldn't have a problem coming here today. In about ten minutes, you can stay or go and get coffee. The programming that needs to be done while its live will take about thirty minutes. Do what you want to do. I'm going to do what I was sent here to do."

Ben and Gabriel talked among themselves. Michael fully knew what they were going to be in discussion about, and this was exactly what they talked about. Ben was exactly what Michael thought him to be, a coward in charge. He used his authority over Gabriel to tell Gabriel to stay with the foreigner. He also told Gabriel that there was no truth to the bomb going live. He tried to convince Gabriel of this while sounding like that was why he had decided to become the errand boy, something that he would never do normally. Michael would have Gabriel to himself shortly.

"I'm there. When I hit the next key on my keyboard, the bomb will be live until I get through this part. Thanks for staying with me, guys."

"I've got to go and make some calls. While I am out, I will get some coffee. How do you like yours?" Ben asked.

"Just get me four shots of expresso. I'm about to do this."

"I'll be back. Gabriel, walk me to the door." Ben and Gabriel walked toward the door away from Michael, and he could not make out what they were saying. When Gabriel returned, Michael stopped typing for a bit and asked Gabriel if he lived in the area.

"No. I am visiting, as you are."

"Are you from the region?"

"Why do you ask?"

"I overheard you and Ben talking earlier. I have been in the region before, but I don't think that I have heard the dialect that you were speaking before." Michael didn't add that he knew the language itself.

"It is not of here. It is from somewhere else."

"Where?"

"It's not important."

"You know that this is a big deal what I am working on. Governments wouldn't want to be associated with this in any way. It could mean that a government gets overthrown or even war. Do you have your own protection in place?"

"What do you mean protection?"

"How many people do you think that will know about the origin of this are going to live? You don't think that the people in charge are going to let any of us live, do you? I'm not worried. I've gotten paid already. It is someplace where my family can get it. I'm dying already. Cancer. I only have six months to live. I took this assignment as an insurance policy payoff for my family. Are you dying or something?"

"No! I'm not dying! I am going home when we are done here today."

"Maybe you got leverage on somebody then since you are not worried." This was where Michael now cast all doubt into Gabriel's mind. "I don't expect to walk out of here today. Ben will kill me. He is the one responsible for keeping the secrets here I guess since I was told that he was my contact. You're probably right. You guys are friends. He wouldn't kill you." Michael knew the threat that Ben had made to Gabriel earlier will disturb Gabriel now.

"Look. We are proud of our work. Nobody will kill me for killing the Zionist right in their so-called homeland of Israel! I am not worried!"

Bingo. Michael had gotten confirmation from Gabriel from what he overheard Gabriel and Ben talking about earlier. The bomb was still intended for Israel. Michael was involved in something now that he didn't want any part of at all. He thought about how he would get out that warehouse and how he would get to any of his exit points. He wondered if he should call the Recruiter first. Whatever he was going to do wouldn't happen until Ben got back. The call would go out on him if he was gone when Ben got back. But if he could disable both Ben and Gabriel, he could gain the time that he would need to get out of the country. He also started to think how he could permanently disable the bomb. He knew that he could put a number of backdoors in place where no one else could get this back online.

"Hey, Gabriel. I'm sorry, I didn't mean to suggest that your friend would kill you. I'm sorry. I talk too much. Let me get back to work. That's why I am here."

"You work. I'm okay. Just don't blow us up."

Michael didn't have the heart to tell him that there was no likelihood of that happening now by this bomb or ever in the future.

CHAPTER 123

While Michael was working on the permanent disabling of the bomb, Ben returned. "Here you go. All four shots in the same cup. I see you still are here. So you didn't blow up. That is good news."

"Yes, it is good news. Thanks for the coffee." Michael took the cup and drank it down all at once. "Soon I will be at a point on this where I need to make a phone call. I'll let you know. It may be about the same time that I will need to go to the bathroom after drinking that down like that."

"I was not told about a need for you to call anyone."

"That doesn't mean that the need doesn't exist. Ben, I can't finish without making that call. I have coded some of my programming so that the person that I need to call can give me the programming language based on what I tell that person. I won't know what that is until I get to a point in the program that I am working on here. Either I get to finish or I don't. I'll let you know when I need to make the call, and you can do what you got to do when I tell you I am ready to make my call."

Ben again looked at Gabriel. Gabriel's eyes didn't give anything back to Ben. Gabriel, thanks to Michael, had doubts on whether or not he would be leaving when this was completed or not. He knew that Ben was going to kill Michael. Why not him?

"I'll let you make your call. Hurry up."

Forty-five minutes later, Michael stopped typing on his laptop, stood up, and stretched. "Where's the restroom?"

"In the office where I got the table and chairs. Are you ready to make your call now?"

"I think so."

Michael walked toward the office. He saw the entrance to the office and a separate door a little farther down the side of the office that had a placard hanging away from the door in Arabic that read "Restroom." He went in and used the urinal. When he was done, he removed from his left boot a .38 caliber handgun. It was what fit in his boot best with the necessary firepower. He pulled his shirt out of his pants and then tucked the gun in the waistband of his pants in back. Before leaving out of the restroom, he called the Recruiter. He quickly told the Recruiter that the destination was still Israel for the bomb. He told the Recruiter that he had disabled the bomb. Then he was shocked. The Recruiter told him to do what he was sent there to do. Michael couldn't process this direction. It couldn't be for national security. It couldn't be that the Recruiter could see this as good for his company. There was no immediate rationale to Michael other than the Recruiter had him on a mercenary mission. "I'm not doing it," was how Michael left it with the Recruiter, and he hung up the phone.

Michael headed out of the restroom and started walking up the side of the office only to be met by a gun pointed at him from Ben. Gabriel was over Ben's shoulder. Ben opened the door to the office with his right hand while the left one was still extended toward Michael with the gun. "In the office."

Michael went toward the door and then sidestepped into the office to never take his eyes off the gun that Ben had pointed at him or to turn his back so that Ben could see his gun. Michael moved into the room and stood in the middle of this office that was now empty of furniture. Ben went in and then Gabriel behind him. The door remained open. "I need you to finish," Ben said to Michael.

"I am done, and why are you pointing that gun at me?"

"You are not done. Or shall I say that you have double-crossed us, and that is why I am pointing the gun at you."

"What makes you think that I double-crossed you?" It was at this moment that Michael was shocked to see the Recruiter enter the small office area. The smallness of the office seemed to get even smaller as he came into the office. It was a twilight-zone moment for Michael. It appeared as if the low ceiling with the waterlines traveling overhead had become lower. The glass-windowed wall behind Ben and Gabriel seemed to move toward their backs and closer to Michael. He felt like he was being squeezed.

"Because you did. I told him as soon as you told me, Michael. We need you to undo what you have done and to make things right," the Recruiter said.

"Did he get direction from you to kill me today when I am done?" Michael asked pointedly toward the Recruiter.

"Michael, no one is going to kill you if you do your job correctly. I can't control these gentlemen if you don't finish your job properly."

"There is nothing else for me to do here today. I guess this is where it ends for Gabriel and me."

"Why are you concerned about Gabriel? He has done his part well. It is Ben's call if he walks out of here."

Ben began to turn to his right where Gabriel was standing with the gun in front of the pivot. Gabriel grabbed the gun. The Recruiter pulled a gun and held it in Michael's direction.

"Don't move, Michael," the Recruiter directed.

Ben and Gabriel wrestled on their feet over the gun with Ben's grip on the gun turning upward into a vertical position between the two of them. It was then that a shot fired. It went between them to the low ceiling and into one of the low-running waterlines. In piercing the hot waterline, it allowed water to come out in a high-pressure stream. The stream of water went directly into the right side of the Recruiter's face and neck area. He screamed as the scalding, hot water burned him. Michael pulled his gun and shot Ben because the Recruiter had dropped his weapon when the stream of water began to cascade down on him. Gabriel now had his hands on Ben's gun. He saw the Recruiter on his knees searching for his weapon with one hand while holding his face with the other hand. Then there were two shots. The Recruiter toppled over. Gabriel had shot him twice.

CHAPTER 124

Michael was going toward the house for Bobby Ashipa from the east. On the same road from the west was another car. This car had turned on its turn signal to turn left at what Michael thought would be the address that he was looking to go to himself. The other car got to the turn-in point with Michael still one hundred feet or so from the driveway leading to the house. That car turned in. Michael turned off his headlights and drove past the turn-in point. There was another driveway on the other side of the road that Michael turned into. Michael got out of the car and, as quietly as possible, closed his car door. Michael jogged back to the main road and then crossed it. There were hedges on either side of the driveway that was the address for Bobby Ashipa. Michael crossed the road. There was a car in the driveway outside of the garage. Michael couldn't tell whether there was someone in the car or not. The garage, unlike the other house that he was at tonight, was a two-car garage. Michael stayed off the path of the driveway, and then he saw the car door open on the driver's side with a left leg stepping out. The light that was cast over the inside of the car from the dome light with the door open showed Michael one head only. Michael moved quickly up the path. The body now had both feet on the ground and was standing. When the driver had closed the door with his left hand and his body facing toward the front of the car, the driver felt something up against his head and heard these words from Michael, "Put both of your hands on top of the car right now and you won't get shot in the head." Both the driver's hands went to the top of the car. "Leave them there and tell me your name," Michael followed up as he began to search the driver for weapons and identification.

"You should know my name if you are on my property."

"What's your name?

"Bobby Ashipa."

Michael had taken a wallet from the back pants pocket and put the wallet into his own front pants pocket. "Who is in the house, Bobby? Tell me exactly or they could die if I don't have them accounted for when you take me into your house."

"No one. Why am I taking you into my house? You got my wallet. My car keys are right here. What kind of early-morning car-jacking is this?"

"I am not here to jack any cars. I'm here to talk to you. Your truthfulness has a great deal to do with whether you will be alive when I leave here. This is the last time that I will ask you any question a second time. Is there anyone in the house?"

"No, there shouldn't be. Sometimes I have a lady friend come by. Sometimes she doesn't call first. But I don't see her car, so she may not be inside. Once in a while, she parks in the garage."

"Do you have an automatic garage door opener?"

"Yes."

"Use it now."

"I was going to do it on the box by the garage door. The batteries are dead on the one in the car."

"Okay. Well, let's go in. Remember, your actions and words have a lot of control in helping you stay alive. Don't make me shoot you. Let's go to the garage."

While walking toward the garage, Michael looked at the outline of the house. It was also different from the first beach house in that there were two stories above the garage—more house to search. The garage went up after Bobby entered some numbers into a pad on the garage. The light came on inside the garage, and there were no other cars in the garage. The garage was sparse in contents. There were two bikes and two Jet Skis in the garage along with a couple of ladders and some tools. At the front end of the garage were some stairs going upward, and Bobby headed toward those stairs. He guided Michael up the stairs to a landing where the light was on and opened the door to the house. He entered and still had not turned to see who was guiding him around. There was a lamp already lit in the room. The rooms that Michael could see seemed to have the right amount of furniture in them, not too little and not too much. None of the areas that Michael could see from this point had anything that made it a personal space. No pictures of people, no clothing laid about, just modern furniture that could have been custom-made. Michael told Bobby to sit in a chair near a column that separated the kitchen from a living room area. Michael pulled a duct tape roll out of his jacket with one hand. The other hand kept the gun trained on Bobby. Michael handed the roll of tape to Bobby. "Pull off about a foot of tape from the roll. Don't tear it off and then hand it back to me."

Bobby did as he was told. Michael then began to roll the tape that was extended around one of Bobby's wrist, and then he told Bobby to stand and hug the column that separated the two areas.

"Now put one arm around the column, and from the other side of the column, put your other wrist up against the one with the tape on it." Once Bobby did this, Michael guided the duct tape around both wrist and hands. Bobby was secured to the column. "I've got to search your place. Are there any alarms that I could trigger?"

"No."

"Give me the layout. What's on this level, and what's on the upper level?"

Bobby gave Michael the full layout, and then Michael duct-taped Bobby's mouth and set out on his search of Bobby's house. The house was not a new home. Bobby or someone must have gotten in another recent trend of purchasing property that was older and on desirable land to tear it down and build a new house on the land. It was a nice home. Besides the rooms that Michael saw as soon as they came into the house, there was a total of three bedrooms, one on the main level and two upstairs. There were three bathrooms total, and upstairs with the bedrooms was a large recreation room that had a patio to it. The master bedroom was on the main level with an exit to a patio on the main level that matched with an exit to the same patio from the dining room. It was nicely done and nicely furnished. No one else was in the home. Michael had found two guns, and he disarmed them and moved their location so that Bobby couldn't even get to them fast if were to get free from Michael.

Michael walked up to Bobby and removed the duct tape from his mouth. He didn't snatch it off, but with duct tape, one could always remove some hair or skin. He looked at the tape, and he had some of Bobby's mustache, and maybe it was skin from his lip. Michael didn't know where the skin came from, but it was skin on the tape. Michael left the hands taped and Bobby standing. He grabbed a chair and put it about eight feet from Bobby. "Remember, I want the truth. Any lies will result in pain that will require a doctor. Full name and occupation?" Michael stated this as a question. He wanted to get Bobby comfortable on easy things before he started with questions that Tammy had provided answers to.

"Bobby Ashipa. I'm a private investigator."

"What did you do prior to that?"

"I was a Gary police officer and detective."

"Where were you coming from tonight? Or better yet, tell me about your last four hours."

"I was out with some friends."

Michael stood and walked toward the kitchen and grabbed a towel and then went back toward Bobby. He reversed the position of the gun in his hand so that the handle was extended from his hand on the top side of his thumb and index finger. He got within one foot of Bobby and smashed the handle into the bridge of Bobby's nose. Michael whipped the towel over Bobby's mouth to muffle his screams. Once Bobby got his breath and began to choke on blood, Michael removed the towel.

"That will be the least amount of pain that you will receive if I need to apply pain again. I told you I will not ask any questions twice. I asked the question, where were you coming from tonight, and you told me something vague about who you were with. I am not going to ask again, so answer my question."

I was in Chicago," Bobby choked the words out.

Michael could slowly play the questions, but it was late, and he didn't want to take the scenic route to his answers. "Were you at the Hilton Towers on Michigan Avenue?"

Bobby lifted his head, and he recognized that this was going to take a direct path. He paused and then said, "Yes."

"Who did you meet at Vic's?"

"An old friend, William Reece."

"Why did you meet him there?" Michael didn't know this answer, so he wouldn't know if he was lying or not. Michael was prepared to put some pain on him if the answer seemed odd.

"I didn't know that I was meeting him there."

Michael stood, flipped the gun around in his hand again, and reached for Bobby's taped hands to pin them on the wall and reared the gun back and was ready to use the handle as a hammer to crush the knuckles on one of Bobby's fingers.

"Wait! Wait! What are you doing? I'm telling you the truth!"

"Why were you there, then? And how did Reece come to be there at the same time that you were?"

"We both got calls from another old friend separately. He told us to meet him there. He never showed."

"Who was this old friend that you were going to meet there?"

"Ron Winston. He was a policeman with us back in the day."

Bobby's answer caught Michael off guard. Michael needed to know why would Ron be wanting to meet them at the Hilton of all places and why he was looking to meet at the same hotel where Michael thought, nearly a day and a half ago, he heard someone calling out to Rick Smalls. Michael didn't show that he was caught off guard, but he did return to his seat. "Why did Ron Winston call you to meet and why there?"

"He said that he needed some help with something. He didn't tell me what. He had told me earlier that he was at that hotel because of a security convention or forum or something."

"Do you work with him often?"

"Not at all. Yesterday morning, he called out of the blue about something from the past, a guy that he knew."

"He wanted you to help him find a guy that he knew, and you went to Chicago for this out of the blue."

"Well, yeah."

Michael got up and went over and smashed the small finger on Bobby's left hand against the wall and stuffed the towel back over Bobby's mouth.

After Bobby settled down, he said, "I'm telling you the truth. I didn't lie to you."

"For what you told me, you did tell the truth. You left something out, and I told you that not answering in full is the same as a lie."

"All right. He and I met up earlier yesterday. We talked some about this guy Rick Smalls from his past. He started asking me questions about an accident that this Rick Smalls's parents had gotten into that caused their deaths. I couldn't help him with that, and we parted. He then called me later to meet him in Chicago."

In hearing that Ron was asking Bobby questions about his parents and knowing that Bobby was the policeman that met with the coroner, Michael wasn't focused because he was wondering if this man had something to do directly with the deaths of his parents. It was room number 2 all over again for Michael. With his face pointed toward Bobby while he was seated, he didn't hear that someone had walked up behind him. He didn't realize that someone was there until he felt the tip of a gun on the back of his head. "Put your gun on the edge of the table. If I have any doubt in your movements, I will not hesitate to shoot you in the back of your head."

Bobby was shocked to see Sarge. One, because he should be dead now, and two, why would he be there at this moment?

"Sarge, cut me loose. This crazy man broke into my house. I don't even know him."

"Bobby, I will get with you. You do as I said and put your gun on the edge of the table."

Michael slowly reached forward to put his gun on the table.

"Now lift your left hand over your head." When Michael had done this, Sarge slapped a handcuff onto that wrist. "Now stand up and keep your back to me and raise your other arm over your head."

Michael did as he was told. After he stood, he was close to Bobby, and Bobby, with his left foot planted, kicked forward like the old-style field-goal kickers that approached the ball straight on and kicked Michael in his groin area. Michael dropped. "Bobby, don't do nothing like that again! You are getting in my way here!" Sarge yelled. "You stand up! Put both of your arms up again with your back to me."

Michael repeated what he had done previously.

"Now go over and face that same column that he is taped to and face it and then connect the cuffs together. Tight."

Michael did as he was told.

"Bobby, I was listening to you on the stairs before I came in here. Were you going to get to the part where you sent someone in the bathroom at that hotel in Chicago to shank me?"

This confirmed to Michael what Tammy had laid out to him earlier.

"What are you talking about?"

"I'll get back with you. You,"—he turned his attention to Michael—"why are you asking questions about earlier tonight?" As William was asking the question, he recognized that this could be Rick Smalls. He had been prepped for this potential from years ago. "Bobby, do you know who this man is?"

"No, I don't. He didn't introduce himself."

"Bobby, I want you to meet Rick Smalls. Rick, there are some people that I need to let know that you are alive and well. Bobby, I'm going to let you go. You cannot touch him. You know who wants him just as he is. This could turn into a profitable day!"

This last statement gave Michael the impression that Reece also might have some relationship to the man that Bobby had met outside of the hotel. Sarge had not cut Bobby loose yet as he sat down in the chair that Michael had been sitting in. He pulled out his phone and dialed. "Hello, sir. I believe that I have Rick Smalls in my custody right now." Sarge was silent for a moment. "Yes. Yes, I do have him. I am certain that it is him. Is that offer still open? Good. You have my account number. Where do you want me to bring him?"

"Bring him to the house. I will be there in three hours. You should arrive about that same time frame." The Voice hung up.

"Bobby, this is a great day! Just think about it. I nearly got shanked by a friend of yours in a hotel bathroom, and now I am having one million dollars deposited in my account because of Rick here." Sarge gestured toward Michael. "And almost as good as the million dollars is that I get to kill you right here in your own house. The house that has been paid in part by the same people that are giving me my million dollars. Isn't it ironic this man's life is worth a million dollars to me while the death of his parents was worth so much to you? Hey"—Sarge again focused on Michael—"did you know that this man that you are facing right now killed your parents? He followed them from your grandmother's house around that road, and as they were rounding that road and slowing down, he sped up in his car and rammed the rear of their car, driving them into a pole. He then got out of his car and walked up to the passenger side first on the side where your mother was and fired two shots into her head. He then walked over to the other side and did the same to your father. He got plenty for it. If I could trust you, I would uncuff you and let you deal with him. Well, it's not that I don't trust you. It's that I want to kill him more because he tried to kill me earlier."

Michael said nothing as he looked at Bobby. While he was looking at Bobby, Michael's head snapped as he heard the sound of the gun. In that same moment, Bobby had the first hole in his head. A moment later, Sarge walked closer and put a second hole in the slumped body whose arms were still anchored to the column.

"We got to go. I've got to prepare you for travel."

CHAPTER 125

Sarge now had Michael bound in the back seat of his car. He had used the duct tape to bind Michael's ankles together first while he was still cuffed around the pole. He then put some duct tape over his mouth. He then bound Michael's waist around the column. He did this so that he could feel some comfort in uncuffing his hands. After securing Michael to the column around his waist, he then uncuffed his hands, and then he recuffed them behind Michael. He then cut the tape from the waist and began to guide Michael slowly through the house to the stairs. Once they were outside of the garage, they went to Sarge's car. Sarge put Michael in the back seat. He put Michael in the back seat on the passenger side. With Michael's hands cuffed behind him, Sarge pulled the seat belt over Michael. He then pushed Michael over on to his left side. He took more duct tape and lapped it around Michael's head at the forehead level, and then before breaking it off, he interlocked it with the armrest in the back seat. He needed to keep Michael down below the window level. He couldn't let Michael be seen by other drivers who would see a man with duct tape over his mouth. Sarge got into the car and drove away. He still had well over two hours before he was to arrive at the destination that he was given, and it was only forty or forty-five minutes away, so he headed to his own house to kill some time. He also knew that he was not going to deliver Rick until he knew that his money was in his account.

CHAPTER 126

Ron didn't sleep much. Instead of sleeping, he was trying to sort out the Bobby thing, how Bobby sounded on the recording that Sarge became aware of what was about to happen to him. But why did Sarge bring someone with him? In Ron's view, there was nothing to alert Sarge to the potential of trouble. When Ron called Sarge to come to Chicago, it was to find out if Sarge was able to reveal anything while talking with Bobby, which was the only known low-level thing coming from Ron. The invite, in of itself, was not something that should lead Sarge to think that he needed his boy with him. He didn't solve anything. The rental car place opened at seven. He had decided to walk over to Grand Avenue from his hotel. It should take just about thirty minutes. As he walked in the summer coolness of the morning, he thought about the last day and a half's events over and over again. If most people were asked what was the thing that surprised them the most about those events, then it would probably be close to unanimous that it would be getting your car shot up while you were in it, only to be saved by someone ramming the rear of your car prior to the shoot-up. Near unanimous was what Ron thought. He would maintain that the thing that surprised him the most was what got all this started: him thinking that he saw Rick Smalls.

CHAPTER 127

Valerie was up and getting ready to go to meet her dad and Dale back over at the Hilton Towers. It wasn't as if she really ever was down. She didn't really sleep. She never did go to bed. If she did sleep at all, it was in an upright position on the couch in her hotel room. At four thirty in the morning, she went down to the exercise facilities and got on the treadmill. She stayed with it for an hour. When she was done, she saw that she had covered eight treadmill miles. She knew she would have done maybe eight and a half miles if she was running outdoors, but she was okay with this exercise. She was able to work through a few things in her mind while she was on the treadmill. She knew that she was being lied to, or she suspected that she was being lied to. The video message that she had received was still on her mind. The message was both terrifying and informative. There was no way that she would normally accept that kind of message and trust in it and use that method of communication to guide her next moves, but it was that something that stood out that gave her reason that she needed to trust in this message. She was out of the shower and getting ready. She didn't dress for business or in, what would be normal business wear for her, heels. She went with a summer sweater and jeans, and she kept with the same running shoes that she had just worn on the treadmill. Her phone rang. She looked at her phone, and it showed that it was six o' seven, and it was from Dave. "They left the hotel. Where are they going?"

"I can't tell you their destination. I can tell you that they are headed south. What do you want to do?"

"Have your guys to keep following them. You come back over this way and pick me up." As soon as Valerie hung up with Dave, she called her dad.

"Good morning, sweetie. I was just about to call you. Can we push our meeting back a bit this morning?" Howard asked.

"Why? What has changed?"

"Nothing has changed that requires the meeting time to change. It is nothing related to Dale meeting with the Programmer. It's just… it's just that I found myself up most of the night. I couldn't sleep, and I was…I was thinking about your mom and how much I miss her. I'm sorry. I shouldn't let my sentimental nature get in the way of your plans. I'm sorry."

"No. No, Dad. No problem. You do what you need to do. Give me a call when you are ready to meet. I love you, Dad!"

"I love you too, sweetie!"

CHAPTER 128

Valerie headed down the hall for the elevator. She took the elevator to the lobby level of the Palomar Hotel. She walked straight through the lobby into what she thought was a cold summer morning. She walked toward the curb to look south. She was looking for Dave's car. Dave pulled up within minutes. She opened the passenger door and got in, and Dave started to pull off.

"Wait a minute. Before you drive, I talked with my dad. It's about my mom. He told me about how he was thinking of her all night and basically how he is missing her. You know, I don't think he comes back to this area too much because his memories for her are still hard on him. Pull your guys off of him. I think I know where he is going, and it should be private. I googled a rental car location. It's a few blocks up on Grand. I'm going to get a car and meet him there."

"I could get out, and you can take this car, Valerie. I can get another one."

"No. Just drop me."

There was no more conversation for the three blocks that they traveled. At Grand Avenue, Dave turned left, and the rental car office was in the middle of the block. Next to the office front was a ramp that came from indoor parking, probably where the rental cars were.

"Thanks, Dave. I will call you later," Valerie said as she was getting out of the car.

"Valerie, are you going to get some flowers for the grave site?" Dave asked as the door was closing and Valerie was walking into the car rental office.

Chapter 129

When Ron had arrived at the rental car office, the door was already open with two people in line for the one clerk at two minutes after seven. He waited his turn. By the time that he was called to the young lady service representative, there were other people in line in a serpentine manner that the chords and posts dictated. He was now glad that he got there when he did. Ron wasn't very good with waiting. "Mr. Winston, I need you to initial in these three boxes, and then you will need to sign the bottom of the form where I have indicated with an X," Jennifer, the service representative, said to Ron. She was pretty cheerful for seven in the morning, Ron thought.

"Okay." Ron initialed to decline the insurance coverage, to acknowledge that the car was not damaged, and to acknowledge that the fuel level was full. He hadn't seen the car, but he just couldn't see Jennifer misleading him. And then he signed the bottom of the form.

"Thank you, Mr. Winston. Here are your keys. Your car is in slot three Charlie. Three-C. You will go through the side door here and turn right for the stairs or elevator. Go to the third level, and it should be in the third slot. Is there anything else that I can help you with?"

"No, Jennifer. You have been very helpful. Have a good day."

Ron turned left to walk parallel with the counter to the side door. He noticed, coming through the front door, a woman that he recognized. He didn't know from where, and in looking at her and not taking his eyes off her, he stumbled into the door that he was going through. This stumble into the glass door brought the attention of everyone in the serpentine line, Jennifer, and the lady who had just entered onto Ron. It was now in this eye-to-eye look at the woman that he knew who she was and what he needed to do next.

CHAPTER 130

The sun was up now. For the last two hours, Sarge had left Michael bound in the back seat of his car in his garage. When Sarge had gone into the house, he didn't try to nap or even to rest by lying down. He saw today as the day that things were changing for the good for him. When he went upstairs after parking his car in the garage, he opened his laptop. He got to the website for his bank account and checked to see if the balance had changed. It had not. He knew that he wasn't going anywhere with Michael until he had control over this new money. He started some coffee. There were things to plan, and sleep could come later. While the coffee was being made, his thoughts were that he was not going to come back to his house again. He wasn't looking at just walking away from the house as an asset because $1 million only went so far. He could still work a sale from his home even when he was not there. His thinking in not coming back there was if this guy Rick Smalls was worth a million dollars, then he didn't want to be in any part of this trail because this Rick Smalls was most likely going to be dead soon. He went to the gun locker that Michael had seen earlier and opened it. He pulled out his own 9mm handgun. He checked the chamber and saw that it had a bullet in it. He then pulled the clip, and he verified that it was full. He sat the handgun on top of the locker and removed a shoulder harness. It fit so that he would be able to have the gun between his left arm and the left side of his chest. Once the harness was secured in place, he put the gun into the harness. He pulled out four more clips of ammunition one by one. As he pulled each one out separately, he inspected them to make certain that they were full. They were. He laid these four clips into his left hand and reached into the locker once again and pulled out his passport.

He came back into the dining room area and set the clips on the table. He went to his bedroom and came out with a backpack. He put one change of clothes in the backpack and a pair of athletic shoes. He brought the backpack to the table and set the backpack next to the clips. Sarge unzipped a lower front compartment on the backpack for storage space for the clips. He picked up the clips and put them into the backpack and zipped that portion close. He went into the kitchen and got a travel mug with a lid out of his cabinet. He removed the lid and then rinsed the mug out with some running water from the sink. With the water still running, he set down the mug and picked up the lid and rinsed it also. He kept the lid in one hand and turned the water off with the other hand. He reached for the coffeepot and poured until the mug was at the fill line. He put the coffeepot back and then screwed the lid onto the mug. He held the coffee mug close to his mouth and blew at the steam coming out of it. He then sat at the kitchen table and refreshed his account information. Still, no change. Sarge got up from the table and started to walk to the sliding doors that led to the patio out front. He stood on the patio, looking out over the new day. He didn't even notice any aspect of the smell of the lakefront, the morning smell of the sand, or the cool morning. He blew at his coffee.

CHAPTER 131

Ron followed Jennifer's directions, and the Hyundai Sonata was waiting on him on the third level in the third space or in three Charlie, as Jennifer said in a morning fresh sort of way. Ron settled in by adjusting the seat and then the mirrors. He backed out of three Charlie and followed the exit signs down the ramps. He approached a booth that had an arm down. He stopped and was asked for his paperwork. He gave it to the attendant that was nowhere near as cheery as Jennifer. The paperwork was handed back to him, and the arm was raised. He pulled forward, and he was able to look into the side glass door to the office, the same door that he had nearly face-planted into earlier when he saw the woman that was now being attended to. The serpentine line was longer now, but at least they had another service representative working with Jennifer now. It was this other representative that was tending to the lady that Ron had recognized. The lady began to walk in the direction of the side door. Ron turned away to look down and played with the car's sun visor to give the appearance that he was not paying attention. The lady came through the door and turned left for the elevator. Ron was trying to determine where the best place was to stage himself to follow her. He thought about sitting right where he was with an incredible act of playing with the driver's side sun visor until he heard the honk of a horn behind him. He then realized that this was not a spot to sit in. It was a single-lane exit from the booth with the arm and a guy who did not have the same disposition as Jennifer. He inched forward to prevent hitting

302

any pedestrians that might be walking by and turned right. He saw that if he was able to pull a U-turn, there was an open parking spot at the moment across the street. That spot would have him pointing back to the east.

CHAPTER 132

The Voice was with the Recruiter, and their car ride had been pretty silent up until now. That was until the Voice broke the silence. "Look, I know you have some payback on your mind to your protégé, but it can't come before we take care of our business. I don't have a problem with you hurting him. He just can't be disabled. I need his mind. I need his ability to type and his fingerprints. I don't know if his eyes are attached to a retina scan, so don't damage or distort his eyes. I am not shocked often, but I thought the old sarge might be good enough to spot him somewhere and then maybe follow him. I never thought that Rick would be captured by someone like Sarge. I guess I am capable of being surprised."

The Recruiter added, "Sir, I will stay mission focused. I don't have any plans to even hurt him prior to the mission being accomplished unless I need to drag something out of him. It has been a long time."

With those last stated words, the Recruiter drifted back to Beirut and the scalding water and the two bullets from Gabriel. He often wondered if Rick thought that he was dead and if that was why he was still alive today. He knew that Rick was more than aware that his life was about to end. So he always assumed that with that knowledge, Rick would want to see him dead as well, and Rick thought that Gabriel had accomplished that for him. Rick never checked. The Recruiter knew that by the time that he and the Voice were done with Rick, he would verify that Rick was dead.

"You know, I may even want a part of this hurting Rick," the Voice interrupted the Recruiter's thoughts of the past and the future. "He cost me dearly. After Beirut, there was a rough patch for the business because our reputation was ruined. While the client base didn't know where we failed, they had heard enough that we had failed on a large contract."

"Sir, there has not been many days that I have not thought about that since then. I let his talents blind me then. It won't happen again with him or any of the operatives that I have contact with. Before Beirut, when I finally found out how he was carving out potential escape plans, I still believe it was right to set him up with an assignment that he wouldn't walk away from. I missed then. I won't miss today."

"You don't sound like you are going to be able to wait through the mission without hurting him bad. Are you sure that you are under control here?"

The Recruiter turned his head toward the Voice and kept the car in its lane and said, "I will not be beaten by Rick Smalls dying too soon today." Then he turned his attention back to the road just before the split of the highway for Interstate 57 to the right and Interstate 94 to the left. He turned his signal on and went to the left.

CHAPTER 133

Valerie came down the ramp, stopped to execute the validation of the rental with the anti-Jennifer, and came through the raised arm and turned right to go west. This was something different. She had reasons to want to know what was going on with her dad. But this was about her mom and her dad. She wanted to support him. Those last years had been rough with her mom's health. She saw the change on both her parents. Her dad even spent more time at the home that they kept back in this area and away from the suburban DC home that they always had. She turned right on Orleans Street and then, shortly after, turned left to get onto the interstate. She figured that she was still a bit ahead of traffic because she was leaving the downtown area. But she had also been in Chicago enough to know that there was no real pattern to being ahead, behind, or in the midst of traffic. Some people said that Chicago had only two seasons: winter and construction. Since it wasn't winter, she knew that she could experience traffic impacted by congestion related to the number of cars on the road or congestion related to fewer lanes being available along with the high number of cars on the road. With any luck, she could be with her dad in forty minutes. She had only gone back here a few times herself since her mom passed away. She hadn't been there with her dad at all. This could be weird. She had her own emotions about this, but she must remember that she was doing this for her dad. She was going to support him. It sounded to her on the phone with him this morning that he could use her on this occasion. It was not his nature to share any aspect of his feelings. He could have gotten out of the meeting without conveying this sentimental reason. That was why she believed that he wanted her there, but he couldn't out-and-out ask her to come.

Traffic was flowing nicely, and Valerie's thoughts began to drift back to business and the video that she had received. The message was startling enough, but the thing that she saw in the video was unmistakable. There was no way to confuse it. It was clear. It was part of the message. She knew that this meant that this whole situation was going to confront her sooner rather than later. She knew that it was inevitable, and she wanted it sooner rather than later. No need in thinking about later. She would be there for her dad this morning and then figure out how to bring the matter of the video forward.

CHAPTER 134

Wouldn't you know it, she went west. Ron only had two directions to choose from, and his staging positions were limited. The lady went west. He had to wait until some traffic had cleared going east before he was only able to start the U-turn. He now had the eastbound lanes on Grand Avenue blocked, but he couldn't enter the westbound lanes until two more cars were to go by. He finished the U-turn in the middle of the block and sped up to get closer to the lady's car. She crossed La Salle on the yellow. He crossed on the red and with horns blaring at him. He thought that in a few short blocks he was already worthy of two tickets. The U-turn he very well could get away with. The running of the red would catch him. Chicago had a pretty aggressive camera system to catch traffic-light violators. That ticket would come his way via the rental car company. Ron was within a reasonable distance of her car now, and she turned right, and he saw her turn signal come on again after they both had made that right turn. She was turning left for the interstate. He followed.

Ron, while following her on the interstate, was trying to compose his own Venn diagram in his head to put the last two days together since he thought he saw Rick. He wondered if this lady was in touch with Rick. He also wondered if they had ever lost touch. They were tight. Ron thought that he and Rick were tight as friends, but he knew that there was some deeper connection between the two of them. He figured that if there was a choice that Rick had to make between him and her, then Rick would be right in choosing her.

What Ron remembered about her was that there was nothing petty about her. He thought then that to say that about any high school person was a remarkable memory. She stood on the ground of trying to be above the matters of pettiness, immaturity, and the normal high school relationship killer of jealousy. Everybody wanted a piece of Rick, and when Ron was in the same place as both of them, she was fine with being right with Rick or peeling off so others could get their face time with Rick. It was like she knew at the end of the night that she and Rick were together, and there was enough of Rick to share with others. She carried herself well beyond her years then. He knew that he would need to confront her at some point. But with all the violence that had shown up, he wanted to make sure that if he was the violence magnet, then he was not going to put her in harm's way.

Traffic was moving well.

CHAPTER 135

Sarge had been refreshing the website that showed his bank account now for the last couple of hours every fifteen minutes. He wasn't getting discouraged that it wasn't there yet, but he was becoming concerned about remaining at his home. He could check the account from his phone. Sarge decided to go mobile. He had everything that he thought he needed in the backpack that he had put together right after getting back to his house, and he had had plenty of coffee in the couple of hours since he had been home. He went to the restroom prior to leaving to get more comfortable. He couldn't help but think about the last time that he went to a restroom and what his old buddy Bobby had led his way.

CHAPTER 136

His old buddy, Bobby Ashipa, had come through the academy one class before Sarge. At the end of Sarge's first year on the force, they were partnered up. Bobby was not necessarily a fast talker trying to sway things his way with Sarge or with others that he came into contact with; instead, he was smoothly matter-of-fact in his approach. They worked together for a couple of years before Bobby got on the path of becoming a detective. Sarge's vision didn't go that way. He thought that becoming a sergeant would be a nice spot to settle into. He worked toward that path. Bobby followed his path, and Sarge followed his. They both landed where they targeted. The Gary Police Department was not a large force; in fact, there was only one reporting station for the entire city at Thirteenth and Broadway. In the area near the police station, there was not a lot going on. This portion of the dividing street that separated east from west in the city of Gary was nearly as desolate as the boarded-up storefronts a few blocks north that represented downtown. Bobby got to know a lot of things about the city and the streets while being a detective. He continued to come to Rudy's. While Rudy's had always been a cop's bar with some cop friends being customers, the pattern of the clientele began to change with Detective Ashipa. Everybody suspected that they knew who those other people were that would flock toward the back of Rudy's where Bobby took on his spot. They were people that worked the streets of the city. They had their hands on the things that the same police officers that trafficked into Rudy's would find in some way in their official duties when they were on their beat. Bobby worked those people, and they looked to draw favor from him. When those folks came in, they all were recognizable in that they all had that street dealmaker look about them apart from this one guy on this one night.

This guy came in and headed straight to the back of Rudy's, then stood for a moment at the edge of the table in the booth that Bobby always sat in, and then he sat down. Sarge and the others would glance back there from time to time when other folks were back there, but when this guy came in, the glances turned into almost a synchronized staring. The staring rotated from different bar seats and tables. If the group was two, then one would look for a bit and then would get relieved by the other one. The same with the larger groups of officers and their friends. The guy that had come in to take this spot opposite of Bobby seemed out of place even to the noncops that were in Rudy's, and that was why they were a part of the synchronized staring. He seemed out of place because he had a governmental, high-business level, professional appearance about him. That was not the normal clientele of Rudy's. He was also not black or brown, which made up ninety percent of the patrons. Rudy's had white customers, but none were policemen. Some of the policemen dated or were friendly with white ladies, and they would be in Rudy's. There were some nonblack or nonbrown clientele that worked their way back to Bobby, but they were not like this guy. They belonged. There was nothing about this guy's appearance that said he belonged. He stayed for a long time compared to the normal revolving visitors that would land next to Bobby. After he left, all the other policemen wanted to head over to Bobby's booth. All the policemen's eyes landed on Sarge. They knew that he was the closest to Bobby. Sarge went over.

Bobby was smart. He knew why Sarge had come over and that anything that he told Sarge, the others would look to pry out of him. Bobby made it a point to make that quick, so by all appearances, nothing of substance could have been conveyed. He said to Sarge pretty quickly after Sarge sat down, "Not now. We need to meet tomorrow." With that being said, Bobby got up and walked out of Rudy's.

Bobby didn't reach out to Sarge the next day or the next few days. Bobby hadn't come back into Rudy's for a few days. About a week after the last time that Bobby and Sarge saw each other, when Sarge was arriving home after his own trip over to Rudy's after work, Bobby walked up on Sarge as he was getting out of his car. At this time, Sarge was not a beachfront homeowner yet. To be as close to Sarge's space when Sarge got out of the car was not the best way to greet somebody that was armed at this time of the night in this neighborhood. It wasn't that the neighborhood over where Sarge lived on Wallace Street near Fifteenth Avenue was a bad neighborhood. It was just a neighborhood in Gary, and most people stayed on edge at night. "What are you trying to do?! Are you trying to get shot? Don't ever walk up on me like that again. I might not be able to control what happens! What are you doing here?" Sarge said intensely.

"My bad, my bad, partner. I didn't mean no harm. Can we go inside and talk?"

Once they had gone inside Sarge's bungalow home with a small front and back yard and a detached garage that Sarge hadn't used, they settled in with beers from Sarge. "Why are you here, Bobby?"

"I wanted to tell you about that meeting that I had the other night at Rudy's."

"Why couldn't you talk about it that night?"

"Because everybody there wanted to know what it was about. Am I wrong? I bet as soon as I left that night that they confronted you, didn't they?"

"Yeah. So what was that about? Who was that man?"

"Before I get into the details of that meeting, I need to find out where you are on some things. If you are where I would hope that you are, then I am going to ask you something. If your answer is the right answer, then I will tell you everything from that meeting, all right?"

"Shoot."

"Sarge, we go back. We spent time together in the same patrol unit. I would like to think that we were not just partners, but we were and are also friends. As a friend, I need a partner with some things. Some of these are things that I have been looking into before that meeting the other night, and some of these things will be related to the meeting from the other night." Bobby paused as he searched the Sarge's eyes. Bobby determined that Sarge was still engaged, so he went on. "You see me in Rudy's. I am working the back of that room. When people come in there to talk to me, they are not worried about being spotted by somebody that might be on the wrong side of the law. They know that there are only cops there for the most part. So when they come to see me and to feed me information, they feel safe. I get good information on the cases that I am working. I am also getting good information about other things that are going on the street. This is where I could use a partner. You and I both know that these streets in Gary are full of people trying to get a leg up on some-body that they are in competition with, and part of getting a leg up on somebody is by taking people out. The shooting and the killing come because of the competitive environment that folks find them-selves in because of the movement of drugs, girls, stolen items, and so on. You and I also know that this the movement of drugs, girls, and stolen stuff is never going to end. What can be reduced is the shoot-ing and the killing. Let me ask you, do you think that the shooting and killing could be reduced if the competition was thinned out?"

"Yeah, of course, it is the competition that brings the violence. They don't know how to settle differences without the violence. What are you getting at, Bobby?"

"I'm almost there. What if we were able to slow down the shoot-ing and killing? Wouldn't this also reduce some of the threats that your boys on the street run up against as people are trying to protect their interests even against cops?"

"Sure. What are you suggesting, the neighborhood cops' guns turned in or some crap like that?"

"Nah, partner. What I am suggesting is that we tilt the coverage of the street units. If we were able to stop some of the shooting and killing by having some focus on some of the competitors, then we could stop some of the territorial fights from happening. I would need your help at the street level, raids on dope houses, or a greater presence in some neighborhoods. I will let you know through some of my contacts where you need to be. Is this something that you can help a friend with, Sarge?"

"This approach benefits somebody, and I don't want to know who they are. I also know that you are not thinking of this from a law-and-order standpoint. What are you getting out of this, *partner*?" Sarge responded with an emphasis on *partner*.

"I might be able to pick up a little something extra hypothetically. That little something extra can be shared with my partner on this also hypothetically."

"Who are you involved with, Bobby?"

"It would be cleaner to provide you full deniability if you didn't know. Do you want a piece of this?"

"I'll try it. I'm not going to commit to the long term until I get a feel that the shooting and killing does slow down. What about the man from the other night? Is he a part of this?"

"He's a totally different deal. He came from out of the blue. I've met with him twice more since the other night when you saw us together. He reached me initially at the station. He told me that he didn't have a crime matter but that he needed some help above the level of a private investigator. He went on to say that this could be career altering. He told me that his client was a multinational businessman that had some local interests that I may be able to help him with. That is when he asked if we could meet. I told him to meet me at Rudy's. You saw him when he came in. You saw how long he stayed. He presented his matter to me on behalf of his client. He finished his presentation and told me that he would be in touch again. That is what led to the other meetings. This guy is interesting. Listen to this. After our second meeting, he gave me a payment for my consulting services. Five grand, cash! Maybe, who knows, I know that I need to know more about the career-altering parts of this man and his client, but I am intrigued. He told me that he needed me and somebody else. I thought about you, Sarge. Do you want to be that somebody else? You got to let me know. I am supposed to have that somebody else with me the next time that I meet with him. What do you think?"

"I don't know what to think. Yeah, I like money. I'm not going to get rich being a cop, but where is this money coming from? What would I need to do to get this money?"

"He told me that there will be a specific job offer when I meet with him the next time. He told me that the payments could be like this five grand, where there are no books or it could be cut through a payroll service. He joked that he didn't know how I might want to handle my income. Hey, man, I thought about you on both of these. Really, you are the only person that I have thought about for this chance, this chance to get a bit for ourselves. You got to let me know what you want to do. Yeah, they are separate things, but I would like to think that if we can partner on one thing, then we should be able to partner on both things. I am meeting him after work tomorrow over in Griffith. You can ride with me. I will pick you up when you finish your shift. It's you only that can help me on the first thing, and I would only do it with you. On this thing, it's only you that I want. Are we partners to the end? What do you say?"

"Bobby, I'll take the ride with you tomorrow. This doesn't mean that I am in or out. When we are done with that meeting in Griffith, I will give you the answer to both of these things, okay?"

"Okay, partner."

CHAPTER 137

The next evening, Bobby and Sarge pulled into the shopping complex parking lot and then did a drive-by on the storefronts to identify the one that Bobby was told that the meeting was to be held at. He spotted it and then turned left to get to the parking slots. Bobby found a spot that was three spots in and then parked. "Let's go see the future, partner!" Bobby bellowed out.

"We'll see. Remember, no promises from me," Sarge countered.

"All right, all right. No promises. Just an open mind, right?"

"Open mind. I can do that."

They walked to the outer door of the business that the guy from Rudy's told Bobby about. They pulled open the door, and a chime sounded. There was a reception area that they were immediately in, and they looked toward the reception desk, and no one was there. Neither was there anyone in the reception area. Bobby walked over to the reception window, and Sarge stayed standing in the center of the room. Bobby leaned into the receptionist's window and called out, "Hello? Anybody here? Hello?" He then turned back toward Sarge. "They must be in the back. They'll probably be back up front in a minute. Let's grab a seat."

"It doesn't seem to be a very busy place, Bobby. Awfully quiet here. Shouldn't there be a sound of something going on?"

"Oh, you're the detective now? I thought you didn't want to be a detective?"

"I'm not detecting anything. I'm simply making an observation."

"Stop trippin'. Grab a seat." Bobby then patted the chair ninety degrees to his, where he had sat, for Sarge to sit.

Sarge shook his head from side to side as he began to sit and said, "Open mind for now." Just as his back side hit the seat, the door leading into the office area was opened, and there stood the man from the bar. "Good evening, Detective. How are you doing?"

Bobby answered, "I'm doing good. This is my associate that I told you about, William Reece."

"Pleased to meet you. Sorry to keep you both waiting. Come on back," the man said. The man walked up to the first door on the left and stopped, opened the door, and turned to them and said, "After you, gentlemen." There were two seats on the one side of the table and one on the other. Bobby and Sarge went toward the side of the table that the two seats were on. Behind them on that side was another door. They were seated, and the man took the other seat on the opposite side of the table from Bobby and Sarge. "Gentlemen, did you have any trouble finding the place?"

Both Bobby and Sarge shook their heads from side to side while basically mumbling no in response to the man.

"Mr. Reece, I have had the opportunity to speak with your colleague, Mr. Ashipa, in broad, general terms of coming into the employ of my client. I will do my best to bring you up to speed. My client has both domestic and international interests and customers. In order for my client to be the leader in his industry, he recruits, and that is where I come in, assets to help to support his information network. While my client's interests in the both of you is as independent consultants, by no means would you be the only independent consultants that he works with. What you both bring potentially is a proximity to a targeted area that my client needs to be prepared to gain information on. My client enlists many law enforcement personnel to support these efforts. My client sees the industry of law enforcement as being underappreciated based on the salaries that they draw. While my client does not need the services of any of the consultants full time, you will find that if you are under the employ of my client as an independent consultant, your pay would be equal to most law enforcement personnel's full-time pay while working very part time. Now there may come a time where more time would be needed from you, and if it was to impact your availability to your full-time employment, my client will look to compensate you appropriately to stay whole for both your current employ and with the established rate that is agreed to as an independent consultant. Through the work that my client can put in front of you, there is a possibility that you would be sometimes, directly or indirectly, be involved in operations with other law enforcement or security organizations. Your ability to maintain professionalism and discretion is a large part of what you will be paid for from my client. There will be times that you may be heavily involved and other times where there may be little to nothing going on. Any questions, Mr. Reece?"

"None yet. Go on, please."

"Thank you. In the current professional positions that you both are in, you have the ability to access sources that could aid the collection of information that is required to meet the objective of my client. Put differently, the fact that you are policemen gives you access to places that private investigators can't get as easily. Besides, you are trained better as well. The assignments that my client will put in front of you, as said before, are to be handled with the highest level of discretion and may require a physical presence from you to complete. There is an initial assignment that will be given. There is no timetable on this assignment. It could end the day after it is given, or you could still be involved in this same assignment five years from now. You may have more than one assignment at one time. Again, your compensation levels will be closely monitored to make sure that you are being paid properly for your commitment to my client. I assume that you both have heard the phrase 'On a need-to-know basis' before." Both Bobby and Sarge nodded. "This is the type of work that you will be involved in with my client. You will certainly be carefully prepared for your assignments. That doesn't mean that you do or do not know everything about the assignment. Staying in your lane or staying with your given assignment is the key to success with my client. If there is a period of time that you do not have a given assignment, then your base compensation will continue." The man then went into explaining the base compensation level and gave examples of how it would spike depending on the time involved. Both Bobby and Sarge were slightly tilted forward in their seats. The man viewed this as a success. Now for the close. "I need to know that the terms presented to you both are acceptable before I go to the next phase. Are you gentlemen in?"

This caught Sarge by surprise more so than Bobby. It wasn't that Bobby knew that they were going to be put on the spot in this meeting. Sarge thought that he controlled his path on this from telling Bobby that he would let Bobby know whether he was in or out after the meeting. This was not between him and Bobby anymore. This was between him and the man on the other side of this table. This man had an attractive deal on the table. The money was nice. Sarge was well aware that he was about to say yes or no to something that could change the financial path of his life without knowing specifically what he was about to get into. Before Bobby could say anything or before he and Bobby made any eye contact, Sarge replied to the man, "I'm in."

Sarge's head turned toward Bobby after he blurted out these two words, and Bobby's head turned toward him. They made eye contact, and then Bobby turned his head toward the man on the other side of the table and said, "Me too."

"Good," was how the man replied before going on. "My client is a private man, and for the sake of his business, he maintains a very private persona. He shows up and is heard by the consultants. But he does not show his face. My client is going to come in through that door in back of you when I stop speaking. He will speak with you, and he will leave. You will not turn to look in his direction. Are we clear?"

"Clear," was said in unison by Bobby and Sarge, and at the moment that the fading sound of "ear" was uttered, the door opened.

CHAPTER 138

"Gentlemen, welcome aboard. You both will be given a card with two phone numbers on it. The first number is for the gentleman across from you. The second is a number for me. He will give you both the description of what should generate a call to him. I will tell you both right now what would generate a call directly to me, any information that leads you to believe that you have some information that brings the possibility of knowing when or where contact can be made with the primary subject of your assignment. The primary subject of your assignment is a man named Rick Smalls." With that being said, the man who had entered behind Ron and Sarge turned and left the room through the same door that he had, just moments ago, entered through.

CHAPTER 139

Sarge was done now in the house. It was time to leave the house now. He knew he was a bit of a sitting duck. It was ironic. The same people that he trusted to put $1 million in his account were the same people that he knew that he needed to keep moving from to make sure that he was safe. Sarge headed down to the car, where Michael was still bound quite well. He got into the car and backed out of the garage. After he tapped the button on the remote control to close the garage door, he just kept looking straight ahead at his house. This could be the last time that he saw this house as his own. He would get it listed remotely to sell. His plan was not to be a sitting duck for the people that were looking for him. It was time to go now. Just before he continued to back up to turn around in his driveway, he realized that he had not brought down his last cup of coffee that he had poured into his mug.

Sarge put the car back into park. He got out of the car and jogged around the side of the house to get back to the stairs in front of the house. He got up and down the stairs now with the mug in his hand. He walked along the side of his house, sipping his coffee. As he cleared the point of the side of his house to cover the last twenty feet to his car, Sarge caught the early morning shadow that was cast on the ground where he was about to step to not quite fast enough. With his mug lowering from his mouth and now his head rocking back into position from the slight backward tilt from sipping his coffee, he caught the shadow on the ground. He turned to his left to see the point of a silencer. If memories could be recounted, that would have been the last memory that Sarge had. The memory would not have gotten to him had he still been alive if he had not gone back into the house for the mug of coffee that he had just sipped from.

CHAPTER 140

"Your previous driver is not going to be able to finish the drive. I am going to finish from here," said the man who had just relieved Sarge off his duties and his life.

Michael saw that the man was different before those words were said through the narrow space of the driver seat and the door panel as the man got into the car. Michael had not seen the path that was going to give him the opportunity to get free prior to getting to the destination that William Reece was going to take him to before William Reece was replaced. The path was less wide now with this relief guy in place. Michael had a pretty good assumption who this guy was, not his name but more of what this guy could do. This guy most likely had some of the same training that Michael had received himself for handling a human package. He might not have been an operator that would infiltrate systems and businesses like Michael, but since he was here at this moment, Michael figured that he could deliver a human package and deliver death. This was still the thing that Michael had going for himself. If he was wanted dead, then he would already be dead. It was that simple. He didn't have any illusion that death wasn't in his near future because to the people that he thought he was about to see, they wanted two things from him, and the second thing was, they wanted to see him dead.

The ride started toward an end that he didn't know where it was and how it was going to be. The last time that Michael had a car ride related to the Recruiter was when he was riding away from that scene in Beirut. Michael hadn't stuck around to find out if the two gunshots had killed the man. Michael was interested in not arming that bomb that was destined for Israel and in getting out of the country of Lebanon. He had snatched a car from near the warehouse that he was taken into and gotten to the city of Tripoli for the ferry to Cyprus. In that car drive and on that ferry trip, he had become Michael Dixon. While he had used other identities since becoming Michael Dixon, he had never stopped being Michael Dixon. He had become Michael Dixon on that day. However, in that trip at that time, he was oddly feeling like Rick Smalls. Rick Smalls was a good kid who worked hard even at things that came to him naturally in academics and through his physical stature. He was never the guy to show up other people. He was the guy who knew that in life, hard work and showing respect to people went a long way. His parents had taught him that. He hadn't thought much about his parents over the years. Here in the last twenty-four hours, it wasn't that there was something that sprung them into the forefront of his life. It was that he came to realize that they lost their lives because of him. They were targeted to lure him into the Recruiter. His parents' lives were not of any value to the Recruiter. Their value was only in death because it was assumed that their deaths were the bait to lure Rick Smalls into the Recruiter's net. Rick knew that the Recruiter played his role for the purpose of the Voice. It was something that Rick was certain that was either initiated by the Voice or signed on by the Voice.

Michael figured that the new driver was taking US Route 12 because it felt as if the traveling speed was fitting to this road, and Michael knew that this road was near where they were leaving from. While the pace of travel and the destination of the travel had some importance to this time in his life, it was still the time of his life with his parents that his mind went back to. Through his choice of giving up his life as Rick Smalls, he was able to provide some benefits to them. He wasn't able to enjoy the fruits of his life directly with them, and that was sad to him at that moment. It wasn't that his parents was hooked on the idea of things for their lives. It was that they had done their best in investing in him with nurturing and love—their best. In life, what was more important than someone doing their best for another was what Michael was thinking about right now. His parents had done their best. Regardless of the assessment of what was accomplished in their actions, the results were their best. Michael thought how rare that might be for most kids growing up. Had their parents tapped into their best for them? Michael believed that he had gotten that rare contribution from his parents, their best.

In the end, they had unknowingly to themselves given their life for him as well—their best and their lives. And he didn't attend their funeral. He had taken up a position near their burial site dressed as a caretaker. His thoughts were that the Recruiter would have knowledge of their deaths and that the Recruiter would be interested in knowing if he showed up. He just had no idea that through the efforts of the Recruiter was why there was a funeral service for his parents. His parents were used as cheese was used to attract a rat—bait. He felt bad at the cemetery on that day then, but he felt far worse today than he did then. He felt bad for himself on that day because of the loss of his parents. He felt bad on this day because of his role in their deaths and for the cowardice that he showed in not respecting their lives on the day of their burial. They gave their best for him, and he realized that he had not given them much in return.

The pace of the car seemed even faster now, and looking up from below the window level to look out, Michael saw the passing of light poles and overpasses. He imagined that he was on an interstate now. His current destination was growing closer. Michael did not feel as if he was dwelling on the past and the what-ifs of his life in thinking about his parents at this moment, but he knew that he needed to figure out something in the present to provide for a future. He knew that he had one point of leverage that could prolong his life, and he needed to know how to use that sliver of leverage to extend his life beyond this day.

Chapter 141

The car had now slowed down. It felt as if the car was in the midst of a circular exit ramp. From there, the speed never picked up to what had been the pace prior to the circular feel of travel. The movement of the car had now turned into stop and go. The stopping was both at the pace of stop signs and perhaps stoplights. This continued for every bit of ten minutes. Now the stopping that might be consistent with stop signs were occurring more frequently. Now there was a turn to the left that had a bump in it, like a driveway. The car moved forward and slowed down. The movement stopped, the car was turned off, and the sound of a garage door lowering could be heard. The space that had some natural light from the daytime skies now dimmed. Michael was hoping to see the light of day again at this point.

CHAPTER 142

"Help me get him in the house. Did you terminate that other matter? Good. After you help me get him into the house, you can leave. I've got it from here."

Michael heard the voice and knew who it was. He didn't like the sounds of what he was hearing.

CHAPTER 143

The Bishop Ford Expressway was a stretch of Interstate 94 that covered 103rd Street to the merging of Interstate 94 with Interstate 80, going from the north to south. This road left Chicago behind and introduced roads to Dolton, Riverdale, Harvey, Calumet City, South Holland, and Lansing, Illinois. It was the exit for Sibley Boulevard that could lead into Riverdale and South Holland that caused Valerie to be somewhat overcome by emotion. She hadn't thought about that exit particularly in years. She had thought about the events of the last time that she took that exit many times over the years. It was on that exit twenty years and a few weeks ago that after attending the prom on her senior year of high school, she was in the car with Rick Smalls when they exited there to go out after the prom. Before getting to this point, they had both gone to her house to change clothes. They wanted to get out of their prom clothes so that wherever they went for the rest of the night, they wouldn't be looked at like high school kids. There was maturity in both their faces and physiques that could cause someone to pause when asking for identification. They both had already come to this club off this exit before, and they liked the nightspot. This was why they were headed here at this point.

Valerie thought about that night as she drove past that exit on her way to meet with her dad. Her dad was so busy back then that he had never met Rick. She knew that he would have liked him. Everybody did. She liked Rick, and right now she wanted to talk to him more than ever. She drove on. She was trying to change her thoughts to her dad, but the thoughts of Rick kept coming back. She remembered how Rick stayed after the deejay at that club on prom night to play an old, slow song. The deejay kept saying that he would, and the longer that he hadn't played it, the more that Rick kept going back near the deejay's booth to encourage the deejay to play that song. The deejay did play the song but not prior to giving it a big introduction. He had come over the live microphone and said, "This song should only start with this one couple dancing. The request for this song has been persistent. The man who kept requesting kept putting me on the spot, and now I am putting him on the spot to dance in front of everyone here tonight. Everybody can join in after we all give him a hard time. This song is for Valerie and Rick! Here you go, player!" She smiled as she thought about the applause that came from the people in the club that night a bit over twenty years ago. There was no remembering anything from anyone shouting out while they were dancing, and if she didn't know that people were there, she would have thought that she and Rick were not only the only people in the club at that moment, but she could also have been convinced that they were the only people in the world! Rick made her feel that way. She always wondered if she made Rick to feel the same way.

She was only fifteen minutes from where her dad was now as Interstate 94 merged with Interstate 80 heading east. She would take the first exit in Indiana south onto Calumet Avenue, a familiar route.

CHAPTER 144

Passing this point of the road caused Ron's mind to drift. It wasn't really a double date. His prom was for his school on that night, and Rick's prom was on this night in another school. They had planned to meet up after the prom with their dates at the Nimbus nightclub off the exit up ahead. They had agreed to be there by eleven that night. He was running a bit late. His date, whose name barely crossed his mind at this point in his life, had slowed him down. While she knew the plan was to change clothes, she tried to convince Ron to keep on the prom clothes. As often as he said that they would not get into the club dressed as high school prom goers, the more that she suggested that they should go somewhere where they could keep on those clothes. There was no way that Ron was going to let her influence him not to meet up with Rick and that girl that he thought was the same lady in that car up ahead. He looked forward to spending the evening with them because he knew that with Rick there was not going to be many more of them ahead.

He remembered telling Rick that he was wasting his time trying to convince the deejay to play an old song. He told him that the deejay wouldn't have that song. He told him that deejays didn't like people telling or suggesting to them what to play. He remembered Rick not stopping in asking the deejay to play the song. The deejay finally gave in, and it seemed as if the deejay thought that he was embarrassing Rick before he played the song by coming on the mic and calling out Rick. It just seemed that they were the only ones in the world once Rick and that girl started to dance. He remembered seeing how the attention was that Rick gave to her, and she to him that nothing else mattered to either of them. It was in that moment that Ron remembered thinking that the date that he had with him was just a girl. He wanted what he saw between his friends out on the dance floor. After a minute or so of the song, he took his date's hand and guided her to the dance floor near where Rick and Valerie were dancing, and he tried to focus on his date the same way he saw them focusing on each other. It didn't work then, and it hadn't worked in his life since, not even through his marriage. His next thought when the car he was following went left to head toward Indiana was, where was this car taking him to?

CHAPTER 145

Michael was taken from the car and into the house through a utility entrance and passed by the laundry room of the house. Once clearing this area, the driver guided him down some stairs into a basement. Once in the basement, it was a space that had some familiarity to Michael. This wasn't at all the furniture that he remembered, but he knew that he had been here before. The space currently was furnished, and laid out was an open area with a pool table, a bar, and some sparse furnishings to sit on. There was a door to the left and a door to the right. It was the open space and the doors in both directions that seemed familiar. "Take him through the door over there and bind him to the first chair that you come to once you are in the room." The speaker of these directions didn't look familiar to Michael, but the sound and cadence of his voice did seem familiar. The driver guided Michael into the room and bound him, as he was told. Once he had completed that task, he came out and told the man that he had bound the man to the chair. He added that he was as secure as anybody could be. There were no concerns that he could get free.

"All right. Go back to the car that you drove over here and get rid of it. I will call you later."

The man headed up the stairs that he had led Michael down, went out through the laundry room into the garage, hit the button just inside of the garage to raise the door, and got into the car. He started the car and backed out of the garage unto the street and then headed in the same direction that he had come from a short time ago.

CHAPTER 146

The door to the room that Michael was in opened, but it did not close. Michael couldn't see that area because of the way that he was bound. He felt the presence of someone in the room, and then he saw the man from the other room walking in front of him. He took a seat in a chair that was placed four feet away from Michael's feet. The man began with, "I am not going to apologize for the binds that you find yourself in at this time. I find them to be necessary. Today can be a long day or a short day for you. If it is a long day, it will be a painful day. If it turns into a short day, then you can expect a great deal less of pain. Who are you? Or better yet, what name are you going by today?"

"I'm not sure what you are talking about," was how Michael responded.

"That is precisely how this can turn into a long, painful day. Now let's try it again. I met you as Rick Smalls and last saw you as Darrell Hunt. So who are you now?"

It was then that it was crystal clear to Michael who this man was. This was the Recruiter. The man from that night toward the end of his junior year of high school. The man that he met with a few times immediately after that first night. The man that had him go into room number 2 at the office. The man who gave him assignments while he was at MIT within his apartment, the assignments in Miami, London, Paris, and other places. The man who gave him the last assignment in Beirut. Michael didn't care about the events of this day and any potential pain that might come his way. There was one thing that needed to be reconciled here today. "Why did you kill my parents?"

Before the man could respond, there was another voice that came from behind him. It was the Voice.

CHAPTER 147

"Rick, it has been quite some time. You have had both of us on edge over the years. Your interests appear to have gone against our interests, and as a result, we are at this crossroads here today. There is much that we want to know about these past years. However, my greatest interests lie in the program that you have been peddling as the Programmer. That is the foremost reason that we have brought you here today. I heard the question that you were asking when I came into the room today. Let me assure you that that question and any others that you have will be answered before you leave here today."

"Sir, I suspected that you wouldn't be far behind once I realized who was hosting me here. I am sure that who you believe me to be is not who I am. I have been looking for this programmer myself. I believe that there is great value in that program that is being purported as a security system for the present and future. I have been looking for it, and that is why I was at the forum. However, my attention has been diverted since I came to town. I have come across information that suggests to me that your man here, my recruiter, has responsibility in the death of my parents. I'm sorry to say that if he has responsibility for their deaths, you couldn't be very far from having responsibility as well."

"Rick, let's try not to get distracted from our foremost reason of this gathering, as I have said before. It is known that you are the Programmer, and it is as the Programmer that this conversation would be fruitful and beneficial to all of us. Your recruiter perhaps has a few things that he would like to say to you with the hope that you would be more compliant with our requests here today. Go ahead."

The Recruiter began as he was walking across the room to a mounted battery on a cart, "Rick, we are not going to be long on patience here today, so let's stop the back and forth of us stating that you are the Programmer and you countering that you are not the Programmer. Seeing that there are no parents or other known loved ones to inflict pain on to help you to speak on the matter of interests, it leaves you as both the receiver of pain and the one who needs to speak truthfully to ease the pain. Perhaps a little clarity of thought can be derived from this here." The Recruiter stopped in front of Michael with the cart. On a built-in shelf from the cart, he removed a pair of scissors and dropped to one knee in front of Michael. Once his balance was steady, he began cutting Michael's pants in a circular manner above the calf on the right leg. Once there was a complete separation of pant material from above the calf and the material below that point, the Recruiter pulled down the material to Michael's ankle. He then did the same with the left pant leg. He then placed the scissors back onto the cart, and he pulled off two Velcro strips. He attached one strip just above the right calf, and the other seemed to be equally positioned above the left calf. The Recruiter, while still on the same one knee, gathered some cables that fed into the battery. On the first cable, there was an offshoot of four cables, each with a small alligator clip of the end. He carefully placed all four on them on small electrode tips that were positioned around the strip on the right leg. Once these four alligator tips were placed securely, the Recruiter followed suit dutifully in his actions to secure alligator tips on the strip on the left leg.

"Rick, I am certain that you know how this works. The voltage level that you will receive to your body is dependent on how high I turn this knob clockwise. I'm not going to ask you about your program right now. Instead, I am going to give you a small sampling of what is in front of you." The Recruiter pressed the on-off switch to bring this battery power to life. At the beginning setting, there was nothing for Michael to feel since the knob was in the home position of zero volts. The Recruiter began slowly turning the knob clockwise to give Michael a feel for the power. Michael began grimacing and tensing up throughout his entire body. The Recruiter leveled off the knob by not continuing to increase the voltage; however, he didn't reduce it. He left it steady at a level where Michael was uncomfortable and feeling his nerves to be somewhat frayed. After ten seconds, the Recruiter returned the knob to the home position, which turned off the power.

"Rick, are you paying attention to what is going on here? I need that program, and you will deliver it to me right now. We have been missing you by mere steps over all of these years, and now that we have you, we are going to get everything that we need from you. You interfered where you had no right to interfere in the plans back in Beirut. Your choice of inaction to not finish your assignment led me to this!" The Recruiter was pointing at the right side of his own face and neck. "You caused this, and I have lived with it all of these years! You did this! Don't think that I haven't looked forward to this moment. I have you exactly where I want you, and you are going to give me what I need!" The Recruiter turned the knob violently in a clockwise manner to three times the voltage that was let loose the first time. He turned it back to the home position much quicker than he did the first time this time. "How was that? Did it burn? Well, this burned when it happened to me! It was a different type of burn, but it was a burn nevertheless!"

The Voice spoke up, "Back off for a moment. Rick, you see how this is going to go, don't you? As it was explained to you earlier, it could be a long, painful day or a short, less painful day. Let's consider this as the potential for the less pain that you will feel here today. I'm going to step out to get some water for you. You catch your breath and think about how you want this day to go from here." The Voice turned his attention to the Recruiter. "Come with me. He can't go anywhere." Once outside of the room that Michael was in, the Voice began to speak to the Recruiter, "Keep it professional. I understand what you went through and maybe Rick does or does not understand it, but for now we must lean all of his attention to the program. If he is not ready to give it to us right now, then yes, apply more stimulus. Don't give him any reason to lock up his mind from us. Are we clear?"

"Yes." This might have been the only time that the Recruiter did not include sir in a response to the Voice. At this moment, neither of them seemed to notice. There was a look of determination beyond the norm in the Recruiter's eyes, and this was recognized by the Voice.

From the refrigerator behind the bar, the Voice grabbed the water and gave it to the Recruiter. They went back into the room with Michael. The Recruiter approached Michael and told him to tilt his head backwards so that he could give him some water. He slowly poured water into Michael's mouth and stopped so that Michael could clear his throat. He then repeated the process. The Recruiter put the cap back on the water and set the bottle on a nearby table. He turned his attention toward the Voice, who was still behind Michael. "Sir, I would like to begin again with Rick. With your consent, I will begin again."

The Voice nodded his approval.

"Rick, you asked me a question earlier. It is the only thing that you have said to me since being here. I will answer your question in time. But I do find it important to know what name you are going by these days. This is where the communication exchange can begin between us. So I will ask you again. What is the name that you are going by these days?"

Michael's eyes were already on the Recruiter with his chin slightly below a perfect horizontal position. At the asking of the from the Recruiter, Michael's eyes grew stronger and tighter. His chin raised to a position just above being horizontal. He licked his lips, stretched his mouth, and said, "My name is Rick Smalls, the proud son of Caeser and Elizabeth Smalls! Now did you have them killed!"

"Your name is not Rick Smalls! You have not been Rick Smalls for twenty years! What's your name?" yelled the Recruiter, showing his rage and short fuse to Michael. From his commitment of remaining professional, he quickly went back to being shortsighted. He turned the knob all the way up for about three seconds and turned it off just as quick. "WHAT IS YOUR NAME?"

Michael, being slow to unclench his teeth from that latest charge, finally composed himself and said, "Rick Smalls is my name, and it is the only name that I will live under for the rest of my life. Do you understand me?"

"I understand that you are not cooperating with me, and your pain threshold will be found. You will give me everything that I want starting with your name, and then you will tell me how to access the program! You don't want to mess with me! Do you hear me? I had no problem seeing to it that your parents died that night, and I won't have a problem seeing you die here tonight! For your information, your parents were not dead from the accident. I was there. They messed up plans, just like you did in Beirut! I put two bullets in the back of both of their heads! Just like I taught you how to double-tap people that you shot! What is your name!"

Chapter 148

Valerie didn't expect this. Why would things be this way? She saw the car that Dave had given the description of, so that wasn't a surprise. Her dad must be really heavily burdened with the thoughts of his wife, her mother. Why would he leave this open like this? As she entered, it had the air of a space that hadn't been opened much or where much air did not circulate. She heard noises. It must be her dad and Dale speaking down below. She headed down the stairs and overheard all the conversation from the room in back between him and someone else. She froze and continued to listen. If she was asked right now why she froze, she wouldn't know if it was to listen better or because nothing on her body could move because of what she was overhearing. She couldn't move, and she didn't know what was going on in there. She clearly recognized two of the voices. The other voice was really strained, and she couldn't make anything out from it for content or distinction. She willed herself forward. Not believing what she was hearing, she inched yet closer. If she wanted to scream out because of the things that she was hearing, she couldn't. Her throat was dry. Her mouth was trembling. Her legs had no strength, yet somehow, she was still standing. There was no potential action from Valerie until she heard these words, "Your parents were not dead from the accident. I was there. They messed up plans, just like you did in Beirut! I put two bullets in the back of both of their heads! Just like I taught you how to double-tap people that you shot! What is your name!"

Valerie willed her way into the doorway. Her eyes only confirmed what she was already afraid of. It was her dad and Dale that she clearly saw. "Dad! Dale! Dad, what is going on? What am I hearing about?"

As her dad turned to face the voice that was bellowing out behind him by turning his torso a quarter turn, it was then that she caught a glimpse of a man bound in a chair with his head back to her. "Sweetie, what are you doing here? You shouldn't be here! You should leave now!" Her dad, the Voice, countered. He stepped toward her with both hands extended.

In a move that would illustrate the application of taking the wax off a car, she knocked his hands lower while sidestepping him. It seemed to her that life was reduced to slow motion as her eyes got closer and closer to getting a viewpoint of the man in the chair. His head was slightly lowered, and his energy had not reemerged from the last jolt yet. As Valerie moved more around the room to get a clear look at the man's face, her knees began to bend to lower herself so that she could get her eyes to his eyes. When she had seen enough of him to know, she screamed out, "Riiiiick! Riiick! Dad, Dale, what is going on here? What are you all doing to him?" She moved quickly over to him and dropped to both her knees while scrambling with her hands on the bindings that have him fixed to the chair. There was recognition in Michael's eyes toward her, but he was not himself from that last surge of voltage.

"Sweetie, sweetie, come here. Let me explain!" her dad called out as he moved for the first time ever into Michael's sight line. The best that Michael was able to do with this was to glance upward toward him.

With Valerie's hands still scrambling around the binds, the Recruiter, Dale Langford, turned the knob up halfway for about three seconds, causing a jolt to both Michael and Valerie. He turned it off nearly as fast as he had suddenly turned it on. Valerie collapsed in front of Michael. Dale reached over and grabbed Valerie around the shoulder of her sweater and pulled her toward him. By the time that Howard had focused on Dale and Valerie and that Michael raised his head in their direction, they both saw that Dale now had a gun pointed at Valerie's head.

"Stop it! Everybody, stop it! This is out of control! It is simple! Rick Smalls, as you want to be called, it is quite simple. You release the program, and your high school sweetheart lives!"

"Dale, you let go of my daughter right now!"

"I'm sorry, sir. Today is the last day that I work for either of you. I have given my life to the best interests of you and your company! I have given dedicated service to all that has been put in front of me! I came this far for that program, and I am going to get it! If Rick there doesn't value his own life, maybe he will value his darling Valerie's life!"

"Dad, Dad, what have you done? You had Rick's parents killed? For what? For what, Daddy?!"

"No, no, you misunderstand, sweetie! That was news to me when he just said that. I had no part in killing them. I admit I wanted to see Rick again. But I wouldn't kill his parents to attract him! I always respected Rick. It was through you speaking about him from high school that first garnered my attention. He always showed respect for you. He cared for you. He showed himself as the perfect guy, not only for you but also for my work. Our work at International Safety Services. He worked to advance many national security projects. Dale led his training. Rick was exceptional. I wanted to get him out of the covert field work. I wanted to see him back in your life. He was going to have one last project in Beirut. It was there that he last worked for me. It was there that things got sideways between both Dale and him."

"Why are you torturing him now? I heard what was being said before I came in here!"

"Shut up! There will be time for you two to catch up after I get that program and get what I am due. Rick, what's it going to be? The program or her life? Decide now. Three, two…"

"Okay. Okay. I'll get it to you. Let her go first."

Dale didn't let her go, but he did loosen his grip on Valerie. "No games. Any games and she dies! Do you understand me?"

"I do."

"Valerie, open up that laptop on the table and turn it on for your boyfriend. Rick, you tell her how to access it. Once I verify it, you all could go," directed Dale.

"What do you mean we could all go? I am not a hostage here. What has gotten into you, Dale?" Howard was asking as he moved across the room toward Dale.

"Stop where you are! Don't come any closer!"

Howard kept moving toward Dale. Dale's gun was between them both. They jostled back and forth, and then there it was, the sound of gun firing in a room that bounced the sound around. From where Valerie and Michael were viewing this, they only saw a pained expression on Dale's face. Both men were currently suspended upon each other. They remained that way for what seemed to be an eternity. It was, however, only seconds later when Howard began to slide down. The pained expression on Dale's face remained. The pain that Howard actually felt was expressed still across Dale's face. Realizing what had happened, Valerie screamed a scream that sounded like the emptying of a person's soul. It was long. It resonated throughout the room. It hurt to hear it because of the sound of despair that came with it. Dale took his eyes off Howard and Valerie and pointed the gun at Valerie while addressing Michael. "See what you caused! Give me that program now! I have no problem killing again!" When he was finishing this statement, he had now placed the gun up against Valerie's head. Valerie hadn't noticed as she was trying grab ahold of her father.

As the gun rested on her head, the room was filled with the cracking sound of two more bullets, filling the room with the echo of shots being fired. Nobody moved. Nobody could move. Michael's eyes were locked on Valerie. Valerie's eyes were locked on her dad. The last thing that Dale saw was his last look at Michael. The shots had come from the doorway where there, standing in a perfect two-point stance with both arms extended to steady the weapon, was Ron. Ron had fired the two shots into the Dale's head. Dale's eyes remained open as his body moved backward and into the wall. They were open, but they saw nothing else ever again. Ron walked into the room with his weapon still extended. When he got to Dale's body, he kicked the gun away and checked for a pulse. There was nothing to be concerned with there. He knelt beside Valerie to check on her dad. There was a pulse. Ron pulled out his cell phone and dialed 911. After stating that he needed an ambulance for a gunshot wound and for another person with unknown injuries, he paused to listen and then turned to Valerie and asked her, "What is the address here?" She gave it to him. Ron then went over to Rick to free him from the chair.

CHAPTER 149

In the emergency room of the community hospital on Calumet Avenue, Ron approached Valerie with a bottled water. "Here you go. I'm sorry. I'm Ron, Ron Winston. You may not remember me, but I grew up with Rick. I haven't seen you since that party after graduation that you had thrown."

"I thought there was something familiar about you. How did you know? What were you doing there? Do you work with Rick or what?"

"No. Several circumstances over the last few days has placed me here, the last of which was seeing you come into the rental car place this morning. You may remember seeing—"

"I saw you. You bumped into the door. How did that get you here or back over at my house?"

"Like I said, several circumstances mounted, and I saw the brochure for your reunion this weekend with your picture in it. I thought your name was familiar. I thought I saw Rick a couple of nights ago, and this crazy ride started."

Valerie sat the bottle of water down on the wide armrest between the chairs and stood up. When she was totally standing, she reached out with both arms to hug Ron. He accepted the hug and hugged her back. They sat and talked for about an hour until they were interrupted by two separate doctors nearly simultaneously. "Excuse me, are you two folks with the two men that came in earlier?" They both stood and barely yielded the word *yes* from their mouths in fear. The two doctors both looked at each other, and the doctor on the right spoke first. "You can go in and see them both right now. Keep it short. They both need to stay overnight. The older gentleman will stay more than overnight."

Valerie turned to Ron and said, "You go see Rick. I'll be over after I check on my dad."

The doctor that spoke before then gave them both directions to where they should go to see the patients, as Valerie had communicated to Ron. Valerie went in to see her dad and then burst into tears to see the tubes and monitors all attached to her dad. He was sedated. She took hold of his hand and held it. She then put her head on the same hand and cried some more. She kept telling her dad that she loved him. There was no response from him. Her only consolation was looking up to see that his pulse was steady. It was lower than it should be, but it was steady. A nurse came into the room and said to Valerie, "We need to let him rest a bit more. We will be moving him to the ICU once they are ready for him. That is for precautionary reasons. If he is able to rest for a few days, he should gain some strength. In gaining strength, we would move him to a regular room, and then he should be able to go home with some limitations."

"Thank you. Thank you for everything. I'll kiss him and then leave. I have a friend down the hall in another room. I want to see him." Valerie kissed her dad. She went into the bathroom in the room that her dad was in and threw some water on her face and patted it dry with some paper towels. She looked at her dad again before leaving the room, and with apprehension, she headed toward the room that she heard the doctor tell Ron that Rick was in. She opened the door and saw Ron sitting there with a look of bewilderment on his face. The bed was empty. "Where? Where is he? What happened?" Valerie shrieked.

"He's gone. When I got in here, he was gone!"

Valerie was stunned by the news. Her heart and mind couldn't handle any more. Ron looked at her and realized that she didn't understand, and he jumped up and went and grabbed her as she teetered on her feet.

"No, no. I mean when I got in here, he was gone. They don't know where he went. He left without anyone noticing him leaving." Ron guided the confused and emotionally empty Valerie to a chair in the room. They sat there for a long time opposite each other. With his right hand, he held her left hand, and with her right hand, she held his left hand. They sat this way for a long time.

CHAPTER 150

The same nurse that told Valerie that they would be moving her dad to the ICU came into the room to tell her that they were moving him now. She also suggested that Valerie should go and get some rest and check back later. She informed Valerie that her dad was going to be sedated for a long period of time and really wouldn't have any prolonged periods of consciousness until later that night. "Is there someplace that I can take you? I followed both of the ambulances here in my car. I know you came in the one with your dad. Where can I take you?"

"Home," was all that Valerie said.

CHAPTER 151

The rest of Wednesday was a blur for Valerie. When Ron dropped her back at the house that she grew up in that she and her father had kept after her mother passed away, she was drained. She was drained from seeing her father in that hospital bed. She was drained from all that was said by Dale and by Dale dying right in front of her, the prospect of dying herself, and seeing Rick bound after all these years. Thankfully, she was drained that Ron walked into that room. But her heart was broken by the absence of Rick from that hospital room. She couldn't understand the prospect of losing him again after all those years. To get the peace off that, she did so from the video that arrived on the phone from the woman in the restaurant. She knew it was him. There was no face or sound on the video. The video captured roughly the torso of a man. The hands signed to her. Without identifying who the person signing was to her, there was so much that was conveyed to her. The message was of a warning about him inviting the VP of her company to meet and for her not to follow, that it could be dangerous, and that this VP had been responsible for the deaths of Vasily and Xi.

Valerie was shocked by the message but even more so by the messenger. It was the angle that the pinky finger on the signer's right hand extended from the hand. It was off-centered in comparison to all the other fingers. She had seen it before when she was teaching her new best friend to sign. She had learned with her Virginia friend Gabriella, and to remember Gabriella, she kept practicing. One day in homeroom in her freshman year, she was practicing, and Rick asked her about it. She began teaching him the alphabet soon thereafter. It was on the letter *Y* that she first noticed the displacement of his pinky. He told her that it was injured in football, and that was the best placement that he was going to get out of the finger for life. When she saw that hand signing, she knew that her friend, the love of her life, was alive. Now he was gone again. When Ron dropped her, they exchanged phone numbers in case one of them heard from Rick. Valerie called Dave after Ron dropped her off and canceled the keynote speech for that night. She only told him for now that her dad was in the hospital. The rest could wait. She went back to the hospital that evening. There was not much change in her dad. She went back to the house. She didn't go back into the basement. She stayed upstairs, remembering her mom, dad, and grandmother. Then her thoughts went back to Rick.

On Thursday morning, she found a local cleaning service from a reference from the police that cleaned scenes like the one in her basement. She went to the hospital again and left them to work. She got a number of calls. She didn't answer her phone. She had made up her mind that the only call that she would answer would be from Ron, if it came. It didn't on Thursday or Friday. When she decided to listen to her voice mails, they were related to work; and between Thursday afternoon, Thursday evening, and Friday morning, there were at least six messages from the head of the reunion committee wanting to talk to her. When she listened to those messages, she thought of Rick and called. The head of the committee didn't mention Rick at all. He was calling initially on Thursday before the welcome party to thank her again for sponsoring it. He called during the event to see if she was going to be there and that he was calling on Friday morning to see if she was going to make it at all. She made mention that her father was in the hospital and that she was going to stay close to him. She did say that if things were to change, she might make it on Saturday night. He thanked her again, and they hung up.

On Friday afternoon, the news became more encouraging about her dad, and he was moved to a regular room to continue his recovery on Friday afternoon. Still, there was no call from Ron or any contact from Rick. Her dad on Friday evening was trying to tell her about how he and Dale and other men like Dale recruited young people like Rick into the organization as assets. She didn't want to hear about the business part of it, but she did want to hear about the recruitment and Rick's life that she knew nothing about. He also told her how he provided for Rick's family before and after he left working for him. He told her that he loved Rick, and he wanted Rick to be with her. They cried together in the hospital, and she said "Me too" after he had said that he wanted her and Rick together. Before she left the hospital that evening, the hospital staff told them both that he could be discharged on Monday with no further complications. They both were delighted. Her phone rang. She didn't answer it. Her dad asked her about it, and she told him that it was someone from the reunion committee probably wanting to know if she was going to come. He thought that that was unusual, and she told him about her contribution, and then he understood. He told her that she should go on Saturday since he was doing better and that she could tell him all about it on Sunday when she came back. Valerie told him that she wasn't up for it. He told her that she should go. They sat and talked for another hour on that Friday evening.

CHAPTER 152

Valerie began her Saturday morning early. She was anticipating that her dad would be recovered enough to travel back to Northern Virginia on Monday after his release from the hospital. While the confirmation of his release had not been stated yet, she believed that he would trend in that direction. Through last night, there had not been a single time that his recovery had stalled or reversed. She knew that he had used his private plane to come into town, and she knew how to reach his pilot. She called the pilot and gave him only the necessary information about her dad because the pilot would take the precautionary preparations for his safe passage. He asked Valerie if she wanted him to arrange for a nurse on the flight, and Valerie told him no. She had taken care of that herself. She had already arranged for a nurse at her dad's home once he was returned there. It was this same nurse that she had flying into the Chicago area on Sunday commercially so that she would be in place when the flight with her dad took place on Monday or Tuesday.

The cleaning crew that the police recommended had done a wonderful job in cleaning the remains of Dale Langford from the room in the basement. The police had spoken with her dad for the first time yesterday, and he explained away how it was, in a home that he owned, that a man could be killed while that same man had another man bound, and he himself was not a part of any of it. While Howard was aware of how Rick had been captured and secured in the basement of his home in Munster, he explained that the man that was killed had done all this and that while they had worked directly on things before, they were not in on this situation together. In his explanation that he expounded upon to the police, he said that he walked into the situation and that Dale Langford had used his home previously when he was in the area, and he had approved of Dale staying at his home on this trip into town. He further explained that he was thinking on his wife, and that was why he went there. He did not have that as a prepared thought because it wasn't on his mind. Valerie planted it inadvertently in his mind when they talked in the hospital before the police questioned him. Howard had asked Valerie how or why she got there at that time. She explained how she heard him speak about his wife and her mom and figured that this was as close as he could get to her in the available time frame. Howard ran with that when asked about it by the police. The police viewed it as sketchy, but they accepted it for now. There was nothing that Valerie said to the police that contradicted her dad's explanation of the events. There were no contradictions from Ron either to the police.

Valerie was tired, however, here on Saturday morning. The week's shocking events was an adrenaline rush—the deaths of Xi, Vasily, and Dale, the thought that her life could have been threatened by Dale with a gun to her head, her dad being shot, and seeing Rick and then losing him again. She couldn't grasp the idea that Rick wouldn't want to see her. Why would he leave like that without talking to her? There was so much that she wanted to say to him, and now he was gone again. This high school reunion had given her a portion of hope about maybe seeing him. She didn't think she would see him by way of Dale. She was still shocked to know that her dad had had a business relationship with him. Over the past few days, she remembered how her dad spoke so glowingly of MIT when she was in high school and before she and Rick went toward the MIT booth that night late into their junior year. Had she been a part of recruiting him through her dad planting MIT subliminally into her mind? It was so much to try to understand. She was exhausted. She had not eaten anything of substance since she woke up on Wednesday morning. She really didn't have an appetite this morning either. She knew she needed something to eat. She would head over to the hospital before noon to visit her dad, and she thought that she should settle down and eat. She also wanted to settle down to cry. All that had transpired had her running empty emotionally. She went into the bedroom that had been her mom's. She sat on the edge of the bed on the side that her mother most frequently slept on. She sat there and cried.

Chapter 153

It had all happened with no opportunity to do anything other than what he had done. The garage was raised. He had seen Valerie go into the house. He waited. He considered ringing the doorbell. There was no reason to think that something was going on in the house. He heard yelling. He heard screaming. He went in and followed the noises. A gun fired. He saw Valerie at gunpoint. He fired his own gun twice. How did this moment arrive? He knew how it began. He had no doubt in his mind that the man that he saw from the mezzanine level was Rick. Rick to Sarge to Bobby and Rick's parents. Since reading the *Post-Tribune* article online about the twenty-year absence of Rick, he had read the daily update of the newspaper online. In yesterday's version of the online publication, he saw that both Sarge and Bobby were found dead. Bobby was found in his house and Sarge outside his house. What had triggered all this? Was it him seeing Rick? There was no way for him to have been there to shoot that man himself if he hadn't been at the car rental office and spotted Valerie. Then again, he wouldn't have been in the rental car office if his own car hadn't been shot. The fact that his car was shot while he was in it was a big deal, and it seemed to not even rank in the craziness of the week.

It all began with a sighting of Rick, and then when he was prepared to go into the hospital room to embrace his best friend, it all faded. Rick was gone. What was that all about? How could he be gone so quickly and easily? Why? What was Rick's life centered on, and where had his life taken him now? Ron himself felt so fragile at this moment. There were some pieces that needed to be picked up and put back into place. He felt alone. He wanted to be talked to, and he wanted to talk, not about anything specifically. He just wanted to be a part of life because right now, life for him was an empty chasm. Ron had driven into the city to see if he could make some connections with his future, and what he walked away with was a future that didn't, a present that hurt really bad, and a crash from the past that left him in no ability to think beyond the very moment that he was in right now.

It was early on Saturday morning, and he hadn't preceded in doing anything other than exchanging phone numbers with Valerie before he left the hospital, calling his insurance company to report his car stolen, calling the rental car company to extend his rental, and driving back downtown to check out of the hotel. Driving into the city did not turn out the way that he thought it would. He drove home that Wednesday night alone and lonely. He got home and did nothing. He did nothing on Thursday with the exception of looking at the *Post-Tribune*'s website. His Friday was nearly identical to his Thursday. His Friday did get his mind churning some after he read about the two former Gary police officers being found dead in what appeared to be unrelated occurrences. Even with the churning of the mind that came with reading about their bodies being found, he still did very little.

Now here on Saturday morning while feeling empty emotionally and nutritionally, he was determined to make this day something bigger than the day before. He did start it by checking the website of the *Post-Tribune* again. There was a small story on the connection in the past about Bobby Ashipa and William Reece and how they had been partners at one point in their careers. There were a few printed testimonials that touched the surface from other policemen that had worked with them, but there was nothing about the investigation into their deaths or how each of them were discovered dead. There was no emptiness today. He thought of calling Valerie. They had committed to call each other if one of them had heard from Rick, and she hadn't called. Maybe she had heard from him and forgot to call him. So he called her.

CHAPTER 154

He was in better shape now than when she saw him a few days ago. He didn't have that "freshly fried from electricity" look about him anymore. He didn't have the involuntary convulsions throughout his body happening anymore. He was able to link multiple words together. He was asleep now in what appeared to be a comfortable rest, no incoherent babbling like the other day. She nudged him gently and then shook him gently to wake him. The shaking had to grow from gentleness to something similar to rocking him. His eyes opened slowly. There was a look of grogginess. Once his eyes opened, then they batted rapidly. His torso began to rise, and his feet swung onto the floor.

"Here, take this."

"Thanks," Michael said very dryly as he accepted the mug of coffee. "What time is it?"

"Just after seven thirty. You finally got some sleep. You went down for good last night around ten."

"What day is it?"

"It's Saturday morning. How do you feel? You look better."

"I feel good. I feel better. What's that that I smell?"

"Breakfast. You should come and get it before it gets cold."

"I'll be right there after I use your bathroom."

"All right. Don't be long."

Rick finished quickly in the bathroom and headed into the kitchen and took a seat. "Tammy, thanks for everything. You have saved me several times this week. I really appreciate everything that you have done for me. You have saved my life and my freedom." He said as he chewed on his toast and scrapped up some eggs on his fork.

"Michael, now that you are coherent, can you tell me what happened and how you got to that White Castle restaurant?"

"Yeah. Let me eat this while it's hot first. Have I eaten since I have been with you?"

"No, you haven't."

"Well, let me get this into me, and then I will tell you everything."

Michael had last spoken to Tammy before he left William Reece's house to go to Bobby Ashipa's house in the early morning hours of Wednesday. He told her about him grabbing Bobby Ashipa and how he was then caught off guard by William Reece, how William Reece killed Bobby Ashipa, how William Reece bound him into the car and then got killed by some unknown person, how that unknown person delivered him to the guy that she had matched the walk to, how that guy had him secured to a chair where he got shocked frequently, how there were other people there and another man came into the room and shot the man with the walk and killed him, and how there was an ambulance ride to the hospital where he was at until he got out of there and over to White Castle. Michael did not touch on the other people in the room with any detail. But now that he paused in speaking to Tammy and was sipping on a fresh cup of coffee, he thought about two of the people that were in that room, and then he felt alive for the first time in days.

"Michael, Michael? Did you hear me?"

"I'm sorry, did you say something, Tammy?"

"I did. What are you going to do now? Is that program that you were peddling real? Where are you going to go? What's next for you?"

The program that he had been peddling was very real. He conceived the idea of it that day when he fled from Beirut. If all things would have followed the script that day, he would have been given access to tap into a satellite to play a role in detonating a bomb. His thoughts coming out of that was to figure out how to tap into any and all satellites worldwide to gain control for whatever reason a country or company might deem necessary. The benefits were numerable. A program that could get you this type of access could be used as it was purposed on that day in Beirut. It could be used to gather information by repositioning satellites. In the world of the companies and people that were at the forum earlier in the week, it could be used to tap into the many closed-circuit monitoring in major cities all over the world. The number of applications were numerable and dangerous. The choice of what to use it for would be the critical thing in anyone should they get their hands on it. Michael knew whom he believed could use it properly. But maybe he would just continue to sit on it for now.

"It's real, Tammy. It can be beneficial for the digital world, but it can also be destructive if the user chose to be destructive with it. Greed could lead someone to use it in a destructive manner."

"Did you think that in floating it out there this week that you would get confronted by the man with the walk? Did you want that to happen? Did you know the risk that led to you"—Tammy waved her hands toward Michael—"like this?"

"Yes, to all of those questions. I had history with him. So yeah. I've got to get back to work. I've got clients around the globe. How would you like to work with me globally? I know that much of what you do can be done from a keyboard anywhere. What I am suggesting is that you and I can approach many of my international clients face-to-face. On assignments where I need cover like this past week, there might even be contributions to make if you were travelling as well. You don't need to answer right now, but let me know what you think. I respect the quality of your work, and I could use someone like you on a more regular basis. Eventually, some of those face-to-face meetings could be yours without me even being present. When you decide and if you decide to do it, you can tell me what you want for a salary, and I will give it to you. I am not going to question your worth. I didn't before this week, and I have no reason to question it now."

Tammy extended her coffee cup toward Michael to cling it with his. Michael extended his likewise. At the moment that they clanged their cups together, Tammy said, "I'm on board."

CHAPTER 155

"Hello. Have you heard from him?" Valerie blurted out as soon as she answered her phone after seeing the contact name, Ron Winston, show up on her phone.

"No, I haven't. I guess you haven't either. How are you doing?"

"Ron, I am moving really slow through things right now. Hey, can you hold for a second? I'm getting another call."

"Sure, go ahead."

Valerie clicked back on after a short break from Ron. "I'm sorry about that. That was the committee head from the class reunion that is finishing up tonight. He wanted to invite me personally to the closeout party tonight. He's doing so because I made a sizeable contribution to the reunion."

"Are you going?"

"I told him no."

"You just told me that you were moving slow. You should go."

"I don't know. Hey, tell me something. You told me the other day that several circumstances had placed you at the rental car place and that you had seen my picture in the reunion brochure. How did that come to happen?"

"I had come into town for the forum. I was a policeman once, and now I run my own PI firm. It's small, and it is not going to carry me much longer. I was hoping to make contacts for a new future at the forum. I really never got a chance to work on that with everything else that was going on."

"I would like to hear more about your background. It was good enough to save my life. I can't talk right now. But we can talk tonight if you were to meet me at the reunion. Can you meet me there at seven for drinks before we go into my reunion?" Valerie asked with more life in her voice since Ron had seen her the other day.

Ron answered with a surge in his voice, "I will be there."

They both hung up.

CHAPTER 156

"Delete everything about Rick Smalls from your database. I am not interested in tracking him ever again," was what Valerie heard her dad say on his cell phone as she entered his hospital room.

"Dad, who was that? What was that about?"

"Sweetie, you heard me say the other day how I respected and liked Rick. I wanted to see him in your life. I have been looking for him for years. I have an operator that is contracted for me, and she does all types of work for me. I called her to tell her that she could stop now. I don't want to interfere in his life anymore. Look what it did. It almost got us all killed!"

"Dad, that is probably for the best. I know that I would like to talk with him. But he's gone, and if he's gone, then he probably wants to be gone. Hey, you look like you are doing better!"

"I feel so much better. They told me that Monday is very realistic to be released."

"That's great, Dad! I have already put things in place for both of us to go back home on Monday or Tuesday. Tomorrow I will firm it up once I know how you rested this evening. I made plans for tonight. Are you going to be okay?"

"I am fine. Do whatever you want to do. You don't have to worry about me. What's your plan?"

"I am going to leave here shortly to go back downtown. I need to shop for a few things for tonight. I am going to the last night of the reunion."

Chapter 157

Valerie and Ron met for drinks back at the Hilton Towers Hotel at seven, as planned that evening. They were not in the reception area, where the reunion was going on. The reunion had their area reserved from six until three in the morning. They met inside Kitty O'Sheas, an Irish pub that would have live music later in the night. This was inside the hotel. Ron had put on a black two-piece suit that had two buttons on the jacket, of which he buttoned only one. His shirt was gray, and he didn't wear a tie. Valerie showed up in three-inch heels and an aqua-colored gown that was narrow throughout and stopped just below the knees. Her hair was recently done, and when she arrived, Ron couldn't help but spontaneously say, "Wow!"

Valerie replied modestly, "Thank you."

They talked and drank for nearly three hours. They got to know each other, and Valerie got to know more of his professional background while telling him of the many divisions of International Safety Services. "Ron, you saved my life, for which I will always be grateful. I want you to work with me and my team, not because you saved my life but because you showed yourself as the type of professional that we want and need. What do you say?"

"I'm saying yes! Thank you. I won't let you down."

"I don't think that you could. Let's finish up here and sneak into the reunion."

They finished their drinks and walked through the main lobby area. They walked up the stairs to the same mezzanine level that Ron was on earlier in the week when his world changed forever. Valerie began to tell a man at the table her name, and he cut her off, telling her that he knew who she was. Her name tag was one of only ten or so remaining on the table. She took the name tag. She didn't peel off the back to stick it on her dress. She kept it in her hand for now as she and Ron went into the ballroom. They cleared the doorway area and moved toward one of the bars. This one was to the right. They went up to the bar to get drinks that they didn't need after the number of drinks that they already had drank, but they got them anyways. Valerie pointed toward a smaller table on the outskirts of the room as a suggested seating spot. Once they were seated, she put her name tag in her clutch. She and Ron sat and chatted, like old friends who hadn't seen each other in a while. They had a good view of the dance floor but never made a move for it. They were happy to be here, and having the company of each other worked well for both.

The night moved on. It was near midnight when a light came on near the deejay stand, and a man began to speak on a microphone to gain everyone's attention. "Thanks for giving me your attention. I won't be long. I wanted to thank you all once again for coming out and making this a wonderful weekend in celebrating our twentieth year since graduating from Bishop Noll High School. Let's give it up for all of you Bishop Noll Warriors!" The room got noisy from applause, screams, and yelping of all sorts. "Look, this is the last time that you are going to hear from me, Terry Vale. That is, until it is time to get the next reunion together." There was some laughter throughout the room. "Listen, many of you have been here for each night of the event, and I want to take the time to make a particular mention of one of our classmates. We were not going to look to these wonderful facilities for our reunion until we got a very generous contribution that allowed us to pick this fine venue. Your classmate that made that possible had not been able to attend before tonight, but she is here tonight, and I would like to get her up here for a moment. Help me to welcome Valerie Benson up here!"

There was a spotlight from the deejay area that shined on the table on the outskirt of the room where Valerie and Ron were seated. The room met the light with applause. Valerie was hesitant in getting up from the table. Ron joined in on the applause and stood up. He moved in behind Valerie to pull her chair away from the table to coax her to go up front. Valerie lowered her head for a moment and then looked up at Ron and smiled, signaling to him to pull out the chair. Valerie rose and headed toward the front. The applause stayed steady. Ron remained standing and clapped from where he was. The light went out from shining on their table. Valerie made it to the front and waved around the room, and the applause died down.

Terry spoke into the microphone again, "Valerie, thank you for coming forward this evening. We all wanted to thank you for your contribution and to let you know how much we care for you in being a part of the Bishop Noll family!" The applause picked up again and died quickly. "I am going to put you on the spot right now by handing you this microphone so that your classmates can hear from you. Let's hear it again for Valerie!"

Valerie reluctantly took the microphone from Terry. She took one step to get slightly in front of Terry and began to speak, "Thank you all for your kindness tonight. I wish that I could have been here on the other nights with you. I had some personal matters that kept me away. It wasn't until I spoke with another friend from years ago that he encouraged me with his kindness to come tonight." She pointed in Ron's direction and said, "Thanks, Ron, thanks for everything." She continued to speak to the room, "A night like tonight helps me to realize the importance of getting the most out of relationships when you can. I am sure that there is somebody that we all are missing that wasn't able to make it over the past few days. We all might even have somebody that we haven't been in touch with for years. I am just thankful for having this time to be here with you all tonight. I wish you all the absolute best! Please enjoy the rest of your evening."

There was applause again as Valerie went to hand the microphone back to Terry. Terry took the microphone but grabbed ahold of her hand also. "Valerie, I am not going to let you get off that easy. We want you to set the pace for the rest of the class for a dance." Valerie was shaking her head no right then. Terry didn't let go of her hand. "Deejay please." The chosen song froze Valerie as she heard the song begin. "Ron, Ron, can you come up here?" Terry called out over the microphone.

From the shadows of the back of the room from where they were seated, Valerie's dance partner moved toward the front of the room. As he walked past tables, some fingers were extended and pointing in his direction. As he cleared the tables and made it to the dance floor, there were now two lights shining in the room, the one over where Terry was standing near Valerie and the other one that picked up Valerie's dance partner. The flicking of the light caused Valerie to squint. It wasn't Ron. After a couple more steps into the light, she recognized that it was Rick. He continued directly over to her and took her hand and pulled her into the middle of the dance floor. The song was the same song that he had requested the night of their prom, "Adore" by Prince. They danced. Their classmates joined in at some point. They didn't know it because they only saw each other in the entire world. "You know, Valerie, when I dance with you, it feels like we are the only people in the world!" It was all that he said during the entire dance, and all that she said, with a broad smile, was, "Me too."

The End

ABOUT THE AUTHOR

Derrick L. Smith is a Chicago area native for most of his life. He has lived with his wife and three sons in North Carolina for the last fifteen years. He had been an executive in various supply-chain, manufacturing, and transportation operations in his adult life. He has a keen interest for the action, suspense, legal, espionage, and thriller genres of fiction. He is a graduate of Indiana State University. The book that you are reading is Derrick's first work.